Killing

for the

Cure

A Biomedical TechnoThriller

By

Andrew P. Smith

BeachHouse Books Chesterfield, MO USA

Copyright

Graphics Credits: Cover design by Dr. Bud Banis using a graphic", royalty free print rights purchased through dreamstime.com for 13421654 Dna©Drizzd | Dreamstime.com and1299268 Man with Gun ©R. M. Hayman | Dreamstime.com

with text enhancements by Dr. Bud Banis.

Publication date June, 2012
ISBN 9781596300781 BeachHouse Books Edition
LCCN 2012941140
Previously published in 2010 as A Cure for Cancer

Library of Congress Cataloging-in-Publication Data
Smith, Andrew P., 1945-
A cure for cancer / by Andrew P. Smith. -- BeachHouse Books ed.
     p. cm.
ISBN 978-1-59630-062-0 (alk. paper)
1. Cancer--Research--Fiction. 2. Kidnapping--Fiction. I. Title.
PS3619.M545C87 2010
813'.6--dc22   2010030497

BeachHouse
Books

www.beachhousebooks.com

an Imprint of
Science & Humanities Press
PO Box 7151
Chesterfield, MO 63006-7151
(636) 394-4950
www.beachhousebooks.com

Killing

for   the

Cure

A Biomedical TechnoThriller

By

Andrew P. Smith

PROLOGUE

I probably shouldn't admit this, but I don't study cancer in order to help the sick and dying. Don't get me wrong, it's a marvelous bonus, and I'm very proud that my research may some day help create new ways to diagnose, treat and I hope cure this terrible disease. But the main reason I investigate cancer is because it taunts, teases, challenges, excites, provokes, puzzles and irritates me. I believe one of the most important differences between our species and all other animals is that we can never accept the world as it presents itself to us. We see mysteries everywhere, and spend our entire lives trying to solve them.

As a scientist, I don't claim to know the truth, nor even to seek it. I'm not sure I would even recognize the truth if I actually stumbled over it. Like all members of my profession, I take a simple oath: to describe the world as simply, clearly, accurately and precisely as possible. And most important, to describe what I have seen in such a way that others can see it, too. To guarantee that I hold these particular truths, partial and imperfect though they may be, to be self-evident.

Francis Bacon, in one of the more famous tributes to science, said that knowledge is power. It's rarely appreciated that this statement should be taken literally; it expresses a relationship of identity. It's not that knowledge discovers or creates power, makes it more apparent or accessible to us. Knowing is the only power of any kind that we have. Everything else is illusion.

It's often said that scientists never ask why. They ask when, where, what and how. But from the answers to these questions we also ask, most of the time without even realizing that this is what we are doing, an even more important question: Who? Who am I? Who are you? Who are we?

1. DISCOVERY

Most people don't find numbers very sexy, but I had never been more turned on by the ones I was looking at now. Just as a plain-looking woman, in the eyes of her lover, might appear to be everything a man could want, I looked at 25.4998, or 26.0273, or 31.8348, or 28.2651, and saw not a row of digits, but the answer to my quest. There was enormous lust in the moment, but also the knowledge that the relationship would grow and deepen, for both of us.

I was alone in the lab. It was almost midnight, though I had long ago lost track of the time. I had begun the experiment that morning, more than twelve hours ago, processing dozens of frozen, stored stool samples, from cancer patients, pre-cancerous patients, and controls. From each sample I first extracted ribonucleic acid, or RNA, which then had to be analyzed to confirm its quantity and purity. I then converted each sample of RNA to DNA by a process known as reverse transcription — reverse, as in the opposite of the normal biological process in which DNA synthesizes RNA.

The climax of the experiment began around nine that evening. Using a procedure called real time quantitative polymerase chain reaction — RT-PCR for short — I would identify and quantitate certain genes in each of the samples of DNA that I had synthesized earlier. I filled each of the 96 tiny cavities in each of two small plastic plates with all the necessary reagents, then placed each plate into a special machine that cycled the samples through several hours of alternating heating and cooling. While the reactions were running,, I sat at my desk, working on a grant proposal, impatiently waiting for the experiment to finish. Now at last I could look at my creation.

Each of the numbers that now appeared on the printouts represented the level of activity of a certain gene in a certain tissue sample. It was like one word in a small text. But just as one is barely aware of reading single words, I was not lingering on individual values, but in a flash grasping the entire pattern they produced. And what that pattern said to me was: *This is cancer.*

This is normal. And this is normal now, but could become cancer. Each sample had a distinct set of numerical values, so distinct that in a flash I could have said to the individual who had donated that sample: You have cancer. You don't. You don't, either, but you have a pre-cancerous condition that we can treat now to prevent the disease from developing.

My pilot study had been successful. A larger follow-up study would be necessary, but there was no longer any reasonable doubt. I had discovered three new genes that could serve as biomarkers for colon cancer. No longer would colonoscopy — expensive, invasive, inconvenient — be necessary to prevent this disease. I was the proud father of a new test that would save thousands of lives, eliminate millions of unnecessary procedures, and make me very rich.

But at that moment, none of the practical consequences of my research mattered to me. I was hardly even aware of them. Because as I was absorbing these data, a new insight suddenly came to me. In a flash, I grasped not simply that these three genes were associated with cancer, but *how* they were involved. A vision of the process now erupted full-blown into my mind, a complicated network of metabolic reactions in the cell. It was so real to me that I could almost reach out and touch them, rearrange them, increase the activity of this gene here, observe the change in that enzyme there. I found myself crawling along the endlessly-branching sequences of reactions, like a child on a jungle gym, exploring each path as it wound and twisted into another, trying to grasp the network in its entirety. It was like being inside a living cell as it gradually became malignant, following in an instant of time, all the metabolic processes that resulted in carcinogenesis.

This is new, I thought. *No one has ever seen this before.*

I wandered about the lab for a few moments, to savor the experience. Though there was not another soul in a large room that, during the day, housed a dozen or more people bustling with activity, the lab had never seemed more alive to me than now. Everything was lit by a soft glow, as if a light had been turned far up in intensity; but not a light from above, nor indeed, from anywhere in the room, but from within every single object in it, from within its very air, within all its empty spaces. This light, bright as it was, did not glare or offend with its intensity, but was as soothing to the eyes as darkness. This light was everywhere, I could even feel it emanating from myself. It made me feel soft, insubstantial, as if I could pass through the walls, yet more real than I had ever felt before in my life.

As I passed by the rows of lab benches, topped by gleaming black Formica, crowded with water baths and small centrifuges, reagent bottles and racks of plastic tubes, everything seemed alive, animated, speaking to me in some language I had never before known existed. Even the most trivial object--a fallen test tube lying a kilter, an orphaned piece of plastic tubing, a crumpled scrap of paper--became *significant*; it stood out before me, announced itself as being as important, as necessary, to existence as absolutely anything else in the universe. Each was unique, totally separate from everything else, yet completely a part of everything as well, as though the entire room were now a living organism. I saw why it was what it was, why it was there where it was at this very moment.

Indeed, I could almost see scientists working at these benches, not just my colleagues, the technicians, postdocs and other graduate students in our group, but my spiritual ancestors. All the investigators whose research I had built upon to develop this new understanding of cancer seemed to be in the room at that moment. Everything they did in the past that had been necessary to what I had done tonight was right there. The past, present and future all seemed to exist together in a single moment that was beyond all the struggles of time. In some strange way I had never encountered before, I felt there were no boundaries to that room, nor to that moment, but that I was one with the entire scientific community that had preceded me. I had never felt more alone, more individual, more apart from the rest of humanity — yet paradoxically, never more connected to all of it.

When I left the lab shortly afterwards, and stepped out into the still warm early summer night, I had so much energy I thought I would explode. I started to unlock my bike to ride it home, but it was too confining. So I left it there, locked near the research building, and began to run across the University of Minnesota campus, screaming like a lunatic. My mind was alive with the ramifications of my discovery. I was already planning six months' worth of follow-up studies, thinking about what each of these genes did, where it was located, what regulated it, how it could be turned on or off. Tonight, I, Alan Rupert, had found a test for cancer. Tomorrow, I would cure it.

I was so ecstatic over my discovery that I hardly noticed the car that pulled up on one of the roads that bordered the quad. Someone opened the passenger door and began to get out. Then my world of light became dark. The infinite expanse became a prison. My expanded consciousness became no consciousness.

2. BOXED IN

When I woke up again, at first I thought I was home in bed. The triumph in the laboratory was still foremost in my mind, and for a few seconds I dreamily returned to planning my next experiments. I could visualize a metabolic pathway that contained the products of each of my three genes, and I was already working out how they must be interacting to produce the results I had observed.

But something was wrong. When I tried to stretch and turn over, I could barely move. Now I was completely awake, and instantly realized I was lying not in bed but on a hard surface. My hands and feet were tied, and I couldn't see a thing, because I was also blindfolded.

I started to panic. Where was I, and why was I tied up? What had happened? Straining to recall my last waking moments, all I could remember was leaving the lab late at night. After that, all was blank.

I squirmed uncomfortably and mostly ineffectively, like a worm caught out of its burrow. I wanted most of all to be able to see where I was, but with my hands firmly bound behind my back, there seemed to be no way to remove the blindfold. I tried to stretch my arms and bring them to the front of my body, but couldn't. I then tried rubbing the blindfold on the floor, but the rag was tightly tied and the bare floor offered no purchase on it.

I had better luck untying my feet. I turned over on my stomach, then bent my knees and arched my back. In this way I could reach the rope tied around my ankles with my hands. It felt like nylon cord, smooth and slippery to my hands. After a few minutes of fumbling around, I got it loose.

With my feet untied, I could now stand up and move around more freely, but I still needed to untie my hands. I tried to get at the knots with my fingers, but could not reach them.

Clumsily, I began exploring my surroundings. I walked slowly in one direction until I bumped into a wall. I then turned around, so my back with my bound hands was touching the wall, and began to move laterally, gradually making a circuit of my confines. I soon came to a corner, and passed it onto another wall, then a second corner and a third wall. I had moved part of the way down this wall when I felt a door. I quickly groped for the doorknob, but the door would not open.

Just beyond the door was what my ever-groping fingers recognized as a light switch. It appeared to be off, the switch pointing down. I didn't bother to turn it on, since I couldn't see with the blindfold, anyway. But as I explored the small plate covering the switch, I realized I had a very lucky break. One of the screws holding it to the wall was loose. Not very loose, but it was protruding just enough to give my fingers some purchase on it. I turned it, wincing as the sharp edges of the screw cut into my thumb, but with effort I was able to pull the screw out. I then pulled that end of the plate away from the wall. It was still fastened down by a screw at the other end, but by yanking hard, I was able to pull the plate free from the wall.

The plate was thin and of metal, and the edges of it fairly sharp, making a crude but effective knife. Indeed, I sliced one of my fingers running it along the edge of the plate, drawing a little blood and feeling joy in that pain. Carefully holding the plate in my fingers to avoid cutting myself any further, I rubbed it back and forth against the cord binding my wrists. It took a while, but finally the cord snapped in one place, and I was soon able to wriggle my hands free.

I immediately undid the covering my eyes and my mouth. At last I could see. Only there was nothing to see.

The room was pitch black, so dark that had I not been holding the blindfold in one hand, I might have thought it was still covering my eyes. I tried flipping the light switch, but it had no effect. Looking towards the bottom of the door, I thought could see just the faintest indication of light, of lesser darkness there.

I spent a few more minutes traversing the room, learning what I could about it by touch. It was about 12 x 10 feet, and though absolutely devoid of furnishings of any kind, I guessed it was a bedroom in a house. I could feel some cracking and flaking of paint in places on the wall, consistent with my growing realization that the house was probably abandoned, far from civilization. The room, of course, had no windows, something obvious from the total lack of light coming to my now highly sensitive retinas.

I quickly took stock of my situation. The door was very solid. I leaned against it a couple of times to test it, then threw my entire weight against it. It didn't budge. I thought about screaming for help, but surely if help were within hearing distance, I would not have been brought here. Much more likely, I feared, one of my captors might be on the premises.

How to get out? To have even the faintest hope of escaping, I needed some kind of tool, but what? I made another slow circuit of the room's walls, feeling carefully with my hands as high as they could reach. Eventually I was rewarded with what I had hoped to find: a nail protruding from the wall. It had probably been used before to hang a picture or something else from the wall. I grasped it and began working it back and forth, until it finally came free.

I groped my way along the walls back to the door. I felt the doorknob. No place for a key to fit in. Were there any screws that might allow me to remove the doorknob? Negative. Could I use the nail to pry the doorknob off? I tried, but to no avail.

I got very frustrated at this point. I started throwing my body against the door, trying to break the goddamned thing down, but it was very strong. I had figured out by now that it was dead-bolted on the other side, maybe also latched. I tried the hinges, but I couldn't get anywhere with them, either.

I stood back for a moment to rest. What was I going to do now? Though I knew it was useless, I returned to the walls, making another circuit of the room, trying to feel a window or any other kind of potential opening. Nothing. Only walls, walls, walls.

My pockets, of course, were empty. My abductors had taken my wallet and cellphone, everything except a single coin nestling in the bottom of one of my pockets. I sat down, feeling depressed, and idly set the coin on the floor, standing on its edge. To my surprise, it began to move. I heard it rolling all the way to one of the walls.

I got up, went over to that wall and groped for the coin in the dark. I then moved all the way to the wall on the opposite side of the room and set the coin down on its edge again. Again, it rolled all the way to the other wall.

I thought about that. The floor was not level. Why? It seemed to be an old house, most likely the foundation on one side was sagging. Or possibly, the sill—the wooden beam that goes on top of the foundation and supports the floor—had started to rot. If the sill had rotted, then maybe the floor had begun to, also?

The floor seemed to be hardwood, as solid as the walls, but I knew if there were any rotting, it would most likely begin in the subfloor below it. Exploring the hardwood with my fingers, which had heightened sensitivity in the dark, I located one of the tiny nails used to fasten the narrow boards to the subfloor.

Using the somewhat larger nail I had removed from the wall, I began to gouge at the nail in the floor, in effect digging a hole all around it. When I had exposed part of the nail in that way, I used the cover of the light switch to pry it loose. I worked at this way for a while, gouging and prying, and eventually was able to remove that nail. I then started on the others.

It must have taken me an hour or more, but eventually I was able to gouge out all the nails on one of the floorboards, and remove it. It was a typical piece of hardwood flooring, about three feet long and two inches wide. Using it as a lever, I now began to loosen the adjacent board. This went much faster, as I could pry it up from the exposed edge. Soon I had loosened enough of the floorboards to expose a broad swath of the subfloor.

My wrists ached from the effort leveraging the nails out of the floorboards. Sitting back for a moment, I wondered what time of day it was. I had left the lab around midnight. I didn't know how long it had taken my captors to drive me to this house, but I guessed it was far outside of Minneapolis, maybe several hours driving. Who knew how long I had been unconscious? Though I could not hear a sound outside, I guessed daybreak could not be too far off.

I turned back to the subfloor, which I guessed was a large plywood panel. Exploring it carefully with my hands, sure enough, I found a soft area where it had begun to rot. Using one of the floorboards as a sort of shovel, I dug away at this spot, creating a small depression in the panel. Then, using the floorboard as a hammer, I pounded away at the relatively thin layer of good wood remaining at the bottom of the depression. Eventually, to my growing excitement, I broke through. A final stab of the board took it through the subfloor and down into the dark, empty space of what I hoped was a basement.

There was still a lot of work to do. The opening I had made in the subfloor was only a few inches across. Large enough to put my hand through, and then pull upwards on the adjacent surface. It didn't budge. I groped around, looking for more soft spots. I found another one, and made another hole. This one was about a foot from the first hole, so I now stood up and stepped on the solid wood between the two, testing its strength. I could feel no give. I raised my foot in the air then slammed it down on this area. Still it didn't give. So I jumped in the air as high as I could, bringing both of my feet down on the targeted area.

There was a loud crack and the wood gave way. One of my legs went clear through the newly made opening, and for a moment I thought I was going to fall into the cellar, or whatever was below. But the hole I had now made was not yet large enough for that. My other leg bent sharply at the knee as my foot caught on the edge of the hole, and for a moment I hung awkwardly, half in and half out of the gap. I gradually extricated myself and proceeded to enlarge the hole by stamping on its edges.

Finally the hole was large enough to let me through—barely. One edge of it was right up against one of the beams holding up the subfloor, and I had to squeeze myself through. As I did so, I felt my dangling legs touching something. At first I thought it was the floor of the cellar, which would mean that there was in fact nothing below but a crawl space. But as I probed further with my feet, the surface below them deformed. It was soft and squishy. I quickly realized it was a cardboard box of some kind. In fact, a stack of them.

So as I slowly squeezed my way through the hole in the floor, I found myself floating on a sea of boxes. They crumpled somewhat under my weight, but the sheer height of the stacks held me far above the floor. This made further progress very slow and difficult, of course. I couldn't stand up and walk on these boxes. It was all I could do to crawl over them, my movements constantly hindered as my shifting weight crumpled and crushed the boxes underneath. Moreover, it was just as dark down here as it had been in the room above me, and of course I had no idea in which direction to move. I was trying, of course, to find a door to the house above.

I don't know how long I wandered about in this way, rather like a bug making its way across a slab of soft butter. But finally, to my immense relief, I came to an end of the stacks. They announced this to me by suddenly giving way completely under my advance, sending me sprawling onto the hard cement floor. I was a little stunned by the fall, and for a moment I feared I had broken my leg, or at the very least sprained something. But after a few seconds, I picked myself up from the floor, and all parts of my body seemed to be in working order.

I felt a little sense of relief to be able to walk again, though it was still pitch black all around me. I was just beginning to grope around for a means of exiting the basement, and hopefully the house, when I heard the sound I most feared. A car was pulling up outside the house.

3. HITCHES

I looked around quickly for an escape from the cellar, not easy to find in the nearly total darkness. I guessed it was morning now, so the lack of any light suggested there were no windows. I seemed to be at one end of the basement, and working my way forward, I found a set of stairs that presumably led up to the main part of the house. That was the last place I wanted to be now, but I realized in a flash that it was my only desperate hope. If I had escaped the house, one of the doors or windows to the outside would be unlocked. But they were surely all locked, so my captors would quickly realize that I was still in here somewhere. With my heart in my mouth, I stumbled as quickly as I could up the darkened stairs and tried the door.

It was locked. Now my hopes really sank. I was trapped. Now they would know for sure I was still in the cellar. Sheerly from my instinct for survival, not any rational plan, I looked around wildly for some place, any place to hide. The obvious place would have been among the stacks of boxes. But they would find me there eventually, and have me trapped.

I felt safest near the door. Right beside me at the top of the stairs there were several wooden storage cabinets. They weren't quite large enough to conceal me completely, but I could squeeze into one far enough to close the door partly. In the dark, I guessed no one would notice that the door was partly ajar, or think anything of it if he did.

Just before I settled in, though, I thought to grope around in the dark for the light switch. Flicking it on for the briefest of moments, I located a light bulb that I could just reach by standing halfway down the stairs and leaning out over the remaining ones. In the dark, I gave the bulb a few quick twists to disconnect it.

A few moments later, I heard the door to the house open, followed by footsteps. Acutely sensitive to sounds because of the darkness and my terror, I detected only a single person, which made me feel a little better. I heard him move about the house for a couple of minutes, then all too soon he approached the cellar door and unlocked it. It let in enough light from the rest of the house for me to confirm a single figure. As I expected, his hand moved immediately to the light switch. He cursed when the light failed to turn on, and took a few tentative steps down the stairs to check the light bulb.

In one move, I burst out of the cabinet and gave him a shove. He toppled down the stairs with a yell. I quickly stepped into the main room above, and shut the door. For a terrifying second or two, my wildly trembling fingers didn't know how to lock it, but then I saw the bolt and turned it.

The guy in the basement, of course, continued to curse in a loud voice, and irrationally, though understandably, soon began to pound on the door and demand that I open it and let him out. I turned and ran towards the front of the house, which I could just make out in the early morning light. I burst outside. I now saw that the house was in a woods, surrounded on all sides by trees. Quickly peering through the foliage in all directions, I could not see any other houses, no sign at all of other inhabitants. A dirt road led up to the house, and the car the man had arrived in was parked on it, near the house. I glanced at it only long enough to confirm that it was unoccupied, then took off down the dirt road.

I didn't run in an all-out sprint, because I had no idea how far I would have to travel before finding another house, a main road, or some other place where there were other people. But I pushed myself at a brisk pace. The guy I had locked in the cellar must have seen the hole in the floor of the room above I had made, and thus knew he could get out of the cellar the same way I got in. Since he would have unlocked the bedroom door, his path of exit was clear.

As it turned out, he got out a lot faster than I would have believed was possible. I had been doing my fast jog down the road for less than five minutes, when to my fear and surprise, I heard a car in the distance, coming from the direction of the house. Instinctively I turned off the road and dove behind the first cover I came upon, a fallen tree about fifty feet off into the forest. Seconds later, the car that had been parked by the house roared by.

As it passed, I peeked out carefully through some branches on the fallen tree. I couldn't be certain at that distance, but I thought I saw two passengers in the car. That gave me a little jolt. It would explain how the man got out of the basement so quickly. His accomplice unlocked the door. But where had the other man been, why hadn't he seen me, and why hadn't the man in the basement immediately called to him for help?

I had no answers to these questions, and no time to mull them over further. As soon as the car was out of sight, I got up and retreated further into the woods. I dared not stay on the road now, but at the same time I was afraid if I didn't keep fairly close to it I would get lost. I still had no idea where I was, how many unbroken square miles of trees might extend beyond this dirt road.

When I was well back in the forest, I stopped and sat down on a small rock for several moments, to catch my breath and to think about my situation. The men in the car knew how much of a head start I had. If they didn't find me on the road ahead of them soon, they would know I had to be in the woods somewhere. At that point, they would probably park the car, and begin to comb the woods on foot, one man on either side of the road. I didn't know how far into the woods they would search, but it would be difficult for me to follow the road without staying fairly close to it.

As my breathing and heart rate returned to normal levels, I felt the peace of the early morning woods. I could hear small birds chirping in the canopy high above, and a squirrel or some mammal rustling in the leaves of the forest floor. It seemed bizarre to be in such a beautiful place, yet terrified, running like a hunted animal.

What to do? My instinct was to keep moving deeper into the forest putting as much distance between these men and myself as I could. But they probably knew this area intimately, whereas I would have no idea where I was going. Once I got really lost, all bets were off.

But what other options did I have? I could stay put. Find a hiding place and outwait them. Eventually they would call off the search, and I could continue on, maybe under the cover of darkness. But I was hungry and my throat parched, and where in this woods could I safely hide?

With desperation comes boldness. Where in the woods were they least likely to look for me? On the road itself. They would assume I would want to stay far from the road, at least as far as I could without losing touch with it. So I would do the opposite. I would return to the road and continue down it towards the highway.

Walking slowly and carefully, as quietly as I could manage on the dry forest floor, I made my way back down to the edge of the road. With my heart in my mouth, I started down it, towards where I had last seen the car. I wasn't sure whether to run, which would be noisier and more noticeable from deep in the woods, or walk, which would increase the length of time of my exposure to the men off the road. I ended up walking very fast.

My worst moment came when I rounded a bend in the road and saw the car directly ahead, parked on the side of the road. It was everything I could do not to turn around and immediately run down the road in the other direction. But I could not see the men anywhere, either in the car, on the road, or in woods nearby. I continued fast walking till I was within about fifty feet of the vehicle, then no longer being able to stand it, broke into a run.

I was just bursting past the parked car, when I almost stepped on a good-sized snake that was writhing in the middle of the road. I should have ignored it, but I couldn't help noticing that part of its body had been crushed. Apparently the car had run over it, and the snake had managed to crawl a little ways beyond it. I actually skidded to a stop, picked up the snake, and carried it hurriedly over to the side of the road, where at least it would be safe from any more traffic that might come by.

What an idiot, I am, I thought. I slaughter mice in the lab, but help a snake that probably won't make it, anyway. I turned and fled.

The road continued for about another mile, then to my intense relief, ended in a paved road, what passed for a highway in this area. But I quickly realized that figuratively if not literally, I was not yet out of the woods. No cars were visible at that moment, from either direction. If I waited on the side of the road for one to come, I risked being seen by my assailants, who would eventually give up searching the woods and drive out to the highway. Though I didn't think they had seen me rush past their car, I couldn't be certain of that.

So I withdrew back into cover, into the woods that bordered the far side of the paved road. From my position there, I could watch the intersection of the unpaved road. As I waited, a few cars came down the paved road, but to flag one down I would have had to rush out of the woods very quickly, and I doubted a driver would stop for someone in those circumstances.

I had to wait for almost an hour, but finally the car with the two men emerged from the dirt road, made a left turn, and drove out of sight down the paved road. Breathing a sigh of relief, I walked out of the woods to the side of the road. I had finally thought to get the license number of the car, which in my panic to escape I had neglected to do earlier, but it was too far away for me to see. However, as the car turned onto the highway, one of the men tossed a small item out the window. Going over to examine it, I discovered it was a small paper bag, stuffed with tissues and other waste. Thinking it might have fingerprints, I carefully collected it, picking it up with a small stick. Having nothing else to wrap it in, I enclosed it in a large leaf, and stuffed the leaf into my pocket.

Taking my bearings from the sun, I guessed the men had gone south, and though I hated to follow in the same direction, that was where home lay. So I stuck out my thumb, and about fifteen minutes later, a driver stopped for me.

He was an older man who said he was going about fifty miles. I wanted to tell him what had happened to me, but decided against it. Would he believe me? I looked a little dirty and unkempt, more like a bum than a scientist, and now that I was safe and sound, sitting in the ordinary seat of an ordinary car, what had just happened seemed improbable even to me. I could have asked him to take me to the police, but what were they going to do at this point? All they could do was record my story and look for the car. I just wanted to go home. Which, I learned, was about two hundred miles away.

We traveled for about forty-five minutes before stopping at a small gas station, the first one I had seen along that road. As we pulled up to the pump, I gagged. There was the car that belonged to the two men! At least it looked like the same car—a red Toyota

Corolla, which at least superficially appeared to be about the same year and condition.

The driver of my car got out, filled up the tank, then went into the little store to pay for the gas. I sat there nervously, scanning the premises for the two men. I saw no one, and guessed they were inside, too.

A few minutes later, the driver of my car returned, and told me he was turning off about a mile down the road.

"I think your best bet is to stay right here, try to catch a ride with someone stopping for gas," he said. "There are a couple of guys in the store who might take you. I heard them asking about some friend of theirs who was hitching in this area."

At those words, I immediately turned my head away from the store, and shrunk down into the seat. All I wanted to do was to get away as quickly as possible. I mumbled something about staying with the driver down to the turnoff, preferring to hitchhike there.

"Suit yourself," he said, starting the car and pulling back onto the road. As we drove on, I turned around to look back, and my heart sank. The other car was following us!

What should I do? I wondered. I could explain my situation to the driver, but wouldn't he wonder why I hadn't said something sooner? And what could he do at this point, anyway? I could ask him to let me come into his house and call the police, but why should he trust the word of some dirty, strange hitch-hiker? And what could the police do, anyway? I had no real evidence against these men, I didn't even know what they looked like.

The driver turned on his right turn signal. "Here's where I turn off," he said. I had to make a decision quickly, and every second that I hesitated, my options narrowed.

"Uhhh...can you just take me down this road a little ways, I want to rest away from the main road for a while."

"OK."

We turned onto another paved road, one going through farmland. I turned to look, and sure enough, the other car turned to follow us. It was about half a mile behind us.

Now I felt trapped. If I asked the driver to take me into his house, and he refused, I was at the mercy of these men, alone out in this country with houses far and few between. We made another right turn. There was a field on the right with some kind of high grass growing in it, bordered by some trees and bushes, so when we turned, we were temporarily out of sight of the following car.

"I'll get out here, thanks" I said quickly, and was out of the car almost before it came to a full stop. I immediately got behind one of the trees, and as soon as the car started to drive away, I rushed into the field and flattened myself in the grass.

A couple of minutes later, I watched from the cover of the field as the other car came to the intersection, and turned right, still following the car I had been in. What to do now? I couldn't stay put. They would follow the other car to the house, which was probably quite nearby, and would see only one person get out of the car. They would quickly realize when and where I had gotten out.

The obvious thing for me to do was to make my way back to the highway, but I couldn't follow the road I had just come down. On the other side of that road was an open, plowed field, bordered at its far side by more bushes and trees that seemed to provide the only cover all the way back to the highway. I sprinted out of the field I was in, across the road, and into the plowed field. Only as my shoes sunk deep into the loose brown soil did I realize I was creating a trail nearly as obvious as one in freshly fallen snow.

I looked around frantically. There was an irrigation pipe further out in the field. If I could get to that without making tracks, I thought. Walking backward, I retraced the several steps I had made into the field, acutely aware that my pursuers would be returning any moment, and I would be a sitting duck out in this field. When I reached the first step I had made in the field, I carefully brushed dirt into it to cover it up, then I started walking forward again, one careful step at a time, stopping to cover each track.

When I got to the irrigation pipe, I stepped on it. It was very narrow, less than two inches in diameter, and I knew I couldn't walk very far on it without falling off. Particularly when I was shaking like a leaf from fear that the men were on their way back. But I knew I didn't have to. I just ran down the pipe as far as I could before losing my balance, about ten feet. I was now well out in the plowed field. I didn't think my tracks would be visible from the road. So I headed across the field in a diagonal, angling towards the highway, but making sure I got out of the bare plowed field and into cover quickly.

Flopping down on my stomach behind some bushes, I looked back where I had come from. Sure enough, a few minutes later the car returned and stopped at the intersection. One of the men got out and started making his way into the grassy field. I realized with a wince that if he had any hunting skills at all, he would be able to tell from the flattened grass not only that I had been there, but where I had exited the field onto the road.

Meanwhile, the other man, still in the car, turned it around and followed the road leading from the highway in the other direction, driving off a ways, then turning around, coming back to the intersection, then turning onto the only one of the four roads meeting at this point that he hadn't been down. Finally, he returned to the intersection. The other man was by that time out of the grassy field and waiting for him. My heart temporarily stopped as I saw him searching carefully along the edge of the plowed field, but I had done my job carefully enough. He didn't find any indication that I had entered the field.

I remained where I was, watching the car as it drove back up to the highway. It moved very slowly, I could easily visualize the two men scanning the fields on both sides looking for me. They knew I had to be very close by, there simply wasn't time for me to have gotten very far on foot. What would they do? Searching the entire area on foot was too difficult. They would wait up at the highway, knowing I had to return there if I was going to get home.

Again I decided to move towards, not away, from them. Staying as much under cover as I could, I made my way through the fields towards the highway. I had to climb over a couple of fences, but otherwise it was fairly easy going in the mostly open country. I was uncomfortably exposed at places, but I couldn't see any sign of the car, and guessed I had not been seen.

When I reached the highway, I was about half a mile further on from where the driver who picked me up had turned off. I hid in some bushes about a hundred feet from the road, praying that my assailants would not decide to comb this area looking for me. I knew I was now very vulnerable. I could have proceeded on foot, following the highway at a safe distance, but I didn't see much point to that. I couldn't walk all the way back to Minneapolis. After all the running I had done that day, I wasn't sure I could walk to the next town.

So I stayed put, hoping that my captors would show themselves. And soon they did. To my surprise, they came from the opposite direction, from further south. So they had driven down in that direction, hoping to find me on the road hitchhiking, and were now heading back the other way. Maybe, I thought, they thought I had returned to the gas station.

As soon as the car was out of sight, I emerged from cover and walked to the side of the road. The traffic was a little heavier here, and I thought I could probably catch a ride sooner. Sure enough, about five minutes later, a small pickup truck pulled up alongside me.

I'm not sure what made me hesitate. I was very tired from all the running I had done that day, and wanted to get as far from my pursuers as I could. But something told me not to get in the truck. Maybe it was the fact that this vehicle, too, contained two men. Maybe it was that they both were wearing sunglasses and had baseball caps pulled down over their faces, so it was hard to see them. Maybe it was because one of the men, in the passenger seat, was starting to open the door even before the truck stopped.

So I froze. I stood there right next to the truck, and without fully understanding why, turned my face partly away from them. The man in the passenger seat rolled down the window and said, rather rudely, I thought, "Come on! You want a ride or not!?"

It could have been my understandably overactive imagination, but I thought he started to reach out the window to grab my arm. I instantly stepped back from the truck. At that moment, very fortuitously, a sheriff 's car appeared on the horizon, fast approaching the car from behind. I waved madly in its direction.

The pickup instantly pulled away from the side of the road and drove on.

As it turned out, the sheriff was chasing a speeder, and either did not see me, or felt he could not stop to investigate. At that point, I was more nervous than ever, wondering if I had over-reacted when the two men had tried to pick me up. Happily, I managed to get a ride a few minutes later with a farmer type in another pickup truck. He only took me a few miles into the next town, but I felt much safer there. I thought of stopping at the local police station, but I really wanted to get home.

I caught another ride, which took me another fifty miles or so. This ride went without incident, and I used the idle time to think about the two men in the pickup. They had definitely wanted me to get in with them, I thought. But what else was it about them that had raised a red flag?

Then it hit me. I had seen the pickup before. While I was waiting for my original pursuers to come out onto the highway, at the point where that side road led to the house where I had been held, a pickup had turned off the highway and gone towards the house. Hadn't it?

Jesus, I thought, who were these other guys? How many people are after me, anyway? And why?

4. PATENTLY OBVIOUS

T he first person I encountered when I returned to the lab the next day was Laurie Gudefrut, one of the new grad students. Like me, she almost always came in early, by seven AM or sooner. In fact, there was a little friendly competition between us on that score, though I usually worked far later than she did.

"Where were you yesterday?" she asked curiously. It was virtually unthinkable for me not to show up at the lab every day.

I looked at her wearily.

"You aren't going to believe this..." I began. I just gave her the bare bones of the story, realizing as I did so that she was the first person I had talked to about it. I told her I had been abducted, locked in house in the northern part of the state, escaped, and managed to hitchhike back to Minneapolis.

She listened with horror.

"My God, Alan! Have you contacted the police?"

"Er..no," I said. "I guess I should do that right now."

"Definitely."

My desk, like that of all the other graduate students and postdocs, was in a cubicle, one of more than a dozen little boxes in a large room adjacent to the lab. As I entered the room, I felt myself growing calmer, more relaxed. This was my real home. Over the past four years, I had spent far more time here, or at my lab bench, than I had in my apartment. I felt very safe in this environment, really much safer than in my apartment. Events in the outside world could not touch me here.

So I thought. Yet as soon as I saw my desk, this growing peace was cut short. Instantly, I felt a sense of unease, though I couldn't for the life of me identify its source. I looked around my desk. Something was changed about it. While I could not put my finger on it, I felt positive that it was not exactly as I had left it two nights earlier.

I instantly went to my notebooks, and all the precious information in them. Most of them were locked in a drawer of my desk, but I had left one, containing my current experimental log, in plain view on my desk. It was still there, and still open to the same page it had been when I left. Picking it up, I riffled through the pages. Nothing missing that I could tell. Likewise with the grant proposal I had been working on the night of the kidnapping. It was right there on my desk where I had left it.

I was puzzled, but there was no time to worry about that now. Picking up my phone, I called the campus police, and briefly explained what had happened to me. The person who answered there told me to come down and file a report in person.

I sighed. I really, really, really wanted to go to work immediately. I hate to miss any time in the lab, and right then I felt an especially strong need to keep busy, as a way of blotting out both my memories and my fears associated with being kidnapped. But of course, I needed those fresh memories to make the best report possible. The longer I put of going to the station, the more those memories would fade.

The campus police office was about a ten minute bike ride from the research building. When I arrived, I locked my bike, and went inside. I walked up to the front desk, and having no idea at all about the procedure involved, began to describe everything that had happened to me to the officer on duty. She quickly cut me off and handed me a form to fill out.

I sat down and spent quite a bit of time on it, mentioning absolutely every detail I could think of, down to the size of the nail I had used to pry loose those floorboards, the size and approximate number of the boxes in the basement, my best estimate of the distance I had gone into the forest after the car had passed by, and the number of tracks I had made and then covered in that plowed field. When I finally finished, I handed the officer the report. She glanced at it briefly, I guess for the first time appreciating that I had actually been kidnapped. She told me I would be interviewed by another officer. That couldn't happen just then, but she made an appointment for later that day. So I gratefully returned to the lab.

I didn't go directly back to my desk, but went to see Mitch Simon, head of the lab and my mentor. He wasn't in his office at the moment I walked in, but Dick Johnstone was, who popped in and out of there so often that we joked that it was his second office. Dick was the Chief Financial Officer, in charge of budgets for not only our research group, but for the half dozen or so other laboratory complexes in our building. I had been seeing quite a bit of him recently, because I was in the process of writing a grant proposal, and I frequently needed his help in estimating projected costs for equipment, laboratory supplies, and so on. The deadline for filing the grant was the end of July, less than two months away, and I needed to finish it a couple of weeks before that, so that it had time to go through various administrative reviews at the University.

"Alan!" he cried upon seeing me. "I just heard a little while ago! My god, my lovely man, is it really true? You were kidnapped the other night? Right here on campus?"

I nodded weakly, and repeated to him a few of the details. Waking up to find myself tied up and locked in a room. Breaking out of the house. Avoiding cars.

He looked me over carefully. His figure was the soft, pudgy kind of people who don't exercise enough, but one hardly noticed it. He was unofficially but almost certainly unanimously considered the best dresser in the group. Marissa Cheng, the gorgeous third year graduate student who I had tried so hard and so unsuccessfully to get to go out with me, frequently complimented him on his clothes. But that didn't bother me, because Dick's interests clearly lay elsewhere.

"Well, I take it they didn't beat you up, thank God for that. But how did you get away? Did you smash down the door or something?"

I told him a few more details. He listened with growing astonishment.

"That is absolutely incredible," he marveled. "I never knew you had it in you, lover boy. I never knew anyone had it in them to do *that.* You're a real hero. You're *my* hero!"

"Thanks, Dick." I didn't feel like a hero. I hadn't saved anyone's skin but my own. I felt like a hero in the lab sometimes, but I saw nothing heroic about not wanting to stay in a locked room and wait for a couple of goons to do who knew what to me.

"Where's Mitch?"

"He'll be back in a jiff."

Dick had been going through the pages of another grant on Mitch's desk, no doubt checking over the budgetary details. But he seemed far more interested in me at the moment.

"You know, lover boy, if I had an absolutely horrific experience like that happen to me, I wouldn't come right back to the lab. I'd take a couple of days off. Go home, get some R&R. You deserve it, poor guy."

I grinned wryly at him. "Actually, I came back just to finish my grant."

Dick, usually the master of pleasantries, couldn't suppress a brief scowl, though he recovered quickly. It was supposed to be a joke. I wanted to learn how to estimate the grant budget accurately, because I expected some day I would be running my own lab. So I frequently asked him for old invoices, so I could compare the budget estimates of previous grants with the actual expenses incurred. Dick would invariably plead with me to let him take care of it, insisting that as a star researcher, I had better things to do with my time.

"Why would anyone do this, lover? What's your theory?"

I was about to reply when Candy Rominger walked in. Like Dick, Candy helped with the preparation of grants. Her job was to make sure all the required sections were filled out and in the right format. When everything was complete, she would print out the final thirty or whatever number of copies always seemed necessary when dealing with the government--each copy nearly one hundred pages long--and ship them off to various places.

"Hi, Can-Can," said Dick. "Our hero is back, and he won't leave these stuffy grants to us. I told him to go get some R&R, but you know our Alan, he never saw work he didn't like."

Candy was a short, energetic woman with a page boy hair cut and a very athletic body who at forty could still turn the heads of many men under twenty-five. I felt a strong affinity towards her, though I had never really understood why, given our differences in views. Despite being an integral part of a high-powered scientific laboratory, Candy's approach to cancer was, to put it as charitably as possible, naive. Eat lots of vitamins, and pray. Literally. She took great delight in finding scientific studies of prayer that she found on the internet, the occasional article that it said it improved someone's health or increased the growth of cells in a Petri dish. "See, Alan, see?" she would exclaim, slapping it down on my desk. "It says the effect was statistically significant. Prayer works! They think it changes the alignment of the water molecules in our cells."

Now, though, she rushed right up to me, her face flooded with sympathy

"Alan, Laurie told me about it a few minutes ago. That's all people are talking about in the lab. This is unbelievable! Why on earth would anyone want to kidnap you? Do you have any idea what this is all about?"

Dick leaned towards me conspiratorially. "Could this be the work of animal rights protesters?" he whispered out loud.

This seemed to me to be a clear shot at Candy, whose sympathies with the movement were fairly well known. Once when they had a demonstration in front of one of the other research buildings at the university, I saw her there, passing out leaflets.

"But I don't even work on animals right now," I protested. "I haven't done any work on mice in almost a year."

"Those morons wouldn't know that—or even care, for that matter."

"Could it have been a case of mistaken identity?" said Candy, ignoring not just Dick's question, but his very presence. "Maybe someone thought you were a—oh, I don't know—some drug dealer who owed money to someone?"

"Oooo," said Dick. "That I likey. I mean, it's horrible, but it's just about the only possible explanation there is, isn't it, Can-Can? I mean, why would anyone want to harm a single brown hair on the head of our dear Alan? Why, why, why?"

As Dick let that question dangle in the air for a while, I thought over Candy's suggestion. "I suppose it's possible," I said finally. "But you wouldn't expect to find someone like that right here on campus, would you? A member of some gang?"

"Where did it actually happen?" asked Dick.

"I'm not really sure. I was on my way home, when boom!"

"Have you reported this to the police?" Candy asked.

"Yeah, just got back from there. I guess I'll be going over the details with some officer later today."

"Good." She gave my shoulder a squeeze. "But if I were you, Alan, I would buy a little can of pepper spray, or something like that. In case it wasn't mistaken identity." She thought a moment about that, then gave a little shiver. "Or in case it was, for that matter."

I wondered which was worse.

Mitch came rambling in a few minutes later, and soon we shared his office alone. He hadn't heard about the kidnapping, so I had to repeat my story.

"Jesus Christ! Are you *serious*!? But why...?"

I hadn't even given him a chance to sit down, and he stood there next to his desk, still holding a valise that I knew was stuffed with articles he was reading. He looked like Ichabod Crane, all arms and legs, each of which seemed to point in a different direction. He had curly, steel-gray hair that had receded almost half way to the back of his head, and glasses that were forever perched on the end of his nose, because he could never get around to buying bifocals. He quivered with energy. Even standing still, he managed to move more than most people would have pacing around the office.

"The patent?" I said tentatively. "Could that possibly be what this is all about?"

Earlier, Mitch and I had applied for a provisional patent, based

26

on my three genes and some others as biomarkers for colon cancer. We had very little evidence for them at the time, most of it coming from work with laboratory mice and cell cultures, and the provisional patent in effect gave us one year to accumulate enough supporting data in humans to file a full patent. The experiment I had completed the night of the kidnapping had been critical to these efforts.

Once we filed the full, regular patent, we would have exclusive rights to develop and market a test for colon cancer based on these three genes. We had already founded a startup company for this purpose. In the meantime, though, we couldn't release the identity of these genes into the public domain, or we would lose the right to patent them. We couldn't publish an article naming them, for example, or give a seminar open to anyone outside of our research group in which these genes were discussed.

Mitch said nothing in response, but finally lowered himself carefully into his chair, as if trying it out for the first time, all the while not taking his eyes off me.

"I mean, why else would anyone kidnap me?" I said helplessly. "It's not like I'm a millionaire, and worth a major ransom." Though I might be in a few years, I thought.

"Well, sure," he said finally, "but *kidnapping*? You said they just left you there tied up. You think someone was going to come back later and demand that you name these biomarkers? *Yikes!*"

Mitch opened his little case and extracted the papers. Several of them were folded back, to where he had currently read. Even now, he couldn't seem to resist glancing at one, as if resuming where he had left off.

"Suppose you did reveal that information to someone," he continued. "Who—let's say--relayed it to some researcher who had hired the kidnapper. How's he going to make use of it? Is he going to announce out of the blue that he discovered these genes on his own?"

I appreciated that Mitch had more on his mind these days than just research, as if that weren't enough. He was going through a difficult divorce. Often when I popped into his office he was on the phone with his lawyer, clearly uncomfortable, almost apologetic, about this interruption of our time. I was wondering now if he were too preoccupied with the divorce to be thinking clearly.

"Why not? Of course it wouldn't be difficult to provide experimental data in support of them. Once you know what they are, it's the easiest thing in the world to do RT-PCR. If someone asked you why you happened to pick those genes, you could whip up some microarray. Hell, you could fudge those data, no one would ever know the difference."

"But if you reported that you had named these genes under duress—"

"What if I never returned to tell anyone that?" I replied, shuddering a little at this new possibility that had not occurred to me before. Maybe they had intended to kill me, after all, but only after I had provided the information to someone knowledgeable enough to understand and use it. Maybe the guy who had entered the house when I was trying to escape had returned for just that purpose. Maybe..."Or even if I was allowed to return, how would I prove that I had been forced to talk? It would be my word against someone else's."

Mitch nodded slowly. "I suppose you're right. Wow..."

An embarrassing silence followed, as neither of us knew what else to say. I looked around the office. In addition to the usual photocopied articles and opened journals strewn around his desk, there were books lying around, on the otherwise empty chairs surrounding his desk, stacked up in a couple of short but already unbalanced piles on the floor, and even on the sill of his one window, which looked out into a courtyard. He had lots of shelf space, they lined two plus walls of the room, extending from knee level to the point where you had to stretch to reach, and many of the shelves were also filled with books.

But he had signs of his other life there, too. Some framed pictures of his kids—I wondered how they were weathering the divorce proceedings—a collection of figurines he had picked up while at some conference in Japan, and a very interesting scale model of a crew shell, complete with all the oars, splayed out on one side so that they dipped over the edge of the shelf. From a distance, it looked like some kind of gigantic insect from a science fiction film. He had rowed in college, one of the Ivy schools, I thought, and though he now preferred a canoe, was often seen on weekends out on one of the city's many lakes.

Finally Mitch noticed the printout in my hand.

"What you got?"

I didn't need any persuading to change the subject. The shock and the horror of the kidnapping had completely blotted out the ecstasy I had felt that night in the lab, but now that I was back in the safe confines of the research building, the significance of what I had discovered returned to me. Though I had not yet had time to analyze the results, I knew that Mitch, like me, could easily see the significance of the numbers. I handed the printout to him across his desk. For a few precious minutes, the kidnapping receded in my mind, like a bad dream.

"Uh-*huh!*" he said, peering over the tops of his glasses at the data. "CRNG-2 is really impressive. Five hundred-fold greater expression in patients with large adenomas."

"And look at these other two genes," I said, reaching across the desk to point out something on the sheet, "their upregulation correlates very closely with CNRG-2, even though they're not as high. All three rise in patients with polyps, then rise further in patients with cancer. I think there's a correlation with the stage of cancer, too, though we don't have enough samples for significance."

"Mm-huh, mm-huh."

We talked for a few more minutes. I excitedly told Mitch my theory about how these three genes interacted in the carcinogenic pathway, grabbing one of his articles and hastily scrawling a diagram on the back. I still had to do a formal analysis of the data, but Mitch agreed with me that we were ready to conduct a much larger trial of these genes, funded by the startup company the two of us had founded.

Twenty minutes later, as we were finishing our discussion, I felt much better. My life was returning to normal. I was getting up to leave when it occurred to me that my latest results were the solution to my other problem as well.

"Mitch, let's say this kidnapping really was an attempt to steal information about these three genes. All we have to do is file for the full patent. Once we do that, we no longer have to hide their identity. That information won't be worth anything to anyone else any more." I took the printout from him. "With these results, there's no reason to wait any longer on the patent, is there?"

But Mitch, to my surprise, shook his head.

"We're not quite ready to do that."

I brandished the printout in the air.

"With *these* data? What more can they want?"

But Mitch brushed me off.

"Let's just get ready for the big study. We can do that now."

I knew I was definitely right about one thing. There were many scientists out there who would have given a lot to know the identity of these three genes. One of them, in fact, worked in another lab located in the same research building we were in. Dr. Alessandro Pignatti, or Alex, as he was comfortable being called, was interested in many of the same cancers we were, and desperately wanted to develop his own screening test for colon cancer. Though that was off the table, other cancers, where neither of us was close to developing a test, were a different story. Beginning about a year before, with Mitch's encouragement, Alex and I had been meeting periodically, to explore possible areas of "fruitful collaboration" between our laboratories.

Our most recent meeting had been a few weeks earlier, outside in one of the courtyards between buildings. May is the most beautiful month in Minneapolis—the only one in which most days are neither too hot nor too cold-- but that was not the main reason we met where we did. Neither of us really felt comfortable, or appreciated, wandering around in the corridors of the other's labs. We needed neutral territory. Oh, and Alex wanted to smoke.

You wouldn't think anyone who knew the first thing about cancer, let alone someone who knew more about the disease than all but perhaps a few hundred other souls on the planet, would get near a cigarette. But smoking, of course, doesn't simply cause disease; it is a disease. Alex had it, and I felt a little sorry for him.

He was waiting for me when I arrived, and he held up one hand in a brief wave, then took a final puff and crushed the cigarette out. He was sitting on one of those little stone walls that rims a raised disc of earth planted with flowers and a small tree. They dotted the courtyard. I sat down next to him.

"Alan, how are you? So good to see you again."

Alex was a skinny, curly-haired kid from Venice, with a broad, flattish face, and the soft eyes of a deer. The kind of man that women all thought they wanted to mother, until they discovered, too late, that they were hooked. Actually, he was much older, and in most respects further along, than I was. He was in his early thirties, and had a solid, if so far unspectacular, record of publications. Despite the background to our meetings—we were like representatives from the Montagues and the Capulets--I liked him. Mostly, I guessed, because he acted as though he liked me. Though he played with my mind like it was some musical instrument, I always left these meetings feeling he was a friend. I had to admit that the music he made was, well, artful.

As always, he began by asking me how my work was going. If anyone else had asked that question, I would have taken as a sign of politeness, like, how's your family? In Alex's case, it was a way of setting me up for what I always knew was coming next.

"But Alan," he began his futile pitch, sounding almost mournful as he spread his hands apart, "surely you can tell me the names of at least one of these genes. We might already be studying it ourselves. How can we know if you won't give us a name?"

"You know I can't do that," I replied.

"Are any of them kinases?"

"I honestly don't know." I had gradually come to realize that I had two stock answers to most of Alex's questions, "I don't know" and "I honestly don't know". I wondered if he had noticed this, too.

"What chromosome are they on?"

31

Jesus, I thought, what kind of question is that? The answer to it doesn't tell you anything about what the gene does. It just eliminates about 98% of the possibilities. Moving you from a situation where you are searching for a needle in a haystack to one where the needle is in a few bales of hay. And of course, I noticed that he used the singular of the word "chromosome". He was fishing, hoping I would at least admit they were all on the same chromosome, without his actually asking that question directly.

"I don't know."

"Where in the colon are the gene products located?"

"I don't know."

"Are they down-regulated under any conditions at all?"

"I don't know."

"Are they upregulated in any other cancers?"

"I honestly don't know."

I knew Alex would tire of this game eventually, and we could get down to business, namely, a joint project to look for gene markers of small cell lung cancer. Neither of our labs had entered this area yet, so we had no data to hide from each other. Of course, my three precious secrets might possibly play a starring role in this cancer, too. I rather doubted this, but we could cross that bridge if and when it became necessary.

Then, out of the blue, he threw me a curveball. He did something I never in a hundred million years would have guessed he would do. It was, for anyone in his position, an audacious move, showing his cards—literally and figuratively—in a way that carried huge risks but also huge rewards. Only much later on, thinking it over, did I realize how much of the risk was based on his judgment of my character.

"Are these the three genes?"

The card he held up was not the Ace of Diamonds—but it was no three of spades, either. It showed the names and accession numbers of three genes. Every human gene is listed in an immense database, which includes its name, its DNA sequence, the tissues it has been isolated from, and other information. The accession

32

number is a tag for the gene, rather like the license plate of a car or the library of congress number for a book.

Bingo! One of my three crown jewels was on that list. Instantaneously, my head exploded into conflict. Did I just answer yes, and refuse to say anything more? Did I say no, and tell a lie — something I had never done in my academic and professional career? Did I say no comment, which would surely be taken as yes? As the alternatives raced through my mind, I was acutely aware of the need to answer quickly. Any hesitation would be taken as a positive response.

"Mmmm...not really," I said.

I rationalized that this was not technically a lie. The gene in question was a variant of one of mine. It had a very slightly different DNA sequence, and a different accession number.

But any scientist would have said they were the same gene. If Alex followed up on this gene, which he might, he would eventually learn that I had lied to him. If he didn't follow up on it, because of what I had said, I was to blame. Wasn't I?

I did some quick thinking. Even if he did follow up on this gene, he was unlikely to beat us to the patent on it. Unless he had already begun the process. I had no way of knowing how much data he had on that gene. But he couldn't know everything I knew about it, or he wouldn't have felt the need to reveal it.

But there was more to it than that. I was in a state of shock, and when my intellect finally began recovering from the shock, I realized why. Alex had taken a big risk here. These three genes, including the two on his list that were new to me, were now out in the public domain of my laboratory. If I wanted to go back to my bench and study them, the two others that I hadn't known about, see if they could improve my colon cancer screening process any further, he couldn't stop me. He had, in effect, offered his jugular to me. Was I going to finish him off?

"What do you know about these genes?" I began tentatively. "Are they all strongly correlated with colon cancer?" As I asked this question, I tried to study Alex's features, to read between the lines. Not easy for me to do, because like most scientists, the lines were generally all I was ever aware of. As soon as someone opens his mouth, and something intelligent comes out of it, I generally become oblivious to all sensory and emotional data. Unless it was Marissa Cheng, of course.

It was Alex's turn to be cagey. "There are suggestions," he said carefully. "We still have more tests to do."

I took the plunge.

"I think you should follow up on these genes, all three of them," I said, emphasizing the last three words. "I definitely think you should."

There was light in Alex's eyes now. I might just as well have said, one of those three is identical to one of mine. He would pretty well guess that it was only one of them. No one would be idiotic enough to give away all three. If that list had contained all three, I would have lied like a son of a bitch, and damn the consequences to my conscience or any personal relationships. Indeed, if I had not lied under those circumstances, I could imagine Mitch, if he ever found out, dropping me from the patent and our startup company. He would have justifiably seen it as a betrayal.

I felt good inside, a warm and fuzzy feeling. Except that the warmth and fuzziness were slowly sinking into my gut. What had I just done? Mitch would have been furious at me if he had known.

Oh, well, I thought, Alex still doesn't have the other two, including the really important one. And hey, I had two new genes to look at. I didn't have time for them now, but one of the other graduate students would. So what if I had just given away a first round draft choice? I got two minor league prospects in return. Not such a bad trade.

After that, we turned to a discussion over collaboration on small lung cell cancer, and it went absolutely swimmingly.

"Why don't we knock the genes out, Alan, and see what effect that has?"

"How about interference RNA?"

"Can't we use fluorescent antibodies to locate them?"

"How about correlating their levels in Min mice?"

"Shouldn't we consider the effects of overexpression of carcinogens?"

"What about the effects of COX2 inhibitors?"

As Andrea Davies and Laurie Godefrut peppered me with questions, research possibilities—some good, some bad, most not immediately technically feasible—I remembered what it had been like to be a first-year graduate student. At that point in our career, we think that anything is possible, that any question that can be asked can be answered. We still haven't lived through months and frustrating months of just trying to set up some system—establish a new cell line, develop a new antibody, construct a DNA vector— before we can even begin to run experiments with it. We haven't spent endless hours preparing reagents, filling tubes, running machines, just to see it all distilled down to a handful of numbers that weren't what we hoped for. We haven't yet learned that while the difference between a scientist and a technician is immense, you can't start at the top. Some of the world's best experimental scientists are klutzes in the lab, but they know that. They had to take the time and trouble to find that out, and they never forget where they came from.

Laurie had the edge on Andrea in that department. Andrea, tall, large-framed, a college basketball player of some accomplishment, had come to us directly after graduating. Laurie, small, slight of build, shy and bespectacled, had gone to work for a few years first. Not a bad idea, I thought. About my age, around twenty-four or twenty-five, she was not simply older and more mature, as if she were some apple that had ripened longer in the sun. She had worked as a technician for several years. She was as familiar with some of the procedures used in our laboratory as I was.

A lot was demanded of both, though. For starters, they had been entrusted with the identity of one of the my three jewels—the 24 carat diamond of the three, the gene that really made the difference, the one I now knew was most associated with colon cancer. They had to know this, since their job was to work with it, to learn more about it. Like me, like Mitch, like everyone else who knew its identity, they were expected to keep quiet about it.

"This doesn't leave the lab, OK?" Mitch emphasized the day he explained to them they would be working with me. "I don't want to sound paranoid, but there are other labs that would be very interested to know what this gene is, and we haven't filed a regular patent for it yet."

"Does that mean we have to keep our notebooks locked up?" asked Laurie, referring to the daily, written records that scientists are supposed to keep of all their experiments.

Mitch shrugged. "It wouldn't be a bad idea to do that, in any case. Of course, you can keep it open and on your desk during the day, when you're working. But when you go home at night, yeah, stick it in a locked drawer." He thought about this for a moment, glancing around unfamiliarly at the lab bench. He didn't come into the lab very often; spotting him there was like seeing a deer in your backyard. Or maybe a heron, which he resembled more closely. "Yeah, why not, why not."

During their first few months in our group, when they weren't taking classes, the two women tagged after me in the lab, two chicks following a mother hen. Andrea told me that she wanted to work for a biotech company after she got her doctorate, and she constantly asked me questions about our company, what it was like to be the discoverer of such a hot property. It was obvious she envied me, and hoped to make such a discovery herself.

"You must be so excited to have discovered these three genes. I mean, a test for colon cancer is a big deal."

"It's just one step," I said. "I don't want to just diagnose cancer, I want to cure it. Hopefully, if we know what these genes actually do, we can start manipulating them."

"Why can't we do that right now? If they cause cancer, knock them out!"

"It's not that simple. I wouldn't say they cause cancer; they're just part of the process. These genes are necessary to the normal growth of the cell. The problem is that at some point they go out of control."

"Sort of like you on the court, Drey," said Laurie. "You shoot too much, when you should be passing. We don't want to bench you, we just want you to be a better team player."

Andrea chuckled at this. "What goes on at those OS meetings?" she asked me, referring to the board of our start-up. "I mean, what do you talk about?"

Our startup was called Oncological Solutions, or OS for short. But since the main project on its agenda was the colon cancer test, which would involve analysis of stool samples, we sometimes referred to it as Oh, Shit! That would have also been an apt answer to Andrea's question, though I didn't say that.

"We're planning the next big study of the three genes," I replied. "Basically the same as the pilot study, but a larger group of subjects."

I was showing her how to prepare a sample for antibody staining. Actually, Laurie was showing her, while I sort of hovered in the background. Laurie seemed more the academic type, more interested in science for the sake of knowledge. Or maybe more interested in me. She liked to stand close to me, and looked me deep in the eyes whenever I was talking, which made me feel powerful but also a little uncomfortable. Definitely not my type.

But I liked her apparent indifference to the commercial side of science. And I felt a strong affinity towards her when she said she had no desire to spend several hours talking with a bunch of business types.

"Are all the other OS members on your patent?" asked Andrea.

I shook my head. "Oh, no, just Mitch and I."

"But they know what your three genes are, don't they?"

"Of course. They have to know, since they're vital to the test."

"So they all signed a non-disclosure—whoops!" Andrea spilled some reagent on the lab bench.

"Klutz!" laughed Laurie. "I thought you had such good hands on the court, Ace."

My appointment at the campus police station was for four o'clock that afternoon. I left the lab before 3:30. I have never been late for anything in my life, and I wasn't going to begin now. Shortly after I arrived, I was shown into a room where I was told to wait for the officer who would take my statement.

The room was bare but for a long table with a few chairs, not enough to go around. The floor was covered with gray, wall-to-wall carpeting, and the walls were painted off-white. Actually, I could have mistaken it for one of the mini-conference rooms in our laboratory suite, which made me feel a little more relaxed and at home. I could almost imagine I was giving a seminar, presenting some interesting new data.

The arrival of Officer Otis Burris, who was ten minutes late, quickly dispelled that feeling. A tall and sparingly built black man with glasses that gave him a naturally inquisitive air, he looked me over rather as though I were some new specimen in a zoo. Though I guessed he was only doing his job, I had somehow expected some sympathy for what had happened to me, and he didn't provide any. Though he was unfailingly polite and respectful to me, he acted as if he didn't necessarily believe without further evidence anything I said to him. This was an attitude I of course admired and expected in scientists. It was the last thing I needed now.

"Can you tell me exactly where this house was?" he asked when I had finished describing what had happened in as much detail as possible.

"Sort of," I replied. Not a great answer, but what was I supposed to say? There were lots of unpaved roads leading off from the highway in that area. Though I had spent over an hour at the intersection when I first emerged from that road, and could visualize it vividly in my mind, I didn't know exactly how far it was from any place else in the area. All I could do was give him a rough description of the place, and an equally rough estimate of its mileage from certain landmarks, like the gas station. I knew I could find it if I returned to that area, but I also knew that wild horses couldn't drag me back there. You could have put a Nobel Prize on the front porch, and I wouldn't have gone back to pick it up.

Burris consulted the notes he had been taking. Of course, the interview was taped as well.

"Did you get the license plate of the car?"

"No." Again, I kicked myself for forgetting to do something so obvious and so critical. But Jesus, I was running for my life, and didn't the bad guys always ditch the car later, anyway?

"Did you or did you not see them come out of the little mini-mart?"

"I saw the door open and I saw a figure begin to come out. But then I immediately turned my head away. I didn't want them to see me." Which they did, anyway, you idiot, I said to myself.

"About how far away were you from the man you saw get out of the car at that corner by the field?"

"More than two hundred yards." I had noticed he was wearing a red shirt or jacket, and that was about it. He was six feet tall, give or take six inches, and had any color hair any length. Truth be told, I wouldn't have sworn in court that it was a man and not a woman.

I was feeling increasingly frustrated and inadequate. I considered telling Burris about the second vehicle that had tried to pick me up, the pickup, but I couldn't say much about those men, either, and anyway, I had no real evidence they were connected to my kidnapping. Then I remembered the small bag of trash I had collected at the scene. When I had returned home the previous evening, I had transferred it to a small cellophane ziplock bag. Now I handed it to Burris, who looked at it speculatively.

"Hmmm," he said. "Worth a try."

He set it aside, consulted his notes in silence for several moments, then giving a grunt, raised his head again to look at me.

"Let's go over the period of time before you were kidnapped," he said. "You were working in the laboratory, you said. Who else was there?"

I named several people in our group I had seen at one time or another earlier in the evening, but emphasized that when I finally left the lab, I was the last one there. There could have been someone in the adjoining room, where our cubicles were located, I certainly didn't check, but that was unlikely at that hour.

"So you don't recall anything unusual, either then or possibly earlier in the day?"

I was about to shake my head when I remembered something. It hadn't seemed important at the time, or even now for that matter, and in any case I had completely forgotten about it after being kidnapped.

"Someone texted my cell phone that night." I paused, trying to recall more clearly. "Maybe around nine or so."

Burris was all attention. "Who? And what did they want?"

"It was someone who worked in the lab. There was a problem down at the Ice, er, another building." I went on to explain to Burris that in addition to our main laboratory complex in the research building, our group maintained space in another building. This was located down near the river, and we nicknamed it the Ice Palace, because there were large freezers there where we stored samples for which there was no room in the main lab. We also kept some old centrifuges and other equipment there.

"What was the problem?"

"One of the freezers had apparently shut down. It was not drawing power. There is a man down there who takes care of such things, but he warns us when there is a problem like this, so if we feel it's necessary, we can come and move the samples to another freezer."

"So this maintenance man texted you?"

I shook my head. "No, someone in our research group did. Apparently the man at the Ice Palace—his name is Bernie—texted someone else about the freezer problem. That someone was busy at the time, maybe not at the lab, whatever, so they texted me and asked me if I could do it. I said I couldn't, I was busy. I offered to go look for someone else, but the person texted back, never mind, I will take care of it."

"I see. But who was this person who texted you?" Burris persisted.

"I don't know. I don't know the cell phone numbers of everyone in the lab, and the person didn't say." I explained that I had the numbers of a few people in the group I worked especially closely with, people I might possibly communicate with when I was not in the lab, but for the rest, didn't bother. There was a list of everyone's cell number posted in the lab and in several other places in our research wing, so it was never difficult to identify someone if necessary.

"Are you certain it was one of your co-workers?"

I looked at Burris in surprise. "It had to be. How else would they know about the freezer, and my number?"

Burris moved his head from side to side, as if considering this answer, but let it pass.

"Have you been back to the lab since this happened?"

"Of course. I've been there the entire day, except now and earlier this morning, when I came down here to file the report."

"And you didn't ask around to see who sent it?"

"No. I just remembered it now. Do you think it's important?"

Even as I asked that question, the answer was dawning on me.

"Don't you understand that this text could be related to the kidnapping?"

"You mean...?"

He got up from his chair, the first time either of us had done this since the interview began. He stood there stretching, doing what looked like some exercise specifically designed to strengthen certain muscles.

"Maybe the text was intended to get you to go to that building. Describe the place to me."

I did, briefly. The Ice Palace was located on a very quiet road down by the river. To get to it, by car at least, you turned off the main road that went through the campus, just before reaching a bridge that crossed the river. The building was actually quite close to that main road, but the road to it was very infrequently used, except by commercial vehicles unloading supplies or arriving to service one of the machines. There were only a couple of other buildings down there. Students, excepting those in research labs like our own, rarely had occasion to be on that road.

Burris nodded.

"In other words, one of the best places on the entire campus to abduct someone. A place where the risk of being spotted by someone else would be minimal. Particularly in the dead of night."

By now, the logic of this conclusion was pretty apparent to me, but it still hit me hard. I couldn't really accept it.

"You mean you think someone I work with was involved in my kidnapping? Actually set it up?"

Officer Burris nodded. "The text could have been a coincidence, of course. We can't rule that out yet. But look at it this way. It actually could have been intended to accomplish two things. Not just lure you to an isolated area, but establish that you were still in the lab at that time. If the kidnappers were certain of that, they could wait for you to come out. They would prefer that you go down to this building by the river, but when that fell through, they went to their backup plan, which was to nab you anywhere on your way home where they felt they wouldn't be seen."

He paused a moment, to let this sink in.

"Do you have your cell phone with you?" he asked.

I shook my head. "The kidnappers took it from me."

Burris nodded. "Of course. No matter. What I think you should do, rather than asking around where you work, is go online first and find out the number of the person who texted you. Then you can look at this list and see who it was. If you're right about it being someone you work with, of course."

I nodded. I understood what he was getting at. Better to know who the potential suspect was before any confrontation with him or her. But realizing that only increased the gravity of the situation.

Burris read this in my expression.

"Don't look so surprised. I don't know why you were kidnapped, but assuming it was not mistaken identity"--I had raised that possibility with him, and he, like myself, was inclined to dismiss it--"it had to be by someone who knew something about you that they considered valuable in some way."

He leaned down over the table and looked through his notes again. "You're a single man who lives alone. Your parents are not particularly wealthy. You said you have very few friends, people you socialize with, outside of where you work..."

He looked up at me again.

"Is there anything about your work that would be valuable to someone? Information, for example?"

In response to this question, I told him about the patent.

"So someone might have wanted to learn what these three genes you discovered are."

I nodded. "It's really the only thing I can think of."

Burris thought this over carefully.

"How much time is left on that provisional patent?"

"A couple of months," I replied.

"OK," he said. "Suppose someone wanted to prevent you from filing the full patent. They kidnap you and hold you for a couple of months until the provisional patent expires."

I hadn't thought of this before. It did seem to fit with the fact that my kidnappers had not seemed interested in extracting any information from me, but were satisfied just to have me locked up in that house. Still, it was not a completely convincing scenario to me.

"I imagine in that case, Mitch—he's the co-applicant of this patent—would carry on without me. It would be a little more difficult without me, I discovered these genes and I know more about them than anyone else, but he could certainly do it."

Burris shrugged. "Well, you're a better judge of this than I, obviously. But it seems to me quite clear that your kidnapping must have had something to do with the patent. Unless there is something else about your life that would be valuable to others."

5. STOOL PIGEON

The following morning there was a board meeting of OS. Everyone had heard about the kidnapping, and yet again I had to describe what had happened, finishing with, no, I don't know why I was kidnapped. Like me, like Burris, they all assumed it had to have something to do with the patent, but looking around at them all, a new question popped into my mind: why me? Yes, I was the discoverer of these three genes, I knew more about them than anyone else, but the bottom line was, every other man and woman in this room knew the identity of these genes. All of them had signed a non-disclosure agreement when they had accepted a position on the board.

If the kidnapping had been carried out with the purpose of obtaining information about my genes, any one of these board members could have been targeted—or, maybe for that matter, bribed or bought off. This seemed to me to provide a little further evidence that my assailants had not intended simply to extract this information from me. Maybe, I thought, I should take Burris' theory more seriously.

Then another, more disturbing thought occurred to me. The text to me the night of the kidnapping, the number of which I had not yet had time to trace, seemed to suggest that someone I worked with was involved. Certainly Burris was pursuing that angle. Could it possibly be someone on the board of OS? Following my conversation with Burris, I had thought about everyone I worked with in the lab. I just found it impossible to believe that any of them could be behind this. It wasn't just that no one seemed to have any strong antagonism towards me. More fundamentally, there was no motive. I was the only one in the group working on colon cancer; no one else, it seemed, could benefit from knowledge of these three genes. Certainly none of the other graduate students, or other members of the lab, was in a position to file a patent of their own.

Except for Mitch, none of the other members of OS was named on the provisional patent, and like the other members of the lab, none would have been able to file a patent. But some of them might have had a motive for seeing me out of the picture. I could hardly attend these meetings without constantly being reminded of that.

With these thoughts in the back of my mind, I briefly presented the results of my pilot study, which I had obtained the night of the kidnapping. The clear success of this study had paved the way for us to carry out a large-scale clinical trial of the colon cancer screening test. The purpose of this trial, which we had in fact been planning for some time, was to verify, using a much larger number of patients, the very promising results of the pilot study. If we could confirm these results, and I had no doubt that we could, the path would be clear to develop and market the test.

Alvin Duistermars, one of the board members, had been responsible for planning the financial aspects of this study, and now he took the floor.

"The stool samples will be collected from a total of three hundred patients at three different hospitals in the Twin Cities area, and sent to the Mayo Clinic for complete analysis," Alvin began. "They will--"

"Three hundred patients are not enough," I interrupted. "We need at least five hundred."

"Why?"

"In order to ensure that the level of significance of the results will be high enough."

"We can't afford to analyze five hundred patients," Alvin said. "It costs too much."

"I don't care how much it costs," I said. "We have to have five hundred."

Alvin looked down at some notes he was holding in one hand.

"We've budgeted one million five hundred thousand dollars for this study," he explained. "Remember, we have to pay the colonoscopists who determine the status of each patient. We have to pay the shipping costs of the stool samples. We have agreed to pay for all the reagents and supplies needed for the tests, and also to reimburse the lab for the time required to use the equipment.

That's all in addition to the actual analysis."

"It's not enough," I repeated.

I looked around the table in the conference room at Alvin and the other board members. As I did so, I had trouble believing that I was at work, in a building that was supposed to be devoted to science. Except for Mitch, of course, there wasn't a soul in view who knew the difference between an intron and an exon, who was constitutionally capable of grasping the most salient facts, such as three PCR cycles represents a difference of 8-fold.

"In the good old days," Mitch had once said to me with a laugh, "the most exotic creature a scientist was likely to encounter during normal working hours was a doctor, an M.D. They don't know jack about basic science, of course, but they think they do. They think because they've been to medical school and putzed around in someone's laboratory, that they're ready to do experiments. They think because they've taken biochemistry and cell biology, and know what a promoter is and what a vector does, and can name half a dozen oncogenes and tumor suppressors, that they're all set to find a cure for cancer. What they can never understand is that 90% of science is knowing the right questions to ask. And that 90% of the questions you want to ask, the questions that beg to be asked, can't be answered, given the limitations of technology at any time."

But at least M.D.s had a solid informational background. They had taken all those courses. They knew the lingo. They could understand what we were talking about, if we didn't talk too fast. These business suits, as far as I was concerned, came from the moon. I had nothing at all against businessmen. My uncle was one, and I thought the world of him. But he didn't try to tell me how to do my experiments.

"Suppose we compromise," suggested another board member. "Suppose we run the study on four hundred patients."

"Uh-uh," I said. "It has to be five hundred. And at least one hundred of those need to be cancer patients, and two hundred patients with polyps." I looked at Alvin. "You better make sure they understand that."

"I don't see why three hundred isn't enough," protested Alvin.

46

"You had only one hundred patients in your pilot study."

Because it *was* a pilot study, you moron, I said to myself. It was large enough to justify a larger, validation study. It wasn't large enough to base a screening test on.

My skirmishing with Alvin had begun over seemingly minor issues, like the size and shape of the tubes that were to hold the stool samples. Alvin wanted a particular brand because they were cheapest available, and could be conveniently packed into a certain type of box for shipment from the hospitals where they were collected to the laboratory where the analysis would be carried out. They would be easier to ship. I pointed out to him that those tubes were completely unsatisfactory, because their dimensions would make it impossible to remove reliably all of the tiny amounts of liquid remaining after the cell isolation process. Ergo, huge variability in the numbers, making it impossible to detect fine statistical differences.

I of course didn't expect him to know this. Even Mitch would not have known this. No one who didn't actually work in the lab every day, who actually had to do the things that all these other jackasses sat around and talked about doing, could possibly know this. But Mitch, like any wise man, knew what he didn't know. He had always left decisions like this up to me. Alvin would not.

I eventually prevailed, but only because I brought one of the technicians to one of our meetings, and had my point clearly demonstrated in front of them. I made damned sure that she held that tube right in front of Alvin's bulbous, hair-encrusted nose, so that even he could see what I was talking about. Actually, I even offered to let him try the procedure. I handed him a micropipetter, tried to, anyway, stuck it right in his face and said, here, you do it. If you think these tubes are so satisfactory, you try it. He politely declined. So did every other member sitting around the table.

"Also," I continued, "I need to know more about the PCR protocols that the Mayo team will be using. What kind of machine are they running? What are the cycling conditions? I need a detailed list of the reagent mix and the primers."

"I'm sure they know what they're doing, Doctor," said Alvin.

"That's not the point," I said. "They have to follow the same protocol I used."

Matters—not to mention my blood--came to a boil when Alvin and the other board members refused to allot funding for a related study I desperately wanted to do. I wanted to determine whether my three genes were useful markers of other kinds of gastrointestinal disease, and analyze not only stool samples, but ones taken from other parts of the GI tract, such as inside the mouth. The study wouldn't have cost that much, and regardless of its outcome, would have provided us with a wealth of useful data on these genes. We would have learned a lot more about their roles in other tissues of the body, which in the long run would have aided our studies of other types of cancer.

But Alvin and Co. would have none of it. They said studies like this weren't "relevant to the company's direction." Like the company had a direction, which it could impose willy-nilly on science. You couldn't tell science what to do, where to go! Science told *you* where to go. It took you by the hand, and if you held on gently, taking one small step at a time, it would lead you to places that you could never have imagined existed. But if you tried to force it, it deserted you.

After a few more minutes of what I could only euphemistically describe as discussion, we took a vote. And I lost. Not close.

As always after such an outcome, Alvin tried to be magnanimous, damning me with not-so-faint praise.

"We are all deeply indebted to you, Doctor, for identifying these genes. But the project has entered a new phase now."

Translation: Step aside, sonny, and let the men take over.

A vote! I imagined myself working in the lab, just finishing a run on the PCR machine, say, and showing the results to others in the lab. What do these results indicate? Let's take a vote. How many think this gene is upregulated four-fold? How many five-fold? Any votes for six?

A vote! A vote! A fucking vote!

The moment the meeting was adjourned, I stalked out of the conference room.

48

Goddamned idiots, I muttered to myself.

I returned to my desk for a while to work on the grant proposal. I pored through a stack of invoices. It was probably not the best way to soothe my frayed nerves. It was not just rather boring, but frustrating as well. I would start with a total of, say, $960 for centrifuge tubes of a certain size for the past month. That was the sum of the invoices. That was what I knew had come into the lab. Then I would leave my desk and go into the lab and look for all these boxes, and all I could come up with was, say, $720 worth of them. So I would check around some more, and sure enough, I had overlooked some, or somebody had forgotten to tell me about an order that had come in, and it would bring the total up to, say, $850. Still short. So I would check some more, and the total would climb higher.

People would forget about an order that had come in. Or no one in the lab was around when it came in, and someone else signed for it, forgetting to tell the people in the lab. Or someone would mislay it. I would find a box hidden under some shelf in the cold room, people didn't even know it was there, they would order more not knowing they already had some. So I would go hunting around for all these lost boxes of tubes, or bottles of reagents, or whatever it was I was checking over at the time. And eventually, after a lot of unbelievably hard work, I would get the numbers to add up, or close enough. They never matched perfectly, but like some mathematical curve, approached the magic number asymptotically.

"Arf, arf!" came a familiar voice from over my shoulder.

It was Dick, holding his hand out. "Please, lover boy, don't strain yourself, let me handle this."

"Well, you can have these," I said, handing him some of the invoices I had validated.

As he took these from me, Dick leaned down and whispered in my ear, "I hear they were very *nasty* to you at the board meeting again today."

I worked on the budget for a little longer, then turned to another part of the grant, the Significance section. This is where the investigator explains why it's important to do these studies, how they will add to our understanding of some process. It's the most literary section of any scientific grant. You can't just cut and paste portions from previous grants, as we frequently do for the Materials and Methods, nor summarize the numbers in a bunch of tables and figures, in the Results. You have to write actual English.

I called Candy, but her phone was busy. I called her about five minutes later. Still busy. So I picked up the grant and went to her office. She was still on the phone, so I stood in the doorway, impatiently waiting for her to finish the call. As she talked on the phone, she sipped that concoction that she seemed to drink by the bucket load, wheatgrass I think it's called.

Candy's office was, well, let's just say it was colorful. Lots of posters of wilderness areas. Several pictures of saints. A couple of Tibetan mandalas. A large Buddha figure, made of some faux-marble substance. Beads hanging in front of the window. She used to have them hanging over the doorway, but so many people complained about having to push their way through them—I think the last person to make that complaint was the fire marshall--that she eventually moved them.

Her office also reeked of aromas. One of the shelves on one side of the office was lined with jars full of incense, spices, dried leaves, dried berries, twigs and many other things I couldn't begin to identify. Plus there were these wax candles that didn't even have to be lit to make their presence known. The fire marshal had had a lot to say about those, too, of course. Candy once told me that she changed the arrangement every day, so that the balance of odors would stay in tune with the universe.

As soon as she put the phone down, I walked in.

"You're in a bad mood, Alan," she said. "Was there another board meeting today?"

I grunted an answer, and slapped the grant down in front of her, and began asking her some questions, speaking very rapidly.

"Alan, calm down, calm down. Take a deep breath. Close your eyes. Try to feel your presence."

"Oh, for God's sakes, Candy, give me a fucking break," I snapped at her. "Just tell me what to do so I can get back to work."

She made no comment, but turned to look at what I had written. Candy was not an editor in the strict sense of the word. She did not know enough about the science to make a major contribution to the writing of a grant proposal. But she did a lot more than formatting. She was very good with language, and had the ability to read a passage with a lot of big words she didn't understand, and say things like, you don't want the passive voice here, or, you're being too repetitive there, or even more helpfully, shouldn't the ideas expressed in this paragraph come before those other paragraphs, or, why don't you break this up here and move it there, or, you refer to something here, but you haven't discussed it there.

Most scientists, I think it's fair to say, don't particularly love writing, and at the graduate student level, hate is not too strong a word. It's not just that it's a pain in the ass, trying to frame your observations in fancy bullshit words. It interferes with lab work. Every hour spent writing is an hour not spent at the bench. Writing, no matter how well done, is a second-class activity in the eyes of scientists. It's parasitic on what happens at the bench. No results, nothing to write about.

I was with Candy for about twenty minutes, and had to admit I felt a little calmer. I thanked her for her help. As I was leaving her desk, she said to me, very quietly, "You know, Alan, anger is a disease, too. And it's very contagious. It doesn't just infect you; it infects the people around you."

I stopped. "I'm sorry," I said, genuinely meaning it. I did like Candy, we disagreed about some things, but she had always treated me kindly. "This is not your fault, and I didn't mean to take it out on you. I've just got a lot on my mind right now."

"Oh, I understand," she said. "But you don't have to worry about me. I can't get the anger disease. I'm immune to it. I have anger-antibodies in my bloodstream. And I can help you develop yours, too, Alan."

I walked out of her office, shaking my head in wonder.

"It's a *disease*, Alan." Her voice, soft but persistent, wafted out of the office along with scents of lavender and cinnamon, haunting the whole hallway. "And it kills just as many people as cancer does."

After lunch I met with Bill Tye. Bill was a new postdoc, had just joined the group about a month earlier. In collaboration with me, he would be searching for genes that were closely associated with other types of cancers, and therefore some day might be used for other screens. Our initial plans were to study ovarian and lung cancer, two major killers that were virtually impossible to diagnose at present.

Bill was a California surfer boy, blonde, hunky, and very good looking, or at least he seemed to think he was. I had seen him preening himself a few times, peering at his reflection on the darkened screen of the computer set up next to one of the PCR machines. I really wouldn't have cared or even noticed, except that to my great chagrin, he was assigned bench space right next to Marissa Cheng, and had already begun chatting her up from time to time.

As if that weren't bad enough, from the moment he joined the lab he seemed to be on a sustained campaign to persuade Mitch to let him join OS.

"Once the colon cancer screen is on the market, what's next?" he had said to Mitch not long after he arrived. "You can't stand pat, you have to move on. The whole future of this company lies in developing tests for other forms of cancer. I should be leading this effort."

He was not blowing smoke. He had been in great demand following his graduate work at Cal Tech, because he had made an important breakthrough in microarray technology. Microarrays are fingernail-sized chips that contain the sequences of thousands of genes, each gene positioned in a known location on the chip. When a solution containing unknown genes is exposed to the chip, these unknown genes match up with their counterparts on the chip. That is, if gene A is in the solution, it attaches itself to gene A on the chip, through basically the same kind of forces that create the famous DNA double helix. If the unknown genes have been previously treated with a fluorescent substance, they're visible.

They light up the chip, with the patterns of light indicating which genes are present.

This was the basic technology I used to find my three genes, and which nearly so many other cancer researchers—indeed, scientists studying a host of other diseases—used. Bill's contribution was to develop a modification of it that greatly increased its sensitivity, its ability to highlight the most important genes. Thus he was very well placed to begin the search for other cancer genes.

He hadn't been particularly pleased, though, when Mitch had told him that he would be collaborating with me on that project.

"I really don't need his help," Bill had said, nodding towards me. "I obviously know microarray technology better than he does. All he's contributing, really, is the three colon cancer genes. Big deal. They're out there now, anyone in this lab can study them. It's unlikely that they're important in any other kinds of cancer, anyway."

I agreed with him on that last point. And anyway, I really didn't give a sh--.

"Fine," I had said. "I've got other things to do to occupy my time."

"No, I want you on this project," Mitch said to me. Turning to Bill he said, "You're right, this is certainly about more, a lot more, than those three genes. But Alan is a genius at this stuff. He just has a way of finding the genes that matter. He did it with colon cancer, and he will do it with these other cancers. You'll see."

Bill shrugged. "OK, but I run the microarrays." He gave that insolent smirk of his. "My array or the highway."

We had the meeting at Bill's cubicle, very informal. Maybe he thought by having it at his desk instead of mine, he was pulling some kind of power trip on me, but I really didn't care. I brought over some of my preliminary data, borrowed an available chair from one of the adjacent desks, and pulled it over next to Bill's. Marissa Cheng's cubicle was in clear view, but no Marissa, which was just as well, I thought.

I noticed some pictures Bill had set up on a shelf over his desk. No babes, which surprised me a little. No pictures of surf, either, though I was quite sure someone had told me he was into that. What there were several pictures of was, of all things, food. A couple of shots of some banquet table, loaded with goodies. Another of Bill holding some casserole or something like that. So he's into cooking, I thought. Interesting.

His desk itself was mostly bare, with very few photocopied articles or journals. In other words, not the workspace of someone embarking on a crash course on cancer. This did not surprise me that much. Most science is heavily dependent on technology, of course, and as a result of that, some scientists become far more interested in the technology itself than in the problems that the technology was actually developed to solve. Bill, I imagined, would have been just as happy studying some other disease — or even some biological phenomenon that had no direct relationship to any known disease — as long as it required the services of his microarrays. He was sort of a scientific mercenary, taking his technology to the highest bidder.

"We really don't have an effective screening procedure for lung cancer," I began. "CT scans are used to locate tumors, but they have far too many false positives. Doctors end up removing a lot of the lung tissue from patients who later turn out to be cancer-free. Most people who are actually diagnosed with this disease have an advanced form of it. It's already metastasized, spread to other tissues of the body. The five year survival rate of these patients is probably down in the single digits."

I thought of Alex Pignatti, who was acutely aware of the risk he was incurring. But I felt far sorrier for the relatively few non-smokers who got this disease. Like the late Dana Reeve, wife of the late Christopher Reeve, and one of the women I most admired. She stuck by him through nine years of what must have been hell, not simply caring for him, seeing to all his needs, but genuinely loving him, setting what I thought was a world-class example of spousal saintliness. After he died, she was just starting to get on with her own life, when she was diagnosed with lung cancer. She didn't smoke. Why, then, did she get disease? Why does any non-smoker get lung cancer? Is it just bad luck?

I next began to describe some of the currently available blood tests, based on some protein marker that increases in people with the disease. The hope was these tests could catch the cancer before it was too late.

"Several groups have reported useful markers. Most of them involve a small panel of different proteins, one or more of which is elevated in concentration the blood. But the sensitivity and specificity haven't really been established. Also, most of them only indicate the cancer at a fairly advanced stage. So I've begun looking for some new candidates."

I now showed him some preliminary results I had obtained. Bill scanned the data very quickly.

"Mitch told me about the statistics you're using. They're kind of out-of-date. Your method of normalization creates a lot of problems when you want to compare—"

"I know what I'm doing. I used this normalization method with the colon cancer project, and it worked fine. Everything from the microarrays has been verified with PCR."

"For those three genes, maybe, but how do you know what other genes you might have missed?" He pointed to some numbers on the data sheets. "Also, you need to eliminate false positives. When you're analyzing thousands of genes—"

"Of course I know that! Believe me, those three genes are not false positives."

Bill patted me rather paternalistically on the shoulder.

"I'm not saying they are, man. I'm saying that some of these genes in *this* study"—he indicated the lung cancer data I had given him—"are sure to be false positives. You need a better statistical method to weed them out. See, I'm developing this new CART system that..."

Even as he was talking, he opened one of his desk drawers and pulled out some of his own data. It was a huge stack of sheets, the size of a small phone book.

"I have data here for twenty different human tissues," he explained. "All controls."

All the genes were listed in a series of tables, each table taking up many pages. Bill began to leaf through it, continuing to explain his statistical procedures. I noticed that several of the listed genes were high-lighted, but he was turning the pages too fast for me to see what they were.

"Oh, I've marked all the genes that are of interest to this lab," he said in response to my question. 'That's one of your colon cancer markers."

I stared at him in astonishment.

"One of mine! I never told you what those three genes are."

Bill didn't even look up.

"Mitch did. Just that one. I could probably figure the other two out easily enough, though."

Bill and I talked for a few more minutes, finally agreeing on a general approach to the lung cancer project. When we were done, I retreated gratefully to my desk and turned my attention to some other work. It was quite peaceful now, and I felt soothed by nearby sounds — the rustle of papers in an adjoining cubicle, someone talking on the phone further away, the soft hum of a large refrigerator positioned in the short hall leading to the main lab. At one point, I heard one of the technicians pass nearby, pushing a small metal cart rattling with freshly autoclaved reagent bottles.

As I started to relax, though, the kidnapping incident, which I had managed to forget or at least bury in the back of my mind during the busy previous hours, returned like a ghost looking over my shoulder. I gradually became aware that I was turning over in my mind my interview with Officer Burris. I was busy analyzing it, detail by detail, even as I was more consciously analyzing some experimental results.

I suddenly remembered the cell phone text I had received that night in the lab. I had been so busy all day that I had not had time to find out who sent it. So I went online and after jumping through some hoops, was allowed to access my account.

Sure enough, I had received a text at 8:39 P.M. that night. But that was not all. To my astonishment, I had also sent a text later that night, at 12:44 A.M. Or rather, someone had sent a text from my phone at that hour, because that had to have occurred after the kidnapping. The two numbers—the one for the incoming text, and the one the outgoing text had been sent to—were different. I could not access the texts themselves.

I was intrigued. I decided to concentrate on the first number, because the latter one, I was quite sure, did not belong to anyone in the group. One of the kidnappers must have used my phone to text to someone else. It seemed like an idiotic thing for them to do, and could quite possibly provide a very important clue, but I would follow up on that later.

I rummaged through some papers on my desk, and quickly found the list of lab cell phone numbers. I scanned the list, and there it was.

Marissa Cheng.

6. BEAUTY AND THE BEAST

I could hardly catalog all the thoughts that flashed through my mind at that moment. The first one, irrationally, was: How could I not know the number of someone on my mind so much of the time? Second, why didn't she identify herself when she texted me? Followed by, finally, the one thought that really mattered: Marissa Cheng played a role in my kidnapping?

Still thinking tangentially as I went to find her, perhaps as a way of avoiding fully acknowledging the anxiety that I was starting to feel, I said to myself, well, I wouldn't mind so much being kidnapped by Marissa. I could enjoy being locked in a room with her. But by the time I finally found her, working at her bench in the main lab, I had sobered up a little. Not that I ever felt completely sober in her presence.

There's something about Asian women, with their midnight black hair, small frames and delicate features, that goes so perfectly with a white laboratory coat. I know I'm not the only guy who feels that way—every issue of Science magazine has a few of them, beaming out at the reader while pointing out the joy of using some centrifuge, PCR machine, or other piece of laboratory equipment. I had long felt that if I ever managed to get a real date with Marissa, she could come in her lab coat, as far as I cared. No matter what she was wearing—well, excepting tight jeans—I had never seen her look any better in anything else.

"Hi...uh, did you text me last Saturday night? About a problem at the Ice Palace?"

She was silent for a moment, concentrating on pipetting some almost incomprehensibly tiny volume of reagent into each of the ninety-six wells of a reaction plate. Having done this countless times myself, I knew how hard it was to talk or do anything else while performing this task, and knew I should have waited till she was finished before opening my mouth. But where Marissa was concerned, I always seemed to do the wrong thing. I just found it impossible to behave around her the way I behaved around everyone else. Clumsy. Awkward. Never my usual suave self.

She finished adding that particular reagent and paused for the very briefest moment before replying.

"No." She resumed what she was doing.

I loved to hear her speak. She had the voice of a four year old, so cute, so preciously high-pitched that she sounded almost like another species to me.

"Well, I received a text sent from your phone—at least, well, I'll wait till you finish with that."

I had to admit that, impatient as I was to find out what if any connection Marissa and her phone had to all this, it was not a difficult wait. I sat down on a nearby stool and watched her, thinking--with the part of my brain not overwhelmed with fantasies--about the implications of that one word answer. She was denying that she had sent that text. Then who did, and why was he or she using her cell phone?

She never actually told me when she was finished. She just sort of stopped work and looked at me questioningly. Not necessarily impatiently, but clearly measuring the passing moments.

"I received a text Monday evening from your cell phone. It said there was a problem with one of the freezers in the Ice Palace and asked me if I could go down there. Do you remember sending me that text?"

She looked puzzled. "I didn't send that text. I didn't know there was a problem down there."

I was proceeding as cautiously as possible. I did not want her to know that I thought the text might have anything to do with my kidnapping. Not yet, anyway.

"OK, but then someone else using your phone must have texted me."

She paused for just a moment, and I saw an expression flash across her face I couldn't quite fathom. Then she said, just a little more quietly.

"Can you show me that text? Is it still on your cell?"

I shook my head. "I don't have that phone any more. The

kidnappers took it."

"Then how do you know I sent it?"

I explained to her that I had checked my account.

She picked up the reaction plate that she had been carrying and carried it over to one of the PCR machines. What did I do now? I hesitated, weighing options and consequences.

"Could you just check your phone now and see if a text was sent to me Saturday night? Something about this freezer came up..." I tailed off, trying to be as vague as possible.

She sighed, and led the way out of the lab to the cubicle area. So she doesn't carry it on her person, I thought. Not a big surprise, actually. Neither did I. I didn't want to be interrupted when I was in the middle of an experiment, so I left my cell phone at my desk. Apparently she did, too. So someone else really could have sent that text. Maybe.

She opened a drawer at her desk — an unlocked drawer, I noticed — and quickly thumbed through the phone's lists.

"Nope. There's nothing there, Alan. I know I never sent you a text that night."

"OK," I said. "But if you check your account, you will be able to verify that someone did send a text to me from your phone then."

I knew I wasn't going to hold her off indefinitely. She finally got curious, turned around. It was so pleasant being able to look directly into her eyes without being guilty of leering.

"Why is this so important, Alan?"

I threw the question right back at her. "Aren't you concerned that someone used your cell phone without telling you?"

She tilted her head to one side, sending her long dark hair cascading down below her shoulder.

"Well, if it was about some problem at the Ice Palace, and this person didn't have their own cell phone, maybe they just borrowed mine."

I thought about that. Bernie might have called the lab that night on one of the landlines, and asked Marissa to come down to the Ice Palace. The person who answered the phone went to tell Marissa. Not finding her there, he picked up her cell phone and...what? Texted me? But I was in the lab then, why not just come and ask? Maybe I had gone out of the main room for a few minutes, the person didn't see me, thought I was around somewhere, was in a hurry, wanted to pass the buck and go?

"Maybe," I said.

I had been to the so-called Ice Palace many times before, but it was a little different making the trip this time. Even if I hadn't been kidnapped here, the possibility that I could have been—that this place was in any way associated with my abduction--put the building and its surroundings in a whole new light. I had never before thought of it as a lonely or scary place, a place where bad things could happen to good people. The old brick building, down by the river on a quiet road not far from the massive bridge leading from campus to the other bank, had always seemed peaceful to me, the slowness of life here in stark contrast to the frenetic rush of the lab. In fact, in the past I had enjoyed coming down here as a change of pace. Now, though, I was only too aware of how perceptive Officer Burris had been. It was a great place to ambush someone, particularly at night.

Bernie Evers was an old, white-haired, hoarse-voiced man who was a little hard of hearing—though some said he could hear perfectly well whenever he really cared to. His office consisted of nothing more than a large, government issue grey metal desk in one corner of a smallish room containing a few old refrigerators and other appliances that were past their time. Pinups of big-boobed women, some of whom looked to me also past their time, decorated the wall above the desk. On the desk itself were some scattered papers, with a large computer sitting in the middle. With the class snobbishness I could never quite erase around people who had spent barely half as many years in school as I had, I wondered if Bernie knew how to use it.

He quickly confirmed that, yes, there had been a freezer failure the previous Monday. He led me out of this room into another one where most of the equipment in operation was kept, over to a large freezer positioned against one wall. The freezer, about eight feet long and four feet wide, opened from the top.

I already knew something about how the freezer worked. It was set to a particular temperature. If the temperature rose above that setting by a certain number of degrees, which could also be adjusted, a siren would go off. Bernie had told me he was on duty when the siren went off about 8:30 Monday night, and he came over to see what the problem was.

"See that light there, the green one?" he rasped. "That means it's drawing power, electricity. But when I'm here that night, the light is red. Meaning no power. Like it's not plugged in."

"So somebody had unplugged it?" I asked.

I vaguely noticed I was already starting to jump to conclusions in a most unscientific manner. I should have said, simply, was it unplugged? What did they call this in court, leading the witness?

Bernie paused and scratched his head. He wore an old pair of army green pants that even I, who could have made anyone's worst-dressed list, could see were too baggy, and clashed with a red checkered shirt. He carried a large ring of keys wherever he went, attached to his pants by a small metal chain, and he periodically dangled the keys by the chain, popping the keys into and out of his hand like a yoyo.

"Well, no, sir, that was the strange part about it. It was plugged in fine, far's I could see. Here, help me with this." He started to pull the freezer out from the wall, so that the plug and the wall jack were accessible to us. "I thought, well, must be some trouble with the wire, the cord. So's I pulled out the plug, to take a better look at the cord, but I couldn't see nothing wrong with it, either. So I put the plug back in, oney I shove it in real hard like, and hold it there, and then that little old green light comes on."

He reached down to the plug to demonstrate.

"Meaning...the plug was just loose? It hadn't been pushed in far enough?"

"What? Well, I dunno about that. The plug sure looked like it was flush to the wall when I first saw it."

"So there was a bad contact, for some reason. Even though the plug was in, for some reason it was not making contact."

"Yep, sir. Cause as soon as I let go of it, the red light comes on agin. Then's when I know we got a problem. I'm thinkin', maybe I can temporarily fix it, but that's when I call your lab."

"I want to ask you about that, too," I said. "But first, how did you finally fix the problem? I see it's working fine now."

"Took me a little while, but I finally figured it out."

He straightened up, holding the plug out for me to examine.

"Once in a while," he explained, "one of these plugs gets a little corroded, you see. So what I did, I got me a file from over in the tool drawer down there"--here he pointed to another part of the room--"and I just filed the prongs of that plug ever so little. Just a touch. And that done it."

I thought about this as Bernie bent down again to put the plug back in. Then I helped him push the freezer back into position. Was it possible someone had done something to the plug to break the contact? It couldn't be that difficult. Just coat the prongs with some clear plastic substance, maybe.

As we walked back to his desk, I said to him, "Let's suppose that at some point the plug failed. No current was getting through. The alarm wouldn't go off immediately, would it? It would take time for the freezer to warm up to the alarm point."

"You're right, sir. That's the way it works."

"How long would that take, do you think?"

Standing over his desk, Bernie jangled his keys. "What? At that setting? I wouldn't know exactly. Coupla hours, I guess, maybe a bit more."

Satisfied that I had learned as much about the freezer failure as I could, I now turned to the issue of the cell phone.

"When you heard the siren go off, and you couldn't fix the problem immediately, you called the lab, correct?"

"Correct, sir."

"Who did you call?"

"What? Oh, why, that cute little Chinese lady, Melissa. She's the one I'm sposed to call."

That I knew was correct. We had set up a rotating list. Every week, a new person was responsible for taking emergency calls from Bernie. Marissa was the one this week. Bernie's words also ruled out, I realized, any scenario involving a landline.

"I talked to her earlier today. She says she never received any call."

Bernie and I were standing in front of his desk. Bernie looked uncomfortable. The keys were jumping up and down. And I had to repeat my question twice.

"Well, now that ain't so. I mean, no one answered my call, that's true enough. But right after I called, I received a text from her, asking what the problem was."

"You mean, you received a text from that number."

"From Melissa, yeah."

"Did the text say it was Marissa?"

"What?" His features relaxed a little. "Oh, I see what you mean. No, the text said, what is the problem, I will take care of it."

He reached into his pocket and pulled out his cell phone. "I still got that text, here, you wanna look at it?

I sure did.

"I see," I said, studying the texts and their date and time. "And I see you texted back."

"Yeah, I guessed there was some problem with the phone, it couldn't take calls. Anyway, I texted back about the freezer. And that was the last I heard from her."

"So no one ever came down here to check on the freezer?"

Bernie shook his head.

"What? No, sir. That nice looking feller showed up the next morning. The new guy with all that blond hair. The pony tail."

I stared at him.

"Bill Tye?"

"Right, sir. He came down here bright and early and was very helpful."

As I walked back to the lab, I tried to sort it all out. The freezer had failed Monday evening, possibly intentionally, an act of sabotage. If it were sabotage, the action had been put into play sometime earlier, maybe several hours earlier. Everyone in our group had access to the Ice Palace, and could probably enter it and move around fairly easily without being noticed. There was no guard at the door, and the building was unlocked during daylight hours. It was probably locked at night, I wasn't sure, but everyone in our group would have a key to the building.

Bernie, alerted to the problem, called Marissa. No answer, but a text a few minutes later. Why no answer? Because her phone couldn't accept calls for some reason, or because whoever used the phone didn't want to reveal his/her identity? Or maybe because whoever sent the text to Bernie just happened to walk past Marissa's desk at the time and heard the phone ring, but not in time to answer it. Or had his or her hands full, literally, with an experiment, and could not answer it at that moment. But if that were the case, why text back instead of calling? Maybe it just seemed simpler, I thought. After all, it couldn't be easy having a phone conversation with Bernie. Texting might be faster in that situation.

I found Bill Tye back at his lab bench. He was talking to one of the technicians, giving her instructions for an experiment. It couldn't be related to our collaboration, it occurred to me, because the lung cancer tissue samples were not ready yet. But like me, he had other irons in the fire.

When he saw me waiting there, he broke off immediately, and looked at me questioningly.

"Did you go down to the Ice Palace Tuesday morning about a

freezer failure?" I asked him.

"What? Oh, yeah. I saw your text from the previous night."

He suddenly slapped his forehead as he realized the significance of the time.

"Oh, *man*! You sent that right before you were kidnapped, didn't you?"

I immediately realized that Bill had to be referring to that other text that had been recorded as being sent from my cell after I had been kidnapped. I had written down both of the cell numbers I had obtained online, the one my phone had received a text from, which had proved to be Marissa's, and the one my phone had sent a text to later. I was about to show Bill the latter, and ask him to confirm it, when I hesitated. Why tell him any more than I had to about what I knew?

"Can you show me that text?" I asked him. "My cell phone was stolen by the kidnappers. I want to check the time."

"Sure, man." I followed him out of the lab back to his cubicle, where we had been talking just a few hours earlier. He opened his desk drawer and took out his cell phone.

I looked at the message of the text, which I had not been able to access online:

Bernie says there's a problem at the Ice Palace. Can you take care of it? – Alan

Even if I hadn't known that I hadn't sent that text, I would have known it wasn't mine. I would have been much briefer, something like: Prob at Ice P. U go der? Whoever sent that text obviously didn't know that, and in any case probably preferred to err on the side of normal English. One would want to make sure the message was clear, so that Bill would definitely go to the Ice Palace. After midnight, there was little chance he would call back for further details, and of course, that was the last thing the text's sender wanted him to do.

66

The next day I received a call from the campus police. They had new information about my case, and wanted me to come down to the station to talk about it. I was so anxious to hear what I hoped was good news that I didn't even care that the appointment was right in the middle of a critical experiment. Ordinarily, I would have simply refused to keep the appointment, but I just left Eleanor Natsuki, a very shy first year grad student who was the only pair of hands I could find on short notice, with instructions on what to do.

I could see the mixed emotions slugging it out on her face when I asked her. She was honored that I would think enough of her to entrust me with this chore. But she was also nervous as hell. She had been in the lab long enough to know that anyone who screwed up one of my experiments would never hear the end of it.

This time Officer Burris was waiting for me in the interview room when I arrived. I thought at first this was encouraging, that maybe the police had actually caught the perpetrators, or at least had some solid leads on them. But even before I sat down across from him and he began speaking, something in the expression on his face suggested otherwise, and his words soon confirmed that.

"We found the house all right," he began. "And the owner of the house confirmed your story of being locked in the basement."

I didn't know quite what to make of this.

"The owner? So he admits that he was one of the guys who kidnapped me?"

Burris shook his head decisively, and shifted his position in his chair, his eyes never moving a millimeter away from mine.

"No, nothing of the kind," he said after a pause too long for my taste. "He says he owns the property, but doesn't live there. He lives fairly nearby, and periodically visits it, just to make sure everything's OK." Another long pause, Burris' stare almost palpably pinning me against my chair. "He says he came over to the house that day, opened the cellar door, and started to go down into it. That was the point, apparently, at which you shoved him down the stairs and locked the door behind him."

I sat in silence, trying to digest this. The story was nothing but facts, a description of the situation that jibed perfectly with mine — yet it wasn't true. How could that be? I wondered. The story was factual, yet not truthful. Here I was confronted with facts — my own observations replicated by someone else's — and I just knew there was something fishy about it all.

"Maybe he's lying," I said defensively. "If he didn't kidnap me, who did? And how did they have a key to his house?"

Burris again said nothing for an uncomfortably long time, leaving me feeling as if I were twisting on my own rope.

"Are you sure about your entire story?" he said finally.

"Of course I'm sure," I snapped irritably. "Why in the world would I make up something like this?"

Burris finally removed his stare from me, and seemed deep in thought for a moment.

"The owner thinks you broke into the house," he said finally, turning back to look at me closely again. "He thinks you were trying to steal something."

"Steal something?! There's nothing to steal in that place! It's empty, at least as far as I could see when I ran out. I mean, I obviously didn't take the time to make a little tour, but every room I saw in that house, including the one I was locked up in, was bare. There was no furniture, there wasn't anything."

"Nothing?"

I thought a moment, then added, "Well, there were some boxes in the basement. I told you about them before. That was about all."

Burris consulted his notes. "The owner didn't say anything about any boxes. Did mention he had some valuable tools down there."

"Maybe," I said. Then I remembered another very relevant fact.

"I couldn't have broken into the house," I pointed out. "The bedroom door was locked from the outside, there was no way that I could get out, that was why I went through the basement. If I had broken into the house, how could I get into a room that was locked behind me?"

"The landlord says that door was not locked."

"Then he's *lying!*" I practically shrieked. "I swear to God it was locked."

"The landlord was pretty upset," Burris continued. "Fortunately, he had his cell phone with him, and was able to call a couple of friends, who came and let him out of the cellar." Again he checked his notes.

"If the bedroom door was unlocked," I pointed out, "why didn't he just climb through the hole I made in the bedroom floor and get out that way? He might not have known at the time that the door was unlocked, but if he really thought I was a burglar, he would have assumed that door was open."

"He said he tried to," replied Burris. "But it was just too hard to squeeze through that hole, and his friends were on the way."

OK, I thought, I could buy that much, at least. I'm tall, but fairly thin, and I barely got through it. A stouter man might have had a lot of trouble, particularly since he was going up, not down. He had to find a stool or something to climb up on, and as he pushed his way through the hole, he wouldn't have had gravity helping him. If he had friends on the way, why bother?

I continued to follow the consequences of the landlord's story.

"So that's why the landlord followed me in his car? Just because he thought I was some burglar? He chased me over half the state, even though I couldn't have taken anything of value from that place?"

Burris shook his head. "The owner says he never followed you."

Now I was really confused.

"He says he never followed me? Then who were those two guys in the car? It was the same car he drove up to the house in."

Burris shook his head again.

"The owner says he came to the house on foot. He lives within walking distance of that property. We confirmed that, he has a little cabin in the woods in that area, maybe a mile and a half away. As I said before, he owns the house where he found you, but doesn't live there, just visits it from time to time. There's a path from his house to the road, then he walks along the road to reach the other house."

"Another lie!" I protested bitterly. "I heard him drive up in a car. I saw the car parked in front of the house. And that same car followed me when I tried to return to Minneapolis."

Burris nodded. "Oh, he did confirm that there was a car parked nearby when he arrived at the house. He just denies that it was his car. He told us that much of the surrounding forest, as well as the road to his house, is public land, and people occasionally park at the end of the road, near the house, then go hiking in the woods. He doesn't recall seeing anyone in the car, or in the area, and assumes they were hikers."

My mind was reeling, trying to make sense of all this information. The kidnappers must have driven up to the house just before the owner arrived. If the owner was telling the truth, and had no involvement with them, they would have waited outside, hoping he might not enter the locked bedroom. They might have done well simply to leave and come back later, except they needed to know whether the owner had found me and released me. But they wouldn't want to be visible if I was released, or for that matter, even if I wasn't. Ergo, they left their car and hid in the woods. They must have seen me come out, but did not give immediate chase, because they thought the owner might see them. So they waited till I had started down the road, then came after me...

That, too, fit all the facts—but couldn't be the truth. Why would the kidnappers take me to a house without the owner's being in on it? If the owner was telling the truth, I would have been released if I had just waited in that room. Or if the kidnappers had come a little sooner, they would have been caught in the act. Why would they take such a risk? Was this just a temporary prison? Were they planning to move me the next day, and came a little too late? Had they perhaps thought the owner of the house was away?

Or was the owner lying? But Burris had verified that the owner did live in a nearby house, and as a police officer, Burris could also verify, and probably had, that the owner did not possess a car that fit the general description of the one that had followed me. Of course, there were two men following me, and if one was the owner of the house, the other could have owned that car.

Burris let me stew in silence for a while, then collected his notes, though he made no move to leave.

There's really nothing more we can do at this point, Mr. Rupert," he concluded. "Without a license plate, there's no way we can track down the owner of the car you said you saw. You clearly can't ID either of the two men you said you saw, either." He paused, then added, "Frankly, Mr. Rupert, the owner could be right. For all you've told me, those two men in the car could have had nothing to do with your kidnapping."

"So you're closing the case?"

"Oh, not yet. But there's not much more we can do until we have more information."

I was getting up to leave when I remembered the paper bag I had given him, the one discarded by my kidnappers. I asked him if he had found any fingerprints.

"Not any usable ones," he said, shaking his head. "Just partials. Not good enough."

"Can I have it back, then?" I asked him.

He looked at me curiously. "I guess so. Why?"

"Ever heard of keratins?" I asked him.

He looked thoughtful for a moment. "Skin proteins?"

"Right. They're known to vary somewhat from one individual to another."

On the way out, Burris spoke to an assistant, who fetched the sample for me.

"I'm going to send it out to a lab that does mass spectrometry," I explained. "It's a long shot, because there will be a mixture of keratins, but I'm hoping to get enough unambiguous sequence to identify one or more variants."

Burris was clearly over his head a little, but one thing he understood well enough.

"And then what? What will you match it against? We don't have a keratin database, you know."

"Give me a protein sequence," I said, "and I will tell you the sequence of DNA that coded for that protein."

He stopped and stared at me. "Are you telling me you can uniquely identify individuals with these keratin profiles?"

"No," I admitted, "but at least it will narrow the field down a little. Give me a line-up of suspects, and I can probably eliminate some of them." He continued to stare at me curiously, so I added, "It's all I can do now, right?"

7. NOT ON THE SCHEDULE

"**A**s a cancer survivor, I can tell you that I never faced a greater challenge in my life than overcoming this disease, not even winning the Tour de France seven times. I have pledged not to rest until all of us are free from this horrible disease, which takes so many individuals at the prime of their life, ending their hopes and dreams..."

The second to last week in June, I went to San Francisco to attend an international conference on cancer. On the opening night of the conference, Lance Armstrong gave one of the keynote speeches. Many of my laboratory colleagues were there, as well as most of the big names in the field. Not long after I arrived at my hotel, I ran into Alex Pignatti. He corralled me in the middle of the lobby.

"Alan, so good to see you. Let's talk."

With that, he led me over to a couple of armchairs.

"What's up?" I asked, as if I didn't know. "You've tested those three genes, right?" I was referring to our earlier meeting in Minneapolis, when he had told me about three genes he was interested in, one of them turning out to be identical to one of my three, but the other two different.

He took a puff of his ever-present cigarette, surreptitiously looking around to see if his violation of the indoor smoking ordinance had been observed.

"Yes. They are very, very good. Better than yours."

I didn't believe it.

"Give me some data." In the elapsed time since our earlier meeting, he could not have carried out a very large study, there simply wasn't enough time. This would have had to be a relatively small pilot study.

He was carrying a briefcase, and he opened it and drew out

some sheets of paper, which he handed over to me. I spent several minutes studying them.

"These results aren't as good as ours," I said finally. "For cancer detection, yes. One hundred percent. Can't do better than that. But for polyps, your figures are a little lower." I looked over at him. "Still very, very good, Alex, great work. But we have a better detection rate for polyps. And that's where the real action is."

He knew what I meant. If detecting cancer is the best you can do, so be it. But detecting cancer may be too late, depending on how far it has progressed. And even if it isn't too late, excising the cancer still requires major surgery. The idea is to detect the polyp before it becomes cancer, when it can be plucked out as part of a routine colonoscopy.

He stubbed out his cigarette.

"Yes, Alan, but we have a lower false positive rate. Yours is about 5%. Ours is 1-2%."

I shrugged. "If it holds up. With such a small study, your level of significance really isn't that good. But even if it pans out, I will trade a higher detection rate for a slightly higher false positive rate any day of the week."

Alex gave me that mournful, basset hound look of his. "Alan, why don't we join forces? Between your genes and my genes, we could develop a super test! One better than either of ours individually."

I wondered if Alex had taken leave of his senses. I hated to remind him of this, it seemed almost impolite, but I held all the cards here.

"I already know what your other two genes are, Alex. Remember? You gave me their names."

In other words, I can develop this test on my own, thank you very much. And thank you very much also for telling me that I should look into the possibility.

Alex shook his head. "No, Alan, you don't know what these other two genes are. I never showed them to you."

Why you son of a bitch! I almost expressed that thought out

loud. I instantly realized what was going on.

When he had showed me those three genes a few months earlier, he had implied that one of the three was one of mine, but he didn't know which one it was. Now, I could see, he had known all along which one of them was mine. The other two were just any old genes that he picked out to cover up that fact. He did have two other genes that were very important, but those he hadn't shown to me.

Why hadn't he shown me just the one gene, and asked me to verify? Because I had nothing to gain from doing that. By including it with two others, he was leading me to believe I was getting something out of the deal. But in fact, he hadn't give me a goddamned thing. The sole effect of the entire transaction was that he got me to admit that the gene he was interested in was one of mine.

It was like a card game we were playing, only with two decks instead of one. Imagine that you hold three really good cards in your hand. Your opponent says he will show you his three best cards, if you will just verify whether one of them is the same as one of your best three. That's all you have to do, you don't have to show any of your cards. You agree to this, and verify that one of his three cards is indeed the same as one of your big three. But later, when you both lay your cards on the table, you learn that the other two were not among his best. They were basically jokers. His best other two he held back.

But I had to be intrigued by his offer, nonetheless.

"How do you know that your other two genes aren't identical to mine?" I asked. Though his detection rates weren't quite as good as mine, that might simply be because   his study was so small. There had to be a sizeable standard error in his results. He might have independently discovered my other two. But the only way we could confirm that was by agreeing to share their identities.

Alex paused a moment, glancing around the lobby again before delivering the knockout blow.

"Because I know what your other two genes are."

As he said that, he held up a card with two names on it. The other two of my crown jewels.

I was in shock. My mind was reeling. Here was the situation as Alex was presenting it to me. He had independently discovered my three genes. He had them all. In addition, he had two other genes that were almost as good. The whole lot of them, all five, could undoubtedly create an even more sensitive colon cancer screening test than mine.

My mind went into overdrive. Had he applied for a patent on them, too? If he had, the game might be over for our test. But if so, why was he seeking my help?

He obviously hadn't approached me to tell me he had scooped me.

"What do you want, Alex?"

"I want to be on your patent, as a co-discoverer of these genes."

I gave a huge sigh of relief, one that he must have noticed. OK, he hadn't applied for a patent yet. So nothing at all had really changed.

"And I get in return?"

"The possibility of adding the two additional genes to the patent, which I alone discovered."

I thought through all this for a moment.

"And if I decline?"

"You won't want to, when you hear what other cancers these genes are associated with."

"I'm all ears, Alex."

He gave me an enigmatic smile. "Come to my poster session. It will be up tomorrow."

We were about to end our little chat, when I did a double take. How did Alex know he had discovered my other two genes? Sure, he could have found them independently, but how could he know they were the same as mine unless we compared notes? He hadn't known for sure he had the first of my three genes until I had agreed

76

to verify that he did. So how could he be so sure he had the other two?

"Wait a minute, Alex, there's something fishy going on here. You couldn't have known for sure that you had my other two genes unless you knew what these other genes were. How did you find out? Somebody had to tell you."

"You just told me," he said.

Goddamn you, I thought. The oldest card trick in the game.

Later that evening, I went to a party. Mitch had rented for the night a large luxury suite on the top floor of one of the major hotels where many of the conference attendees were staying. All of us in his lab who were at the conference were of course invited, as well as many other researchers, and their colleagues, whom Mitch knew.

I brought Alex along with me. When we arrived there about nine, the place was packed, at least forty to fifty people, I guessed. Some were sitting on a couple of plush couches and armchairs in the main room, many others standing. From where I stood at the entrance, I could see at least two other rooms, plus beyond one of them a balcony, providing a spectacular view of San Francisco, with the bay in the distance. How much did this place cost a night? I wondered idly. One thousand dollars, at least? Did Mitch dare count that as travel expenses on the grant? Had he persuaded the stingy board members of OS to foot the bill? Or was he paying out of his own pocket?

Looking around at the people, I saw many other than my lab mates whom I recognized. When I had attended my first scientific conference, three years earlier, I hadn't known anyone outside of my own lab, but now I had fairly extensive contacts. Research was a large family. We got to become quite familiar with people we might see only two or three times a year, because in addition to such personal meetings, we were constantly communicating through email, phone calls, and just by reading their latest publications.

There was a large buffet table at one side of the room in which we entered, loaded with meats, pasta, fruits, several kinds of desserts, and all the usual alcoholic beverages. As we headed towards that, Alex stopped briefly and said, "Who is she? *Bellissima!*"

Following his gaze, I saw that he had spotted Marissa Cheng. Damn, I thought, just what I need, another rival. She did look absolutely radiant, in a long, powder blue dress that fitted the curves of her body perfectly. Her hair was unbound and fell almost to her waist. She was on the far side of the room, talking with Mitch and a couple of other people.

One of Alex's lab mates, Franklin Saito, came up to us just as we were moving on from the buffet with loaded paper plates. He was getting a refill on his glass of wine.

"Alex! Wondered when you would get here. And you're Alan, of course. Great work you're doing. I know we've met before." He would have offered a hand to shake but could see mine were occupied. As the three of us snaked our way through the crush of people, Franklin gave me a wink. "This guy," he said, referring to Alex, "is the ultimate chick magnet. I guarantee you he won't go home alone tonight."

Great, I thought, miserably, great. First he gets my genes, now he's going to get my girl.

Sure enough, he made a beeline towards Marissa, so Franklin and I followed and joined the little circle around her and Mitch. Alex injected himself into the conversation immediately, and was introducing himself to Marissa within seconds, but to my secret pleasure, that was as far as he got with her. While she chatted freely with him and everyone else, she politely declined his invitation to accompany him out on the balcony. Alex, I was interested to see, didn't seem particularly upset about the rejection; he soon drifted off in search of another conquest. Watching him go, I immediately felt better disposed to him; I sensed a bond between us that in some strange way seemed even stronger than that provided by our common research goals. Tell me about it, brother, tell me about it.

I, too, drifted off, knowing I wasn't going to get anywhere with her, either. I was in that sort of in-between groups limbo that cocktail party goers know so well when someone I didn't recognize at all came up to me. He was a somewhat short, thin man with sharp features, including a long, straight nose. He was dressed, overdressed, really, in a very good suit and tie.

"Excuse me," he said. "Are you Alan Rupert?"

"Yes," I said, turning to him.

"I'm Ed Cole, and I've heard you're doing great work!"

"Well, thank you!" I said. "What group are you in?" I was referring to whose laboratory he worked in. Just from looking around at the crowd, I could see that at least four other research groups had members present, and I didn't know which one he belonged to.

He gave a sort of faux-guilty smile. "To be honest about it," he said, "I'm not in research. I'm just a high school science teacher. But I try to keep up with things best that I can, and I have a particular interest in cancer. I'm not attending the conference officially, of course, but I'm going to all the lectures that are open to the public."

"Why, good for you!" I exclaimed. "I think it's great that you're introducing high school kids to this kind of stuff. And I'm very flattered that you've even heard of me." Gesturing around the room, I added, "There are some very big names here in this crowd. Some scientists much better known than I am."

"You're all big names to me. Tell me about your work. I'm trying to teach my students a little about cancer research."

"Love it, love it," I said. "Where do you teach high school?"

"In Lincoln, Nebraska, believe it or not."

"And you flew out here just to attend the conference? The parts of it you can?"

"Well, and to see this lovely city, too. First time I've ever been here."

"One of my favorite places", I said.

"I'm still learning my way around," Ed replied. "Where are you staying, by the way?"

I told him the name of my hotel.

"Oh, yeah," he said. "I think I know where that is. Do they have a shuttle there, that takes you to the other conference events?"

"Sure do. Why?"

"Well, I'm staying in one of these hole-in-the-wall budget places, if you can call one hundred a night a budget price. Welcome to San Francisco, I guess. Anyway, I thought if I could get to one of these hotels, I could get around to the other conference sites by shuttle. I am renting a car, but you know how impossible it is to find parking in this city."

"Right," I said.

Ed and I chatted a little longer, then saying he felt a little guilty monopolizing all my time, he left my side, and made his way onward through the crowd. I didn't see him again.

I looked around and saw Bill Tye nearby, and joined his little group. I was relieved to see that he was nowhere near Marissa, and seemed to have no particular interest in her. Bill was standing next to Walter Cho. Walter was the colonoscopist we had used in our pilot colon cancer studies. He was the one who determined which of our experimental subjects had colon cancer or polyps, and which were free of any abnormalities and could serve as controls.

As I came up to the group, Bill, holding a drink in one hand, clapped his other hand over Walter Cho's shoulder. Bill had his hair down now, and I noticed it flowed half way down his back. "Hey, Walter," he said, "how does it feel to be going out of business? When we get this test on the market, what will you do for a living?"

Walter smiled. "Maybe you can tell us if a polyp is in there, but we still have to go in there and remove it."

"Yeah, but how many people actually have polyps? It's only like one or two percent, isn't it? It's that other ninety-nine percent you make a living on."

I knew that the proportion of people with intestinal polyps was considerably higher than that. Bill again was revealing a little ignorance about the diseases he was boasting he was going to cure.

But still, his point was well taken. Most colonoscopies were, in retrospect, unnecessary. They were performed on people who had no polyps, and who currently, had no way of being certain of that without submitting to the procedure.

"And in a few years," commented someone else in the group, "when you have re-engineered the genes, there won't be anyone with polyps. There won't be any need for GI surgeons at all."

The person who made that comment, Sabita Chatterjee, was joking. She knew it would be a very long time before we reached that stage — if we ever really did. But Bill, who had probably had more than his share of the punch by then, happily took the bait.

"Oh," he replied airily, "it will take more than a few years, but the day is not far off." He waved his glass of punch around at everyone in the circle. "I mean, the time is coming when we won't need surgeons at all. Everyone who cuts up bodies for a living will be gone. All medicine will be at the molecular level."

"That's OK with me," said Walter. "Every doctor out there is some other doctor's patient."

I spent the next couple of hours like that, moving from one group to another. Periodically, I would look around to see where Marissa Cheng was. She was always with Mitch, which greatly relieved me. He would keep her out of the clutches of wolves like Alex and Bill, I thought.

Later, I ran into Andrea Davies. As a first year graduate student, she was attending her first scientific conference ever, and was clearly having the time of her life. She had already been picked up by some guy, another young graduate student apparently, a member of one of the other research groups.

"Hi, Alan!" she said gaily. "This is Steve Perez, Steve, meet Alan Rupert."

Steve was at least 6'6", so I had to look up as I shook his hand.

"You must be a basketball player, too," I remarked.

"Yeah," he said with a grin. "Andrea and I have been comparing moves." He winked at her.

"Andrea has told me all about you," he continued. "How you're going to be rich and famous very soon."

"Well..." I said. I never knew how to respond to a comment like that. I guessed it was true, the test would make me wealthy and well-known, but I never thought of that as the same as rich and famous. It was not like I was some hot new rock star.

"Come on, Alan," teased Andrea. "Don't be shy. Everyone's talking about it, you know."

"Talking about what? That I'm going to be rich and famous?"

"The test. People are taking bets about how long it will be before it hits the market."

I laughed a little nervously. "I wouldn't put any of my money into that pool, and I would guess I have more inside information than anyone else."

"Andrea says you've got these three marker genes for colon cancer," Steve went on. "She was telling me all about one of them."

My party face froze instantly. What exactly had Andrea told him? If she wanted to describe her experiments, how she was trying to localize the gene and determine some of its functions, that was no problem. Everyone knew we would be doing that, it was a logical step. But if she went into any detail about the results, detail that might provide hints about what the gene was, she was walking dangerously close to a line. And if she actually told him what the gene was, she had crossed that line.

I looked at her carefully. She obviously liked Steve a lot. Like most party time relationships, moreover, this one was being lubricated by alcohol. Tongues loosened.

"Ummm, Andrea," I began. "I hope you haven't been..."

She smiled at me and held up her right hand. "I know the rules, Alan. Scouts' honor.

I breathed a little easier, but not too easy. War was not the only game in which all was fair.

I finally left the party around midnight. By that time it had pretty much wound down. After all, we all had to get up fairly early the next morning. The sessions began at nine. As I walked out, alone, I saw that Marissa was still there, one of the very few people left. Well, I thought, I guess she's going home alone, too.

When it comes to women and sex, my attitude is pretty much the same as it is in most of the rest of my life: perfectionist. If I can't have a really hot babe, I would rather not bother. Since hot babes aren't particularly interested in me—exhibit A, Marissa--I can get pretty frustrated. Every once in a while—say, annually—I can't take it any more, and grab just about anyone I can get. It must have been about that time of the year again when I returned to my hotel that night, because as I entered the lobby, and saw Laurie Godefrut on the far side waiting for the elevator, I made sure I got there before the elevator did. By the time we reached the fifth floor, where both of our rooms were, the only question left to settle was, you know. We took mine.

Laurie was about as far from my ideal woman as you can get. It wasn't just that her face was plain, to be generous. She was totally flat. I mean, she had the body of a twelve year old boy. The body is very important to me, particularly in the dark when you know that so much better than the face.

I did understand, of course, that there is more to any woman than the surface, than what meets the eye. What I did not appreciate until I got into bed naked with Laurie is that there is more to the surface than what meets the eye. All you can really tell about a woman's body for sure by looking at it is its shape. It takes touch to know its texture.

Laurie had what I still consider today the gold standard in body tone. She was hard, not like a rock, not like some female body builder, but like hard rubber. Firm enough to repel any touch that was timid and tentative, but yielding enough to give in grudgingly to hands that were not going to take no for an answer.

She also had the silkiest skin I had ever encountered, the kind your hands slide over effortlessly. You can't fail to recognize this kind of skin. If you happen to touch a strange women by accident, say bump into her in a crowded subway, you can always tell, because the frictional coefficient, as some physicist would say, approaches zero. There is just enough resistance to tell you that it is skin, that there is something there — and absolutely nothing else. If you could put skin like this in a package and sell it, it would put Teflon out of business.

Then there was her hair. I had sort of noticed in the lab that her hair was thick and shiny, but I could never really tell how good it was, because she almost always tied it up in all the myriad ways that women, for reasons beyond my comprehension, do. When she undid it, before she got undressed, I immediately stopped worrying about how I was going to get turned on by her.

Hair to a woman is sort of like a kitchen to a house. If you want to renovate, upgrade, you get the maximum bang for your buck by starting there. A woman can be as ugly as sin, but if she has gorgeous hair she will be at the very least passable, if not attractive. And Laurie's hair was gorgeous. It was not just thick and soft, but strong, like a good mattress; I could push as hard on it as I wanted and still not feel the scalp underneath. I could bury my head in it and probably die from strangulation, but what a way to go.

So I got a lot more turned on by her than I thought I would. I thought I would have to pump myself up by imagining she was Marissa, but to my utter amazement, all thoughts of Marissa disappeared the moment I touched her naked body. It was just her, that was all that was there.

When it was over, I felt very peaceful and satisfied — for about ten minutes. Then reality began to kick back in. This had been wonderful, but what next? What was I getting into? This was not some babe from some other lab, someone I would see only two or three times a year, at most. This one was home grown. Even worse, I was her mentor. I was at her side constantly, she depended on my advice and my trust. How could I just say, this was great for one night, but I'm not interested in doing it again?

"Has it been a while for you?"

"The first since my boyfriend left."

"You have a boyfriend? Has he ever come to the lab? I don't remember seeing him."

84

"He's in Wisconsin. He's doing a postdoc there."

"Do you like him a lot?"

"Of course I like him a lot! He wouldn't be my boyfriend if I didn't."

"Then why did you go to bed with me?"

"Alan, do you really have to ask that question?"

I rolled over and we both went to sleep.

The next day was a busy one. The morning sessions went on till noon, followed by a one hour break for lunch. Further sessions were held from one till four. And if I had any idle time at all, I would be hanging out at the poster sessions, which were up all day and could be visited at any time.

It was never possible, of course, to attend every session. One had to make a choice. During any particular time slot there were several options, tailored to the diverse backgrounds or interests of the attendees. For example, there were molecular/genetic approaches to cancer, where my own work fitted; there were physiological approaches; pathological approaches; clinical approaches; epidemiological approaches, and on and on. Not to mention that there are dozens and dozens of different kinds of cancer, all of them attracting specialists. It's truly humbling to realize that there are dozens if not hundreds of categories of cancer studies, and that no one on earth is very familiar with more than a handful of them. And cancer, of course, is only one disease among many.

Not wanting to miss any more than I could, I didn't get to the poster sessions until lunchtime. They had a box lunch deal available for those of us who wanted to eat on the run. I took one of the Styrofoam packets containing a tuna sandwich, salad, fruit and a cookie, and headed to one of the large atria in the hotel. There, in a space that seemed almost the size of a football field, had been set up hundreds of poster stations. Each station featured a large standalone cork board, on which were pinned what amounted to the pages of a mini-scientific paper. There usually was an Abstract, Introduction, Methods, Results and Discussion, complete with supporting figures and tables.

Poster sessions are immensely popular at scientific and I suppose other conferences because the audience can move at its own pace. You can pick and choose which posters to read, and spend as much or as little time as you want with each. If you have trouble understanding some point, you reread it carefully. If you still don't get it, you ask the author, who is on hand much of the time, though not always. I felt this made them an especially good place to learn about areas outside my own specialty, research I might lack even the basic background in and therefore would require some time to absorb. Thus I paid particular attention to some studies on types of cancer I was not so familiar with, because if I was going to try to develop new molecular screens for these cancers, I needed to know as much as possible about them.

Poster presentations are generally not considered as prestigious as formal, speaking presentations, and they tend to be dominated by young graduate students and other relative unknowns who may be publishing research for the first time. But just for this reason, they often turn up surprises, new discoveries that very few people are aware of. One such surprise was Alex Pignatti's poster.

It wasn't a complete surprise for me, of course. Alex had told me about it the previous day. But he hadn't shown me any actual data. These were not my three genes—our three genes I guessed I now had to call them—but his two new genes, the ones I knew nothing about. And what I saw now was impressive, to say the least. I stood there reading through it in silence, because Alex's student, who was actually presenting the poster, was not around, nor was Alex himself.

The two genes were closely associated with lung cancer, of all things. This was very surprising to me. It was not immediately obvious why genes associated with colon cancer should also turn up in lung cancer. It did suggest that the relationship was something very fundamental, and likely would turn up in other cancers as well.

Alex was right. I couldn't pass this up. I would have to speak to Mitch about it.

That evening, we all attended one of the major events of the conference, a talk given by Goren Chambers. He was one of the grand old men of cancer research, having given more than fifty years of his professional life to the field, and the recipient of numerous awards, including election to the highly prestigious National Academy of Sciences. His talk was open to the general public, and was heavily attended by the press. I looked around for Ed Cole, hoping to see him there, but I never did, and figured he was just lost somewhere in the huge crowd.

The speech was part science, part exhortation, summarizing in the most general terms the progress that had been made in the past several decades in understanding cancer, the obstacles that still lay ahead, and the hope that continued research held out for millions of patients around the world.

Following the speech, questions were taken from the audience. One man asked Dr. Chambers if he thought that a general goal of science was to eradicate all disease, and if so, whether it would ever be successful.

"It's certainly a goal of science to eradicate every disease afflicting the human species," Chambers responded. "Is that actually possible? That's a difficult question to answer. As you all know, we have eliminated many, many diseases that used to terrify our predecessors, reduced them to nothing but a footnote in some history book. And we will eradicate cancer, I promise you that."

This last statement was interrupted by impromptu applause.

"But we have seen that diseases, like life itself, are not fixed entities. They come and go; they evolve. When I began my scientific career, no one had ever heard of the AIDS virus, or SARS, or Ebola, or any number of highly pathogenic bacteria.

"My best guess is that while we can suppress disease to a minimum level, we will never eliminate it entirely. A major goal of this century, I think, will be to establish some kind of early warning system, so that we can identify and deal with new infectious diseases as they emerge, before they have a chance to spread throughout the population."

The questioner posed a follow-up.

"All right," he said, "Let's assume that we actually accomplish that. But of course that doesn't mean that no one will die from disease. It just means that we delay the day of reckoning. I mean, as we are today, if someone dies of heart failure, or cancer, or neurological disease at age fifty, we consider that tragic, and we fund research aimed to prevent that. But if someone dies from one of those same diseases at age eighty or ninety, we consider that natural. We call it old age. But from the viewpoint of science and medicine, isn't death the ultimate disease? Will science take it upon itself to try to conquer death itself?"

This was one of those questions, of course, that has no simple answer, and Dr. Chambers was old enough and wise enough — close enough to his own passing, one might say — not to try to provide one. But the audience buzzed about the exchange for a long time after.

The conference was scheduled to end Sunday morning, so that researchers could make arrangements to fly back to their home cities by Sunday night. The main business of the conference was actually finished by Saturday afternoon, and Saturday night there was to be a catered banquet at the hotel where the conference activities were centered.

After the last of the Saturday afternoon sessions, I returned to my hotel to get dressed for the banquet. My thoughts turned to my kidnapping case. I had made no further progress in solving it, except to analyze the keratins present in the small trash bag.

Identifying a protein by mass spectrometry is rather like identifying a book by random passages lifted from its pages. A specific short string of words will probably be found in several if not many books, but several such strings, occurring in different parts of the book, are very likely to be unique. The same is true of proteins. A short string of amino acids might be found in several different proteins, but only one protein is likely to make a perfect match with several such strings.

Analysis is much more complicated if one has a protein mixture, though, just as it would be if one had several unknown books, with the words from all of them somewhat jumbled up. Not only does every individual have about thirty different keratins, each of which is very similar yet not identical in sequence to the others, but some or all of the samples I was analyzing might contain keratins from both of the men. It was rather as though one had two authors, each of whom had written thirty different versions of the same book. To get unambiguous data, I needed to purify the keratins, separate them cleanly from each other, as well as from any other proteins that might be present in the sample.

Back in Minneapolis, before the conference, I had first soaked the samples—the bag, and several of the waste tissues inside separately—in a medium to extract all the proteins. Then I concentrated the medium to a very small volume, and applied each concentrated extract to a gel, which was subjected to an electrical current. Each of the proteins in the mixture differed from the others in its size and charge, and thus migrated differently on the gel.

I was working with such small quantities that I couldn't even visualize the proteins on the gel by staining them in the conventional manner. But I didn't worry about that, because I knew from using standards where they were supposed to be. So I just cut out the appropriate sections of the gel, and sent them to the lab.

As I had anticipated, some of the gel segments contained undetectable quantities of protein, and in those cases where there was enough for analysis, the results were often ambiguous, because the protein was insufficiently pure. But I did get a few definite sequences, which I had used to search a database of all human proteins. I had been able to identify several different keratins, including two forms of the same one, which strongly suggested that I was looking at profiles from each of the two men.

Still, as I had conceded to Burris before I even began the analysis, this didn't tell me a lot. Based on these sequences, I could distinguish each of the men from the other, and probably from many other individuals, but I could not identify either uniquely. What else could I do?

Using my laptop there in my hotel room, I went online, doing some more comparisons with the sequences in the database. Now I found something I hadn't noticed in my more preliminary investigations back in Minneapolis. One of the sequences had a fairly rare mutation in it, in which one amino acid was substituted by another. Searching for information on this mutation, I discovered it resulted in a disease called Messmann's corneal dystrophy. Not a serious disease, I learned, not always even symptomatic, but it frequently resulted in visual impairment. Interesting, I thought, but could it help me?

I left about 7:30. The instant I stepped outside of the hotel, a van pulled up. I suppose I should have been a little suspicious of such perfect timing, but the van looked like a shuttle. It was the right size and color, and had markings on the side that at a superficial glance indicated it was the hotel shuttle.

But the moment I stepped inside I regretted it. There were no other passengers inside. The sliding door closed behind me without my help, and as it did, I heard a loud click, suggesting it was locked. The windows were as opaque as walls, I couldn't see a thing outside. And I couldn't see the driver, either He was separated from the rear of the van where I was by an opaque partition.

Had I not been kidnapped before I might not have noticed all this immediately. As it was, I was much more attuned to anything out of the ordinary. I instantly tried the doors on both sides, confirming that both were locked. I banged on the partition. No response. The van had already begun pulling away from the hotel, out into traffic I assumed, on Van Ness Ave. I guessed I was again being taken to some hideout in the country. I knew whoever it was would take even greater precautions against my escape this time.

Well, I thought, at least I wasn't tied up this time. I tried waving at anyone who might be outside, though I knew it was futile. Of course the windows would be opaque in both directions.

I sat back in the seat, which at least was very comfortable. How was I going to get out of here? I studied the barrier in front of me carefully, where the driver and any of his accomplices had to be. There was no way I could break through or in any other manner penetrate it, but it occurred to me the reverse was also true. The only way my abductors could get to me was by stopping the car and opening one of the side doors to my compartment.

The barrier had a couple of small vents at the top and either side, a sort of meshwork that allowed air to circulate between the two compartments. Peering through one of these vents, I could not make out much of anything, but I could see just enough flashes of color and movement to be certain that it did go all the way through to the front. I searched my pockets. Normally I have no reason to carry matches, but at dinner the previous night, I had grabbed a small packet of them to write down the email address of a scientist I was interested in communicating with again. I also had plenty of papers with me. I wasn't thrilled about destroying them, of course, but I could at least start with some that were definitely dispensable, like the program of events for the preceding three days.

I rolled up one sheet into a narrow tube, then flattened it out. I lit one end of this flattened tube, and held it up to the vent, hoping that some of the smoke would waft into the front compartment. I let the flattened sheet burn down almost to my fingers before flicking the ash on the floor. No response. Clearly most of the smoke was not getting through. It was just building up in my own compartment.

I looked down at the seats and the floor. They were covered with a material that I was sure was flame-retardant. Indeed, the burning remnants of paper I had dropped on the floor smoldered out, barely even scarring the carpet.

I turned around. The back of the seat, at the top, was covered with a clear plastic. Pulling out a ball point pen, I used it to puncture this plastic in several places. Working at it for several minutes, I was eventually able to make a small tear in it. Getting a purchase on this with my hand, I pulled hard, ripping the tear further open. Finally I was able to pull away a small sheet of plastic.

I shaped this plastic into a convex or bowl like form, which I could cup over the vent, sealing it from the rest of the compartment. I took several more sheets of paper, wadded them up and stuffed them inside the hollow space between the plastic and the vent. I lit them with another match.

It was tricky, because I had to unseal the plastic a little bit from the vent to give the flame enough air. But eventually I found a way to hold the plastic such that the papers burned well, with most of the smoke going through the vent. As a bonus, the plastic melted a little, giving out a very distinctive smell that I hoped would be much more noticeable in front.

At first, it didn't seem to work. No response. The wadded up papers burned to black ash. But I couldn't think of anything else to try, so I pulled out some more papers and refueled my little fire. And again. And again.

My patience finally paid off. The van pulled over. As it came to a halt, I held my breath. One question was about to be answered. Were there two men in front, or only the driver? If there were two, the passenger would get out and open the door on my right side. However I managed to handle him, I would still have to deal with the driver. Not a very promising situation. If there were only the driver, though, he would open the door on the left side. One on one, I thought I had at least a fighting chance.

I positioned myself in the center of the seat, ready to move instantly to either side depending on which door opened. As it happened, I actually heard the door on the driver's side open, and gave a little sigh of relief. I could not see him get out of the van, of course, but he couldn't see me, either, which gave me a little advantage. I wondered if he were armed.

He was. The first thing I saw, as the door was tentatively opened just a sliver, was the barrel of a gun. I was ready for this. I had lit another rolled tube of paper, and as soon as I saw daylight, such at it was at this hour, I thrust the flame towards it, through the crack in the door so that it would reach his hand.

He gave a yelp of pain and reflexively withdrew his hand and the gun. At the same moment, I dropped my little torch, grabbed hold of the edge of the sliding door, and shoved it open with all my might. I then crashed out of the van, bowling my assailant over onto the ground.

For what seemed like an eternity, we lay tangled up together on the ground. I had already decided that if he had a gun I would not try to grab it from him, because even if I were ultimately successful in subduing him, I might get shot in the process. I was thinking only one thing: escape.

I scrambled to my feet, scanning the dark surroundings wildly. There simply was no time at all to consider options, so I took the plunge, literally. I jumped off a cliff.

8. THE DEVIL AND THE DEEP BLUE SEA

It was a long way down to the ocean, where I could hear the surf pounding the rocks, but fortunately I didn't fall all the way. About twenty bone-bruising, skin-scraping feet below the edge of the road, I slammed to a halt on a large rock outcropping. Before I could even feel the dull, aching pain deep inside my ribs, I was scrambling around below it, so I could shield myself from the man holding the gun above me.

I was familiar enough with northern California to guess where I was. On Route 1, one of the most scenic highways in the world. The road winds along the Pacific coast, at places climbing far above the ocean. It's a very popular tourist spot, and though I was sure a car or two would drive by eventually, it was after dark and I doubted any of them would stop.

My kidnapper had recovered. Though hidden from my view, he made his displeasure clearly known.

"If you climb up here right now I won't kill you," he shouted down in my general direction. This was followed by several stones that he apparently tossed like birdshot, hoping to get a lucky hit and maybe a response. None landed very close to me, at which point it occurred to me that he didn't know exactly where I was. He might even not be sure that I hadn't fallen all the way into the ocean, and perhaps now was lying dead or dying on some surf-slopped rock.

A moment later I heard the door of the van open, and for a brief moment of joy, I thought he was actually giving up and leaving. A classic case of wishful thinking, of course. I never heard the car start, and too soon I understood why. The area all around me was flooded with the beam of a very powerful flashlight.

He still couldn't see me, but I guessed he could see clearly enough right down to the water to confirm that I had not fallen all the way down. Therefore, he knew I was hiding, probably within yards of him. I didn't have to wait long to see what he would do

94

next. There was a sharp report and a bullet whistled by, ricocheting off the rocks further below.

"If you want to get out of here alive, climb back up here now," he repeated. Silence. The surf, at least fifty feet below me, was very loud and actually felt soothing, when I didn't think about what would happen if I lost my desperate, nail-scratching grip on the rock. There was no way I was going to reveal myself. If he wanted me, he was going to have to come down and get me. Would he really do that? I wondered. It would be dangerous for both of us. If I were willing to risk my own neck, I could risk his, too. If he managed to make it down to where I was, and there was a struggle, there was a good chance both of us would fall. I didn't want to take that chance, but surely if he had any sense, neither did he. He had more to lose at this point than I did.

What if I surrendered? Would they kill me eventually? It all depended, of course, on why I was being kidnapped. How high were the stakes involved? Were they really willing to kill me for them? Had they intended to do so before?

Surely all they wanted was the identity of those three genes. They didn't want any harm to come to me, they were just trying to get me to talk. But what if I refused? How far would they go? Would they try to torture it out of me? The whole notion seemed absurd—I was not some kind of military agent or spy, I was just a young scientist.

But if that were really the case, why not just give them what they want? Why not climb up right now and say to this thug, OK, I'll talk. Whatever it is you want, I'll give it to you. You want to know the identity of these genes? No problem, I'll write down all the information you need.

Suddenly I became very angry. Not because I would be forced into surrendering a discovery that was rightfully mine, jeopardizing my chances of getting a patent on a highly successful colon cancer screening test. Not that, but because the extraordinary secrecy that had come to shroud so much of science, bordering on paranoia, could lead to a situation like this. Cancer was public enemy no. 1, and we should all be working in unison to beat it. When I had discovered these three genes I should have proudly announced their identity to the entire scientific world. This should have become public, immediately.

Maybe if I had done that—if I had been allowed to do that—some other group would have beat us to the draw. Taking advantage of better facilities, more influential contacts, greater funding, or unique access to other critical information, another group might get a test on the market sooner, and maybe an even better test at that. And we were supposed to *resist* that? We were supposed to do everything possible to make sure that a test that would save thousands of lives, and make millions of others a little more worry-free, would be *delayed*, would take *longer* to go on the market?

For a moment, I quite forgot where I was: cringing behind a rock, barely keeping myself from plunging into the sea, while some rent-a-goon above me, some asshole who almost certainly didn't have the foggiest understanding of my research, threatened to blow my brains out. The sheer idiocy of it all made my limbs, already sapped to near exhaustion from clinging for dear life to the rock, weak to the point where I almost let go. If this stupid game is so important to you goddamned idiots, I thought, then go ahead, you can have it. I'm outta here.

But of course I didn't let go. And a moment later, my tenacity paid off. I heard another car stop on the road above. By now I had guessed that the van I had been abducted in had pulled into one of the numerous turnouts along highway one, spaces just off the road where two or three cars could park while their passengers got out to marvel at the ocean. He really had no choice. But now he had company.

I listened carefully for the sound of a car door opening, but with the surf pounding below, noises from above were indistinct. Then I heard the sweetest sound in the world, even if the information it contained terrorized me.

"Man, you shouldn't be climbing down there!"

The words couldn't have been directed to me, of course. I was invisible to anyone up on the road. My assailant must have climbed over the stone wall and started down towards me. Now he would be trying to get back up.

With all the strength I had left in my failing grasp, I raised my head above the rock and screamed at the top of my voice, "HELP! That guy in the van is trying to kidnap me. PLEASE HELP ME!"

I considered warning them that he had a gun. It seemed only fair. On the other hand, he would probably hide it and challenge my credibility. For all these new people on the scene knew, I was some loony who had gone climbing down the cliff. I wanted to keep the situation as simple as possible.

There was a pregnant pause, then a male voice said, "Are you serious? Where the hell are you? I can't see you."

This was followed instantly by another voice, a woman's.

"Dave, get in the car, NOW. I'm calling 911."

My kidnapper was no fool. He was not about to use his gun on these two innocents. A moment later I heard him open the van door, start the engine, and pull away screaming into the night. At least I prayed it was he that had left. I still did not budge from my position, waiting for positive confirmation.

"Where are you? Can you climb back up?

Now relief poured unrestrainedly into every pore of my body.

"Yeah, I think so. You wouldn't happen to have a rope in your car, would you?"

Dave and Samantha were very nice. They let me sit in the car with them while we waited for the police. I briefly told them what happened, not mentioning the previous kidnapping, or giving them any indication I had any clue over why I was being targeted. Only right before the police arrived did I think to ask Dave a critical question.

"Did you happen to see the license plate on that van?"

He shook his head with frustration.

"Shit, no. We were parked front to front, and there was no plate on the front of the van, that much I remember.

Damn it, I thought. Another draw.

When the police arrived, we gave them a description of the van, and the direction it had been heading in. I could say virtually nothing about the kidnapper himself, other than his general size, because it had been dark when we struggled outside the van, and I was in a panic to get away. In fact I thought he had a mask on. Dave had seen a little more, but not much more, not only because of the dark, but because the kidnapper had been some distance away from him, and Dave also thought, was wearing a mask or some kind of headgear that obscured his face. The cops told me they would send a team to the site the next day to search for the bullet that had been fired. They took me to a local station where I filled out a full report of the incident.

When I was finally done there at the police station, one of the officers kindly offered to drive me back to the city, all the way to my hotel. I felt absolutely exhilarated to be cocooned in the safety of a police car, and the officer was very friendly, asking me with interest about my work in cancer research and about the conference I had been attending. It was a long ride, nearly two hours, and I ended up spilling my guts to her. I told her all about the other kidnapping and the evidence that someone I worked with might be involved. Jesus, I even told her about Marissa Cheng, not just about the key role of her cell phone, but about my interest in her. I don't know why in the hell I talked about that, except that I felt a strange and heady sense of freedom, of not having or wanting to have any secrets any more. I really think I would have told Officer Hamilton the identity of the three genes if she had asked, not that the names would have meant anything to her.

There was a pleasant silence after I had told her the entire story. At one point the police radio crackled, but she did not answer it.

"Well, you know the old saying," she said finally. "Follow the money."

Officer Hamilton, whom I was very soon calling Iris, was short and compact, not what I would call pretty, though sexy in a sort of sensual, cuddly way. She was slow and deliberate in her speech, and seemed almost too sensitive for a member of her profession. I took an instant liking to her, and as the ride proceeded, I quite forgot that she was a police officer at all.

"Follow the money?" I echoed. "The problem is that money is everywhere. This patent is worth millions of dollars. I don't want to sound melodramatic, but the information I'm carrying around with me is worth a fortune to anyone who knows enough to make use of it. Even if our test is the first on the market, these genes might be critical to other types of cancer as well. We don't know at this point whether we can patent them for that purpose, so the door is wide open for someone working on another type of cancer."

Iris nodded, getting the gist if not the details of what I was saying. "My husband had a colonoscopy last year. It wasn't that bad, but he said the worst part was the preparation. He had to drink gallons of fluids to flush out his system." She paused to check another message crackling over the police radio. "Hell, if you eliminate that, I'll take your test right now. And I'm only forty-three, with no family history of cancer as far as I know."

We were crossing the Golden Gate Bridge, and it was a perfectly lovely evening, with none of that Bay Area trademark, "patchy fog", to spoil the view. I could look out on the Bay for miles, seeing little lights winking in the distance.

"Cancer," Iris murmured. "It doesn't always kill people, does it? One of the officers in our department had a tumor in his neck. He had it removed eventually, but the doctor said that, cosmetic reasons aside, he could have lived with it for years."

"That's right," I said quickly. "Not all cancers spread, or metastasize, to other parts of the body. Some stay put. They grow very slowly, diverting just enough blood to nourish their cells, but leave the rest of the body alone."

"Many crooks I've run up against are like that," said Iris. "In fact, most of the really successful ones—the ones that get away with it for years or years, maybe never get caught—are probably like that. They find a way to steal what they need without calling a lot of attention to it. They're smart enough not to kill the goose that lays the golden eggs."

I still hoped I wasn't that goose.

9. SEQUENCE ANALYSIS

U pon arriving back in Minneapolis on Sunday afternoon, I went straight to the lab. I had another lead on my case, one I hoped would pan out better than the keratins had. When I had tussled with my kidnapper north of San Francisco, I had stabbed him with a pen. Before Iris Hamilton had dropped me off at my hotel in the city that night, I had realized the potential value of the tiny sample of blood on its tip, and had kept it refrigerated. I knew what I planned to do with it was still something of a long shot, so I didn't tell anyone about it, not even Officer Hamilton.

The first thing I did in the lab was extract DNA from the sample. It contained a very tiny amount, a little less than one microgram. This was not enough to do much analysis on, so I then proceeded to amplify it. The same property of DNA that allows it be passed down from generation to generation in all species of life — the ability to reproduce exact copies of itself, which it parcels to daughter cells during mitotic division — also allows the investigator to make more of it. In fact, I followed a procedure very similar to the PCR or polymerase chain reaction that I used to amplify the gene messages in my cancer research. In principle, there's no limit to how much DNA one can create from any starting sample.

While I was running the amplification reaction, I went online and followed up another hunch. I had begun to wonder about Ed Cole, the man who had approached me at Mitch's party during the conference. Was he really a high school science teacher, as he claimed to be, or was it possible he had something to do with the kidnapping? I didn't think a man who was planning to kidnap me shortly thereafter would want to present himself to me so brazenly, and thinking it over, I felt quite sure that Cole did not fit the physical impression, sketchy as it was, I had of the man who had driven that van. But remembering that Cole had asked me what hotel I was staying in, it occurred to me that he might have been working with the driver of the van.

It was not an easy search, because the name Ed Cole is quite common, but to my mild surprise I did find a man of that name listed as a teacher at a high school in Lincoln, Nebraska. That seemed to clear Cole. But I still wanted to talk with him. He had no phone number or email address listed at the website, so I sent an email to a general address of the high school. I just said that I had met Cole at a party in San Francisco, where he had expressed an interest in cancer research.

If Ed Cole had in fact been working for the kidnapper, though, it seemed a little less likely that anyone I worked with in the lab would be involved. Laurie—not that I had ever suspected her—had stayed on the same floor as I, so she obviously had known where I was. Several others, including Bill Tye, had also stayed in that hotel, and probably had seen me there. And almost anyone in the group might have casually asked me where I was staying without attracting any attention. Likewise for any rival scientist who had attended the conference, including Alex, who in fact did know where I was staying.

So who wouldn't know where I was staying? Maybe someone on the board at OS, I supposed. Perhaps this latest kidnapping pointed a finger at one of them? Granted, it seemed highly unlikely that any of them could have sent that text to me on Marissa's cell phone, which more and more appeared to be the biggest clue in the entire case. But then again, I had had no luck pinning that text on anyone who might have been in the lab at that time, either.

In any case, I felt I had nothing to lose by trying to learn more about Ed Cole. In the meantime, I decided not to tell anyone in the lab about this second kidnapping. Maybe whoever was behind it would betray some surprise at learning that I had again escaped. Anyway, I was tired of telling the same story over and over to everyone who asked, and I didn't see that doing so was going to bring me any closer to identifying my assailants.

While I was in the lab, I called the campus police station. As it happened, Officer Burris was around, and when he heard that I had been abducted a second time, he invited me to come over to talk with him. I visited him in the late afternoon, when I was done for the time being in the lab.

It was pretty obvious to Burris as well as me that the two kidnappings had to be connected, and after listening to the details of this second attempt, he returned the discussion to the first one. I told him what I had learned about the cell phone text I had received the evening of the first kidnapping. Actually, I had known most of these details at the time I had last seen Burris, but I had been so disappointed to learn that the owner of the house where I had been taken denied all knowledge of the crime that I hadn't bothered to share this information with him. Now I told him all about my discussions with Marissa Cheng, Bernie Evers and Bill Tye.

"There's just one thing I don't understand," I said when I was finished. "If someone wanted me to go to the Ice Palace that night, why go to all the trouble of sabotaging the freezer, ensuring that Bernie would text Marissa's cell phone? Why not just text me about a phony problem, from Marissa's phone or some other phone they felt wasn't traceable to them?"

"I can see a reason," said Burris. "Think about it this way. Whoever planned the kidnapping couldn't be certain of pulling it off. Suppose you don't go to this Ice Palace, what you call it, and they don't manage to nab you somewhere else. Even worse, suppose you do go there, but they bungle the job, and you get away. At that point, you naturally begin to wonder if the text about the freezer problem was just a way of setting you up."

I now saw the point Burris was making. "So by having a real problem, whoever sent that text is not implicated. He or she could even freely confess to having sent it, and Bill would back up the story that there really was a problem."

"Exactly. And even if the kidnapping were successful, there's always the chance that the text will be discovered. Maybe Ms., er Cheng, is checking her account and she discovers a text that night from her phone to yours that is deleted. She tells the police. If there really was a problem at the Ice Palace, it will appear less likely that that text had anything to do with the kidnapping."

Burris got up from the table and began to pace around the room. Periodically he would stop to do his stretching exercises.

"So there are three people involved in this chain of texts— besides you, of course. It begins with Mr. Evers, goes to Ms. Cheng,

102

or at least to her phone, then to Dr. Tye."

I nodded, now beginning to get into the flow of logic. "Bernie has to be clear—not that I could see a motive for him, anyway. Because if he wanted to get me to come down to the Ice Palace, why didn't he text me directly? True, he was supposed to text Marissa first under those circumstances, but he claimed there was no immediate reply from her, and Marissa herself says she never texted him. He could have then texted me, but he didn't."

Burris nodded. "What about Ms. Cheng?"

"She denies sending that text to me, and there's no record of it on her cell phone. I suppose someone else could have accessed her phone that night. On the other hand, she didn't seem particularly upset to learn that someone did."

"She doesn't carry it with her?"

"Apparently not. She leaves it at her desk. Actually, I do the same thing. I don't want someone calling or texting me in the middle of an experiment."

I explained to Burris that security in our wing of the research building was very good. Because of that, and because we generally trusted our co-workers, many of us did not lock up semi-valuable items like cell phones, flash drives, and even laptops, but just put them in a desk drawer.

"Also," I continued, "Marissa claims she wasn't around then. She also told me that she doesn't take that cell phone home with her, so anyone could have taken it from her desk."

"Who was in the laboratory at that time?"

"I really don't know. As I just said, Marissa claims she wasn't there, for what that's worth. I believe Bill Tye was there. I remember seeing him at one point, though I couldn't swear he was around when that text was sent." I looked at Burris. "What do you make of the fact that someone texted him later from my cell phone?"

"I don't see anything definitely suspicious there," replied Burris, still pacing. "You said he volunteered the information that he had received a text from your phone, before you actually knew that. Then he showed you the text. He also confirmed Mr. Evers's story that he, Dr. Tye, had gone to the Ice Palace."

"But then why is Bill involved in this at all? Assume someone else did this. Why did he or she text Bill?"

Burris stopped pacing, lost in thought.

"I'm thinking to get Ms. Cheng's phone out of the loop," he said finally. "If you're kidnapped successfully, and no one goes to this Ice Palace to see about the problem, then the next day Mr. Evers might call Ms. Cheng and say, why didn't you send someone down here? At that point, she will realize someone used her cell phone, and when your disappearance becomes known, we may realize that's a clue."

"That makes sense," I replied. "And I guess that might also explain why they used my cell phone to text Bill, rather than Marissa's. The only people who know that Marissa's phone was an intermediary in this chain are the person who used it, and me, and I'm supposed to be safely out of the picture."

"Exactly," Burris replied, "and no one will even connect the kidnapping to the Ice Palace, because the text that was sent from your phone to Dr. Tye's implies that you never went there — that you just stayed in the laboratory, then went home later."

For the first time, it began to dawn on me how cleverly this had been set up. Of course, given that the exact time of the freezer failure would be difficult to predict, the ploy might not have worked — and indeed it hadn't. But there was virtually no downside to it. Nothing to lose — or wouldn't have been if I hadn't escaped that house.

"Have you talked to others in your research group about that text?" Burris asked me.

"No. Do you think I should?"

Burris, still standing still on the far side of the table from me, thought this over in silence for a moment.

"I think you should ask Ms. Cheng to do the questioning. After all, it was her cell phone that was used. She ought to want to know who did it. If she doesn't seem to care — well, that's a little suspicious in itself, isn't it?"

I nodded. "I guess it is." I still couldn't imagine why Marissa of all people would want to see me kidnapped.

Burris returned to the table and sat down again. "Now let's talk about motive," he began. "I assume this has to have something to do with the patent you told me about — at least until you can give me some other reason why someone would want you out of the way. Who in your laboratory would stand to gain if you weren't around?"

I mentioned Bill Tye and his interest in OS. I also told Burris a little about my troubles with the other board members at OS, how some of them might have loved to have me out of the picture. But I felt it was unlikely any of them would have been around to use Marissa's cell phone that night, even assuming they knew where to find it. The same with Alex Pignatti, who seemed to have an excellent motive, but who, again, had no reason or business to be in our laboratory that night.

Burris thought this over. "If I understand you correctly, a competing scientist outside your research group — someone like Dr. Pignatti — would have the most to gain by your disappearance. Suppose someone like that was working with someone inside your research group."

I stared at him. "What do you mean? How?"

Burris looked down at his notes for a moment. "You told me these three genes you discovered are critical to the success of your patent, right?"

"Yes, absolutely."

"Suppose someone inside your research group, one of your colleagues, offered to sell that information to someone outside the group."

"But most people in the lab don't know what these genes are," I protested. "Only Mitch and I, and the other board members of OS, know the identity of all three. Two of the new graduate students I work with know one of the genes. Plus Bill. That's it."

"But wouldn't it be possible to find out?" persisted Burris. "Go through your computer files, or laboratory records, you must have this information recorded somewhere."

"I suppose it's possible, sure, if someone wants that information badly enough." I thought about that. "But even supposing that were the case, why have me kidnapped?"

"Maybe it would be easier to go through your files when you were gone for an extended period of time," suggested Burris. "Or maybe the information has already been transferred, sold to someone outside the group, and he now wants you out of the way so that he can make use of it."

Noting the look of puzzlement on my face, he continued.

"It still goes back to the patent, Mr., er Alan. Suppose someone has sold the needed information to a rival scientist. This scientist wants to patent this information himself, but he can't beat you to it unless he manages to prevent you from finishing your patenting process, or at least delay it."

I had already explained to Burris, at my first meeting with him, that even in my absence, Mitch would be able to go forward on the patent process easily on his own. Still, I thought, my absence might slow things down. After all, I was the only one on top of every last detail.

"Is there anyone in your research group who would be in a particularly good position to obtain the needed information?" he asked me.

I told Burris about the grant I was working on. It didn't name the three genes I had discovered, but it did provide a lot of useful information related to them. Knowing this information, a scientist working in this field would at the very least have a better idea what these genes might be. And he might be able to guide or direct someone in my group where to look next.

"Who else in your research group has access to this grant?"

I told him about Dick and Candy. Dick was responsible for just the budget, but he did have access to the entire proposal at one time or another. Candy of course definitely had access to the entire proposal, as she was responsible for editing it.

"OK," said Burris. "Suppose Mr. Johnstone or Ms. Rominger offered the information in the grant to some rival scientist. Maybe this information is enough for them to discover these three genes, given enough time. Or maybe it isn't, and they ask the person in your group who sold this information to get some more. In either case, I can see how it might be very helpful not to have you around for a while."

I nodded. It all made about as much sense as any other hypothesis, I thought. I found it very hard to believe either Dick or Candy would be involved in having me kidnapped, but then neither did I think anyone else in the lab would.

"Do they have access to the laboratory itself?" Burris asked. "Could they have been around that night and obtained that cell phone?"

"Sure, they come into the lab from time to time. Both of them are working late a lot now, because this grant is due at the end of July. I don't know if either one was around that night, but it's certainly possible."

"Fine," said Burris. "If you can find out, maybe not by asking them directly but by asking someone else, you might try to do that. You might also want to think about specific researchers who might be interested in this information. I guess Dr. Pignatti is the one you can be certain about at this point."

I hadn't told Burris about my latest talk with Alex in San Francisco, and how complicated the situation had become with him. But I spared him those details, and just said I would think about that.

"Is there anything else I should do or could do?"

Burris frowned. "Watch your back, that's for sure. I can't offer you police protection at this point, I'm not sure you would want it, but you need to be with someone when you are outside on the street, at all times, if possible."

10. EXPERIMENTAL ERRORS

Monday morning, I met alone with Mitch in his office. He was aware of Alex Pignatti's latest work; he had seen the poster session at the conference. What Mitch did not yet know was Alex's proposed deal. He would allow us to join him on the patent he was filing for these two new genes, in return for a reciprocal arrangement in which he would be a co-discoverer listed on the patent of my three genes. Alex had not told anyone but me that these two new genes were important to colon cancer — that information had not been in his poster presentation. So they were still patentable.

I had put off until now to inform Mitch of this because I knew it would come as a shock to him. Not simply that Alex had independently discovered my three genes, but that I could even be sure of this. Though it was Mitch who had encouraged me to talk with Alex from time to time, it went without saying that we were not supposed to discuss anything related to my work on colon cancer. Our discussions were supposed to be solely about other types of cancer, studies of which neither lab had begun and were therefore not in competition over. If Mitch had known the full extent of what had transpired between Alex and me over the past few weeks, he would have shit in his pants. I knew I had to choose my words with care, yet I could think of no way to cushion the blow.

"Mitch," I began, " when I was at the conference I talked to Alex privately. He has our three genes now."

Mitch had been perusing a journal article when I walked in. But now I had his complete attention. He stopped abruptly and looked up at me sharply. "How do you know?"

"Because he named them to me."

At this point, I expected Mitch to react with several emotions, beginning, but by no means ending, with astonishment. Because Alex had not only found these genes, but had got me to admit that they were in fact the same as the ones I had discovered. That I had spilled the beans, or at least hadn't picked them up off the floor when they were knocked out of my hands. But to my surprise,

Mitch took this news rather calmly.

"Well, I knew he had one of them. I suppose it was only a matter of time before he found the other two."

Suddenly I was the one caught of guard.

"You knew that Alex had identified one of these genes? How?"

"He told me."

Mitch set the article back down on his desk and proceeded as if he didn't know everything he was going to say would shock the hell out of me.

"One day several months ago, Alex visited me here in my office. He told me he was pretty sure one of the genes he had identified was the same as one of your three. He wanted me to confirm this."

So he was playing his little game with both of us, I thought. Figured if he couldn't worm the information out of me, he would try Mitch.

"So he told you he would give you the name of this gene if you would just tell him if it was one of my three, right?"

Now Mitch did look surprised. "Exactly. How did you know?"

I waved him off, indicating he should just go on for now. I was busy with chronology. Alex came to me first, I guessed, with his three-gene card trick. When he knew for sure that the gene he was interested in was one of mine, he was then in a position to approach Mitch more confidently.

"Did you agree to do this?" I asked Mitch. I was very curious to see if he had succumbed to Alex's little tricks as easily as I had.

"Not at first. But then Alex said something else, which changed everything."

"What was that?"

"He told me he had already filed a provisional patent for this gene."

Jesus, I thought, of course he would do that. How could have I been so naïve? I had assumed when I had talked to Alex that day that he hadn't filed a patent on it, because he didn't know as much about as I did. But of course, that would not stop him.

"At that point," Mitch continued, "there was no reason not to tell him. If his gene was different, it didn't help us, we couldn't use it, maybe add it to our test, because he had already started the patent process. I mean, technically we could have, because his patent was only provisional, but in that situation I wouldn't have. On the other hand, if it was the same gene as one of ours, his knowing that wouldn't give him anything he didn't already have. It was really more for our benefit than his at that point."

"Wait a minute," I interrupted. "When exactly did he file this provisional patent? It must have been after we did."

Mitch nodded. "Yes, but Alex claimed that didn't matter."

"Doesn't matter? Why the hell not?"

Mitch frowned, took off his glasses and toyed with them for a moment.

"Alan, I'm not sure if I told you this before or not? In the U.S., priority is not determined by the date at which a patent application is filed. It's determined by the date at which the discovery or invention was first conceived. Alex claimed that he discovered this gene before you did. He has records establishing that he identified this gene more than a year ago."

I did a lightning-quick recall process of all my research that had led to the discovery of the three genes. I couldn't remember the exact date at which I had first noticed this one gene's potential, of course. I would have to go through my own notebooks to see. But it was obvious we had a problem which might take some time to resolve. Now at last I understood why our application for a full patent had been held up. Why Mitch kept insisting that all the data I had accumulated showing the involvement of my three genes in colon cancer were not enough.

I gave a long sigh. "So the ownership of one of my three genes is under challenge. And until that is settled, our hands are tied."

Mitch nodded. "Yes, but the situation is even worse than that. Alex is not actually the one who is challenging us. Not any more."

I stared at him, puzzled. "*What?* You mean there is some *other* researcher involved?"

"No, the federal government is. The government is claiming that it owns this gene."

Now I was really confused.

"*Huh*? How did the federal government get involved in this?"

Mitch picked up the article he had been reading and flapped it around helplessly.

"Goddamn it," he said. "Alex's research was funded by a federal grant, and—"

"But so was mine, Mitch!" I interrupted in protest. "You told me that the way patent law works is that if the investigator makes a discovery while being funded by the government, he's still allowed to keep it."

"Oh, yes, as long as we notify the government at every step of the way. Remember that meeting we had with the university's lawyers and research administrator? Remember how they kept emphasizing that the federal government had to be informed about everything?"

"And Alex *didn't*?" I found this hard to believe. Whatever his faults, Alex was not careless about anything, at least he never gave me that impression.

Mitch sighed, and motioned me to sit down. I had been so transfixed by hearing these developments that I had remained standing in front of his desk up until now. "It seems to be one of those unfortunate glitches that really is nobody's fault. You see, Alex, like us, has several sources of funding; not just federal, but also from private organizations and the university itself. The grants which supported his work on this particular gene were supposed to be entirely private. But apparently they ran out of funds near the end of the term, and Dick Johnstone dipped into a federal grant that Alex had to make up the difference."

"And he didn't tell Alex that he was doing this?"

Mitch shook his head. "He didn't think he needed to. Dick is accustomed to making cost transfers, using excess funds from one grant to pay off a shortfall on another. Normally, there's nothing wrong with that if the two grants are working in closely-related areas. It's allowable. But once the federal government has any financial interest in a project, it has to be informed about any patents."

My mind was in turmoil as I thought through the implications of this.

"We can still apply for a patent for my three genes together, can't we? Our test requires a combination of the three. Any single gene is not sufficient as a colon cancer marker."

Mitch got up from his desk, something he rarely did when were talking, and sort of loped around the small quarters of his office, bobbing up and down.

"At the moment, that's unclear. The government is claiming something called prior art. The idea is that once they hold a patent to one gene, adding a couple of others is considered a derivative. It's not a genuinely new advance, but a modification of a previously patented idea. We—the university and its lawyers—are objecting to this, on the grounds that one gene is useless for a test, that all three are needed. But at the moment the whole thing is sort of in limbo."

"You mean we can only patent two of the genes, rather than three?" I said. "But the test will lose a lot of its sensitivity if we can't use all three. It won't be any better than some of the other tests that are already out there. We need them all."

Mitch stopped, and softly pounded his hand on one of the bookshelves.

"Of course, of course, Alan. But you see, the federal government is in the same boat, since the one gene they're claiming title to doesn't help them, either. It's clearly not good enough by itself as a marker for colon cancer. So now they're talking about making a deal with us. They're willing to let us apply for a patent for all three genes if they can be on the patent, too. In other words, they give up some of their rights to one of the genes in return for some of the rights to the other two."

"How would that work, exactly?"

"Right now, the university lawyers are haggling over this. As I

112

told you before, the way this usually works is that the university gets about sixty percent of the royalties from a patent, while the discoverer gets the remaining forty percent. The government, having one of these three genes, wants thirty-three percent. But we're refusing that offer, because the gene they have is not the most important of the three. We don't think it really contributes one-third of the value of the test. So we've offered them twenty percent. Then the university would get fifty percent, and we would get thirty percent."

And of course, I thought, the federal government was taking a very keen interest in our upcoming validation study. Because that study would not only establish once and for all that the three genes could be used to screen successfully for colon cancer. It would also indicate, in quantitative precision, the relative contribution of each gene. I had no doubt that those numbers would be critical in determining just how large a piece of any patent pie the federal government finally claimed title to.

Not that I cared how much pie they eventually crammed their greedy fingers into. No matter what the final percentages, I was going to make a lot of money. What I did care about was getting the full patent application underway. Now that I had been kidnapped a second time, I had begun to feel an urgency to the situation. As long as ownership of these genes was up in the air, I was a target. Surely once our claim to these genes was firmly established, whoever was trying to get me out of the picture would cease and desist. I almost broke my little vow not to tell anyone in the lab that I had been kidnapped in San Francisco.

"But couldn't we apply for a patent right now for the other two genes? Suppose someone else comes along and beats us to it? Then they would be in a position to bargain with the government instead of us."

Mitch returned to his seat.

"We're safe on that score. As I told you earlier, priority is determined by the date at which the discovery or invention was first conceived. In other words, as long as we can establish that you identified those two genes first, it doesn't matter if we aren't the first to apply for a patent."

"It's really that simple?"

Mitch made a gesture with one of his hands, as if to say, sort of.

"The discoverer or inventor of some idea does have to demonstrate what the law refers to as "reasonable diligence". That is, if after identifying those genes you had made no attempt to patent them or commercialize them, then someone who later identified them and did make such attempts could be awarded the patent. But the existence of our startup, OS, plus our ongoing negotiations with the government over the status of the other gene, make it clear that we have exercised 'reasonable diligence.' Not to mention the provisional patent, of course. We have attempted to derive practical applications from the identification of these genes."

"OK," I said, "but how exactly do we prove that I identified these genes first?"

"Generally by what is called physical evidence. Not computer files, for example, which can be altered, but entries into lab notebooks. If the notebook is bound, so that one page clearly follows another, and each day's entry is dated, the law says that can be used to establish priority."

He looked at me sharply.

"So it's a very good thing you have those lab notebooks, Alan. Just make sure they're all safe, sound and intact."

Mitch and I were not finished yet, though. In fact, we still hadn't discussed what I had come to his office to discuss in the first place: Alex's role.

"He wants to be on the patent, too, Mitch. His deal is if we do that for him, he will let us share the patent of his two new genes."

Mitch looked puzzled.

"That doesn't sound to me like much of an offer. What's in it for us? They may have some promise for lung cancer, but so what?"

In response, I told him about my private talk with Alex in the hotel lobby in San Francisco, on the opening day of the conference. In that discussion, Alex had shown me data indicating that his two

114

new genes, together with the one of mine, were almost as good as my three together as colon cancer markers. The implication being that if we used all five together, we would have an even better screening test.

"Alex has not patented their use for colon cancer, because at the time he discovered them, he didn't know of their value in that regard," I continued. "But we can find out easily enough. We can just expand this study we're planning at the Mayo clinic. We'll ask them to analyze all the stool samples for these two additional genes. If they improve the sensitivity of the test, we can add them in. If it turns out they really don't make much more difference, we can leave them out."

"And leave Alex out, too, in that case."

Somewhat to my surprise, I found myself defending Alex.

"Remember, Mitch, these genes are also associated with lung cancer. That was the whole point of the poster presentation. So they would be useful to the studies I'm doing with Bill Tye."

Mitch started to shrug, as if to say, big deal, when a light went on in his eyes.

"Hey!" he almost shouted. "Suppose these two genes of Alex's really add sensitivity to the colon cancer screening test! We can tell the federal government to kiss off! We can just use his two genes and your other two. We won't need the one that the federal government owns! The four might be good enough by themselves."

"Sounds good," I replied. 'Let's hope Alex learned his lesson on his first patent application, and hasn't handed these genes over to the federal government, too. Because if he has, they might not need us. They might be the ones ending up with the only marketable colon cancer test."

I returned to my desk with a lot to mull over. Alex, it seemed to me now, looked much less like a suspect in my kidnapping. I was his lifeline to a patent. I was the only person he had given the critical information that his two genes were associated with colon cancer. Obviously he had told me this in San Francisco with the objective of getting me to tell Mitch. Had I been kidnapped, Mitch never would have known this. Of course, Alex could have approached Mitch instead of me, but the point was, he didn't. And because he didn't, because he went out of his way to entrust me with this valuable information, it made no sense for him to have me kidnapped subsequently.

Of course, Alex had not been entirely forthcoming with me. He hadn't told me about his claim to prior discovery of one of my genes. But presumably that had been Mitch's idea. Mitch would not want to burden me with this bureaucratic nightmare until the point came when I had to know about it.

What about other possible suspects? If my claim to the other two genes was as certain as Mitch had implied, there would be no real value in stealing the identity of the three genes. But maybe not everyone understood patent law that well, and assumed that if we hadn't filed a patent on the genes, there was still open season on them. Or maybe the idea was to find the notebook in which I had recorded the identity of these genes, and destroy the evidence. Or maybe even someone thought I might have made some key progress on another cancer test, and just wanted to find out once and for all everything I had done. But again, did I really have to be kidnapped to further that aim? How much time did someone need either to find that notebook, or conclude that it couldn't be found?

That particular notebook, like all of the others except the ones I was currently using, was locked in my desk. Someone who wanted it badly enough could break into my desk, I was sure, but so far, no one had tried. On the face of it, it did not seem that whoever had me kidnapped was interested in that notebook, or at the very least, knew enough about my work to know where it would most likely be.

After lunch I visited Dick Johnstone's office. Until I had heard Alex's sad story, I had been considering letting Dick handle the remaining budget details of my grant proposal. But now I felt it was more important than ever to make sure I understood the budgeting process. There was no possibility of what had happened to Alex happening to me; since I was applying for a federal grant, I would of course keep the government informed about any new discoveries that might be patentable. Still, the fact that something like that had slipped through made me concerned that there might be other crucial details that could be missed.

Dick acted uncharacteristically embarrassed when I told him I had heard what had happened. He said he felt some personal responsibility for the government's claim on the patent, even if no one was blaming him.

"It won't happen again, lover boy, cross my heart and hope to die," he said, going reluctantly to his files. "Yours truly was a stupid idiot, and he learned his lesson. I'm a sad, sad camper."

"I know it won't happen again, Dick. But I have to learn how this is done."

I felt a little sorry for Dick, asking him for more invoices, as though I didn't trust him not to screw up again. But following my talk with Burris the day before, I had realized that I had to consider Dick a suspect in my kidnapping. Could he possibly be selling information from the grant to some rival scientist? Even before I walked into his office, I had formulated a little plan to test that. I thought I would see how he would react if he thought I was thinking along those lines.

It was probably a dumb thing to do. I'm not a detective, and I had no experience in questioning suspects, particularly in approaching them in a way that would not raise their suspicions. I did realize that, that my questions could just have the effect of warning someone off, telling him to be more careful. But after the second kidnapping, I was getting desperate to know what was going on, to find out who was trying to destroy my life, and I really didn't know what else to do.

As it turned out, Dick himself provided me with an opening. He asked me if I was making any progress in solving my kidnap case.

I shrugged and said, "The question is motive. I guess it must have something to do with my work. The valuable information I have."

"You have valuable information?"

Dick was magnificently dressed, as always. He was wearing

charcoal pants with broad, barely visible gray vertical strips that ran their length. He had a pink long-sleeved shirt with some sort of black flower—an orchid, maybe?—pinned to one of the pockets. His shoes were as black, smooth and shiny as a seal, and alone would easily cost five times as much as all the clothes I had hanging in the closet of my apartment. He had taken off his coat and tie, and hung them very carefully in a small cabinet at one side of his office.

He always had a small pot of coffee brewing on a lovely little glass-topped table at the front of his office, right next to the door. I declined some, as usual, but did help myself to some exquisitely delicious cookies, the kind that came in a metal box and were imported from some Asian country. On his desk there were some framed pictures, Dick at all ages of his life, and with all kinds of people. Many of them were taken on a small boat which I knew Dick owned and liked to take on little outings at various lakes in the Twin Cities area.

I nodded. "Related to this colon cancer test we're developing. Other groups are trying to develop the same kind of test, and they would love to know what we know."

If this blunt talk bothered Dick, made him uncomfortable, he sure didn't show it. On the contrary, he seemed intrigued by it.

"Really, lover boy? Oooo, that's exciting! You mean someone might actually want to abduct you and—what?—torture it out of you? But you can't be serious!"

I shook my head. "I don't think anyone wants to torture me. You're right, that is a bit much. I think they just want me out of the way."

Dick raised his eyebrows at that. "What do you mean, out of the way?"

I explained the scenario as vaguely as I could. I didn't suggest the possibility that the information was in my grant, or that someone in the lab might be offering it for sale. I just said that anyone who got a peek at some of this information would want more, which could only be obtained by getting hold of my lab notebooks or computer files. Maybe they would even want to destroy the original evidence, to prevent my patent from being accepted. To do this might require a lot of time and effort, and would be much easier to accomplish with me out of the way.

Dick's eyes lit up. "I see! But has anyone tampered with your notebooks or computer files yet?"

I shook my head. "Not yet, as far as I can tell. But then, maybe they would have tried if I had been away longer."

"You just got back from several days at the conference," Dick pointed out. "How much time would they need?"

Very good question. "Maybe that's not enough time. I really don't know."

A little later, when I visited Candy in her office, I tried the same approach on her. Her reaction was quite different. But then again, I sort of went too far with her. I really couldn't help it. As soon I said the word "information", she could figure out what I was talking about. After all, unlike Dick, who was concerned only with the financial aspects of my grant, Candy looked at the parts where my results were actually presented. She could guess very easily what I was talking about.

"OK," she said, after I had described the scenario, "let's suppose someone in the group has information about your research. It could be anyone, I suppose." She gave a nervous little laugh. "It could even be me, couldn't it? But how would they find a buyer for this information? I mean, how would they know whom to contact? And how to approach them?"

I was taken completely aback by this point. It was really a very good question. In my own case, of course, it would have been no problem. I knew what other laboratories were working on a similar test. Mitch, of course, knew too, as did Bill Tye. Same with some of the older graduate students, like Marissa. The younger students, like Andrea and Laurie, might have a little more difficult time, but no doubt they had the skills and resources. After all, at our group meetings, we often mentioned the related work of other groups.

But for people like Dick and Candy, who were not familiar with the research at all, this would be a major problem. They would not know who these interested parties were, and even if they did know, it would be difficult to approach them. They did not generally attend scientific meetings, so had little chance to rub shoulders with other researchers.

On the other hand, I thought, it didn't have to be initiated by someone in our group. It could start at the other end.

"This person in our lab might not have to know anyone," I pointed out. "Someone might approach him. Someone in some other group might come up to someone in our group and make an offer. You tell me what you know about what Alan has found, I'll pay you for it."

Candy was dressed in jeans and a long, pale blue T-shirt that had a Navajo design on it. She was wearing a necklace with little bells or something on it that jingled whenever she moved. There were large floppy bracelets on both her wrists. She had a couple of jars of scent-emitting substances on her desk—carefully positioned, I knew, because once I had idly moved one a few inches and she told me very solemnly that I had misaligned it.

"But how would this someone, this outsider, know who to approach? I mean, I guess there are a lot of people in the lab who might have some knowledge of your work that might be worth something to someone. But who can someone on the outside trust to be willing to sell that information? What if he asks the wrong person? He not only doesn't get what he wants, but he's exposed."

"Come on, Candy, I'm not saying this person is going to walk right up to someone in our lab, and say, will you sell me some information that I need? Obviously, it would be more subtle than that. He would test the waters, maybe ask some indirect questions. Before he actually got around to stating his purpose, he could have a very good idea of what the person's answer would be."

Candy looked up at me. She was a pretty unflappable person. She hadn't been kidding when she told me before that she never got angry. At least, I had never seen her angry. She might not be at one with the universe, or whatever it was she often claimed to me she was, but she rarely showed signs of stress. Now, though, Miss Peace and Harmony seemed just a little flustered by the conversation.

"Alan, are you implying that I might sell information on one of your grants to someone outside the lab? Then have you kidnapped so that this person could go through all your files and get still more information? Is that what you're trying to say?"

"Well, I didn't mean to accuse you specifically. I'm just saying, maybe this is what someone is doing, or trying to do."

She handed the grant back to me.

"I swear to you, Alan, I would never, never, never sell any information I have about this lab to anyone. Not for any amount of money! Now I'm busy right now."

That afternoon, there was another board meeting of OS. As I looked around the room, I wondered again if my enemy could be in their midst. If Mitch were right about the security of the patent, then my kidnapping was not about learning the identity of the three genes nor of delaying that patent. The fact that no one so far had tried to access my notebooks or computer files provided further support for that. So the motive might be a lot less complicated: get me out of the way. And here was a roomful of people, most or all of whom, as far as I could see, wanted exactly that.

I couldn't really believe that anyone in this room, no matter how much they all seemed to hate my guts, would want to see me dead. That was a little extreme. But if I were out of the way for a little while, they could move on without me. By the time I was set free and allowed to return, the major issues that we were battling over would all be resolved in their favor. Or better yet, maybe they would take the opportunity opened by my absence to appoint someone else, another research scientist more to their liking. Someone who basically went along with all the main decisions of the board. In other words, I thought bitterly, a goddamned puppet.

Anyway, desperate times demand desperate measures. I decided to go on the offensive again, to try to draw out a reaction. Clumsy as my attempts to do this seemed to be so far, I felt I could no longer go along passively, until the kidnapper struck again. So I opened the meeting with a real stunner: I offered my resignation.

I didn't really intend to resign, of course. I wasn't going to let these bozos bully me out of a company that wouldn't have existed if not for my research. But I wanted them, all of them, to think I was going to resign. I was hoping and expecting to see some smiles of smug satisfaction when they suddenly realized they didn't have Alan Rupert to kick around any more.

There was none. The room fell deathly silent.

"You can't be serious," said Mitch finally.

"I just don't think I belong here," I said. "You all have your own ideas about this company's goals, the kind of studies it should conduct and the way those studies should be conducted. Maybe you're all right, and this is the way the company should be run." Bullshit, I thought. Bullshit, bullshit, bullshit. "But it's not the way I think it should be run. I have tried to be totally honest with you about what we need to do and how to do it. I'm sorry I can't see it your way, I've tried very hard to, but I just can't."

As I talked, I scanned the table so I could look each of them in the eyes, trying to see some sign of secret glee. I couldn't, and regretted again that I wasn't more experienced at this, able to see through someone's little act.

"So maybe it would be better for all of us if I just left. No hard feelings" — oh, right, I thought — "but we all move on. I could still be available as a consultant, whenever you wanted to ask me my opinion on something."

At this point, total chaos emerged. Everyone seemed to talk at once. One member said they all understood I was the real founder of the company, but for my work it never would have come into existence, and that they couldn't possible continue in my absence. Another said he really respected my ideas, and always argued on my behalf for them, if not always at the meetings, then afterwards one-on-one with individual board members. Still another said better he resign than I. That he was dispensable, that everyone there except me was dispensable.

After a few minutes of this cacophony, Alvin Duistermars, my *bete noire* himself, rapped the table for silence.

"Doctor, I'm sure I speak for everyone in this room when I say we don't want you to resign. Every one of us, to a man and woman, wants you here on this board. And if you want proof, want a show of support, well, then…"

He raised one hand in the air, and looked around the table. Everyone else raised his or her hand. Immediately. No hesitation.

I was truly stunned. My eyes actually misted over a little. I had never, ever expected this reaction. Even before the kidnappings occurred, I felt I was a marked man here, that everyone wanted me out. To learn just how completely I had misjudged them all, that behind all the shit I experienced in this room they really cared about me…

There was another long silence. Again it was Mitch who broke it.

"Poor Alan. Voted down again."

Everyone cracked up. Even me, a little.

You might think that after that, everything was lovey-dovey between me and the rest of them. Actually, the honeymoon lasted about five minutes. Then Alvin and I were at each other's throats, just like old times, just as though the preceding events had never occurred. Like a couple of boxers who shook hands before the match, acting for all the world like they were the best of friends, then as soon as the bell rang proceeded to beat the shit out of each other.

"You can't have this, you can't have that," he would growl at me, or words to that effect. He was an ancient wreck of a man, eighty if he was a day, with a mane of snowy hair and a face that looked like Niagara Falls. I had been told he was from Texas, had run a very successful manufacturing business, and though he spared us all the cowboy hat and boots, there was a definite swagger to him that even sitting in a chair couldn't contain.

I thought he was the classic example of a miser, someone who thinks money has intrinsic worth beyond what it can buy, who would keep a chest of gold coins under his bed, deriving the most sensuous of pleasures raking his stubby grasping fingers through them from time to time. He had definitely gotten into my head. I

123

would be in the lab, doing an experiment, and make a little mistake, put the wrong volume of some reagent in a tube. So of course I had to discard the tube and repeat the procedure. This was a plastic micro-centrifuge tube, they probably cost about five cents apiece, and all I could think of was, Alvin won't like this, Alvin says you're being wasteful, Alvin says be careful.

After the board had given me their vote of confidence, Mitch had told the others about Alex Pignatti's offer. Since the other members of the board were not on the patent, our decision whether or not to accept him was not relevant to their interests. But if we were going to test his two new genes, along with the original three, that would mean more analyses, and of course, more money.

"I thought the test was good enough as it was," rumbled Alvin. "Why in tarnation are we now adding two more genes?"

"Because they might make the test even better," I explained. "No test for cancer is ever going to be perfect, but if we can detect, say, 90% of people with small polyps instead of 85%, that's a significant improvement. Remember, the earlier the stage we can detect these polyps, the better. And Alex's studies indicate that his genes may give a lower false positive rate. If only two or three people out of a hundred who are clean test positive instead of five or six, that makes the test more attractive, too. It means fewer unnecessary colonoscopies. It also means fewer people worrying unnecessarily about getting cancer, when in fact they may have nothing to worry about."

"OK," said Alvin, "I can understand that. But I ain't real worried about these false positives, what you call them. We can live with them. What I wanna know is, if we fund these new tests, for these other genes, can we be sure we're catching more cases of cancer? Are we gonna save more lives, or not?"

I sighed. Wished that science were so simple.

"I don't know, sir. Nobody knows. That's why we need to do these tests. To find out."

I felt exhausted after the meeting. One of the many little discoveries I had made since joining the board—something I never would have thought was possible before then-- was that I could get more physically tired sitting and talking with these people for one hour than I could working on my feet all day in the laboratory. Whenever I left that room, I felt I needed a very long vacation. From the entire human race.

I was walking out of the conference room when I felt a huge, hammy hand clamp down on my shoulder. It was Alvin.

"Sorry to give you a hard time in there, doctor, I just had to make sure I follow what we're doin'."

He stopped walking, and through a power I really didn't understand, made it clear I should, too. I found myself standing there, face to face with him. Alvin in his off-white shirt, charcoal trousers and red suspenders.

"Doctor, there's just one thing I want you to understand, to be clear about. I'm not in this for the money. I have all the money I need, thank the good lord for that, I'm not asking no one for more. When Mitch and some others asked me to join the board, I told them right at the outset, I don't want a salary, I don't want a commission, and I don't even want stock options, and I won't accept none of it if you try to give it to me."

He reached into his back pocket and pulled out his wallet. Opening it, he revealed pictures of two women, both, I guessed, very roughly around fifty years old. He pointed to the one on the left.

"This here's my Mom, the gal who taught me never to give up, never to stop pushing for what I wanted in life. She supported me and my five brothers and sisters, all by herself, because my Dad…well, best not to speak of him here."

He tapped the picture for emphasis.

"She died of breast cancer when I was fifteen years old. Hell, I'd a never even heard o' cancer before she got it. I din't even know what it was." He gazed in silence at the picture for a moment. "We weren't allowed to talk about it at all. Couldn't tell my best friends at school that my Mom had this disease. Couldn't tell nobody. We were all so ashamed."

His rough, horny finger slid over to the other picture. There was a definite resemblance to the first picture.

"And this un's my older sister, Jessabel. After Mom died, she was my mother. She took care of this rowdy, badass teenage boy, made sure he got to school every day, did his homework, din't get in no trouble. She gave up goin' to college just so's she could get a job and help support me an' the rest of us. And it was the proudest day of my life when I made enough money to send her to college, 'cause she was always the brains in the family. Lord knows, I weren't particularly blessed in that regard."

He lingered over her picture.

"She died of breast cancer, too. More'n thirty years ago."

He snapped the wallet shut, as though he could take only so much exposure from its contents, and replaced it in his back pocket.

"When Jess died, I made a promise to myself. I was goin' to do something about this disease. If I had to spend every goddamned last cent of my money, I was goin' to do something about it."

He grip on my shoulder tightened.

"I can't understand cancer like you can, doctor. I wish the hell I could, but that just ain't my calling. But one thing I do understand is money. I ain't braggin' when I say I understand money like you understand cancer. Better even, 'cause I been studying it all my life, and just like you could study cancer all your life and not ever understand it all, so you can study money all your life and not understand it all. But there's one thing I do understand about it, and I want you to understand it too, son."

He loosened his grip but continued to confront me.

"It all starts with money. Everythin' does. You can have money without science. But you cain't have science without money."

He left me and made his way alone down the hall. Maybe it was just me, but he seemed to have lost a little of his swagger.

11. SEEING IS NOT BELIEVING

The second kidnapping had definitely changed me. It should have frightened me more, I suppose, but it had the opposite effect. It made me angry, and emboldened. I was a little more familiar with my kidnappers now, and therefore less in awe of them. Having seen, if only briefly, the man who had abducted me in the van, and having managed to overcome him to escape, I no longer regarded him, and whoever had put him up to it, as invulnerable or unchallengeable. He was just another flesh-and-blood human, who moaned when he was hit and bled when he was stabbed. And though he had fired a gun at me, I was also becoming convinced that, whatever the reason for the kidnappings, the intent was not to harm me. In other words, I now saw them as more of an annoyance than a threat.

Thus it was that I decided to do what had previously been unthinkable: revisit the scene of the original crime. On the Sunday following my return from the San Francisco conference, the end of June, I drove up north to see the house where I had been temporarily imprisoned. I was not so rash as to go alone, though my companion was hardly the bodyguard type: Laurie. I thought it was a great way to spend some more time with her, even if it did make for a rather unusual kind of date.

"Don't you think you should tell the police what you're doing?" she asked me when I invited her to go along.

"Probably," I said. "But frankly, I think they're an obstacle at this point. I want to talk to the owner of that house. I think—hell, I know—that he knows more about my kidnapping than he told the police."

"But aren't you afraid of meeting him up there, in the woods, far from any possible help? What if he was involved in the kidnapping?"

I shook my head. "I'm sure he's not. I mean, of course it was his house, but I'm convinced he didn't know it was being used for that purpose."

"How can you be so certain?"

I was talking to her out in one of the courtyards outside our research building. We were eating lunch. I made a point of bringing up the subject here and now, because I did not want other people in the lab to hear what I was saying.

"Because of what happened that day when he came into the house," I replied. "I remember thinking at the time that it was a little odd, but of course I was scared out of my wits at that point, and so focused on escaping, that I didn't dwell on it."

"What was odd?"

"When he entered the house, he went straight to the basement. Why would he do that? If he was one of my kidnappers, or if he just was letting them use his house for that purpose, don't you think he would check on me first? At least make sure that the door to the room I was in was still locked. For that matter, if he knew I was locked in that room, why would he come into the house, anyway? If he had some deal with the kidnappers, allowing them to lock me up in one of the rooms, would he really continue to use that house for other purposes? Wouldn't it be understood that he should steer clear of the place? And if he wasn't directly involved, wouldn't he want to, anyway? If something went wrong—as of course it did, from their point of view—wouldn't it be much easier for him to deny any involvement if he hadn't been in the house?"

Laurie heard me out, then said, "So you're not afraid at all to go back there and confront this guy?"

"Nope."

She started to laugh.

"What's so funny?"

"Honestly, Alan, I think you would jump off a cliff if you had a theory that gravity didn't exist."

She slept over at my place Saturday night, and we left about eight the next morning. It was a beautiful early summer day, and I enjoyed getting out of the city. We had brought some food so that we could have a picnic later. We chatted a little about science, about the project I was helping her with, but in the circumstances, it was natural that the conversation would turn back to my kidnapping. I told her all about the second abduction—making her the first person in the lab I had confided in—before turning back to the first one.

I wanted her help on unraveling the significance of the cell phone call I had received from Marissa's phone earlier that evening. Laurie was in fact the first person in the lab I had mentioned that to, except of course Marissa herself, and Bill Tye, who were both directly involved. I told Laurie basically everything I knew, all my conversations with Marissa, Bernie and Bill. I also told her about my latest conversation with Burris, and his thoughts on the matter.

She listened to all of this with great interest.

"I guess the text couldn't have been faked, could it?" she said finally.

I turned to stare at her in astonishment, almost forgetting to watch the road. "*Faked*? What do you mean? *How?*"

"It's quite easy, actually. There's a simple service that allows you to make calls and send texts so that they appear to be coming from another number. It's called ID spoofing."

"And it will appear in my records as coming from that fake number?"

"Yep."

I groaned, briefly sagging against the steering wheel. "Great. So that means that *anyone* could have sent that text."

She reached over to stroke me lightly on the shoulder. "No, I think we can rule that out. You said you received two texts from Marissa's number, the second one being in response to your text to that number. If someone had sent you the first text from another cell phone faking Marissa's number, they would not have been able to receive your reply to Marissa's phone. In fact, the more I think about it, for a text like that, where you expect a quick response, it would be vital to be using the phone with the real number."

"Well, that's a relief, I guess," I said, though I really wasn't sure how much difference it mattered. "So it really does seem that it had to be someone in the lab at the time."

"Assuming Marissa is telling the truth, yes. Assuming her phone was really sitting in her desk drawer all this time."

I flushed a little, and wondered if Laurie noticed. As good as the sex with her had been, I still lusted after Marissa. It was very hard for me to talk about her objectively, and particularly difficult in front of Laurie. I was well aware that even now, Marissa could have snapped one of her elegantly ringed fingers, and I would have discarded Laurie like a batch of radioactive waste.

To change the subject a little, I told her about Burris' theory that someone in the lab might have been trying to sell information about my work to someone on the outside. I explained to her how that possibly brought both Dick and Candy into the picture. Finding it impossible not to pour out everything to her sympathetic ears, I went on to tell her about the little tests I had performed on the two of them. Dick had been intrigued by the idea that someone might be trying to sell information to someone outside the lab. Candy, in contrast, had reacted defensively, but I didn't know why.

"You think she's hiding something?"

"I don't know. She just seemed upset that I would accuse her of something so horrific. I thought she overreacted, but then again, if someone accused me of a crime like that, I would probably be upset, too."

"Who else have you wondered about?"

I shrugged. "In my darker moments, just about everyone in the lab." I took one hand off the steering wheel and reached over to squeeze her thigh. "Except you."

To my surprise, she turned very serious. "Alan, I can prove that I was not in the lab that night. Neither was Andrea, for that matter. I was with her then."

"I know," I replied. "That's one of the main reasons why I trust you."

I regretted saying those words, at least putting it so bluntly, even if it was true. But she said nothing. We had brought a map with us, and though we didn't need it at the moment, she picked it up and began to study it in silence. Several minutes passed, and I thought she was going to drop the subject.

"What about Mitch?" she said, seemingly out of the blue.

"*Mitch?*" I had never thought of him as a suspect. "What would he have to gain by my being kidnapped? He's already on the patent."

"But if you weren't around, he would be the sole beneficiary, wouldn't he?"

That hadn't occurred to me.

"If I really did die or disappear, my share of the patent royalties would go to my will," I pointed out. "And I don't even have one. I guess they would go to the government."

"But you told me you haven't filed the full patent yet," Laurie countered, "just the provisional one." She glanced back at the map. "Seems to me that if you disappeared now, anyone who plans to be on that full patent has a lot to gain if you disappear."

I was surprised at how easily I found the side road off the main highway. Though there were several somewhat similar-looking secondary roads in the vicinity, I recognized the right one instantly. My memory of sitting on the far side of the entrance, waiting for my pursuers to drive out, was still vivid. And when I turned off the highway, I felt the fear welling up in me. Memories of the entire sequence of events, from waking up in that house to evading the pursuers as I hitchhiked back home, were so fresh that I almost felt I was re-living the events. And it did not help knowing that, if my assailants were still around, I really might re-live them.

As we approached the house, it looked as I remembered it, an old wood frame structure at the end of the road, set in a small clearing of the surrounding forest. I parked on the far side of the drive from it, right where the car had been when I had escaped.

"So that's the place," Laurie said.

"Yeah," I replied quietly, almost reverentially. I paused for a moment, remaining in the car, while I let the immensity of my memories of this place soak in. We had already agreed that I would get out of the car alone. Though I felt very confident no one would be around, I wanted Laurie to stay in the car, with a cell phone, just in case worse came to worst. And despite my confidence — my rational, scientific brain telling me that it had figured out to better than 99% probability that my kidnappers were nowhere in the vicinity--I still felt myself trembling a little. I could not suppress a vision of two men rushing out of the house, one of them grabbing me while the other began smashing in the window of the car.

But all was quiet and still, but for the pleasant sounds of birds in the nearby woods. I crossed the drive, the gravel scrunching under my feet, and ascended the steps to the front porch. The creaking of the boards seemed as loud as gunshots in such a quiet setting. I felt anyone within a mile would know someone was here. Shading my eyes, I peered inside one of the windows. The house was still empty, it looked just as it had when I had left it. Gently, I tried the door. It was locked, just as I had expected it to be.

I turned around, descended back to the driveway, and began to circle around the house. This was the real reason I had returned to this house, so I took my time, inspecting it very carefully. There was a little backyard, devoid of any furniture or other objects, invaded by weeds.

A couple of minutes later, I returned to the car, feeling more relaxed than at any time since I had turned off the highway.

"OK," I said to her, "I found out what I wanted to."

"What's that?"

"That there are no windows in the basement. And the walls of it are very thick and solid."

"So no one could get out."

"Yes." I smiled, "but more important, so no one can get in."

She asked me what I meant by that, but I waved her off.

"Now we go see the owner," I said.

I turned the car around and drove back down the road, towards the highway, but slowly, on the lookout for a path that might lead to the man's house. From my previous time here, I well knew there were no houses within sight of the road, so if the owner lived in the woods, he had to have some kind of access to the road.

I found what I was looking for about a mile up the road, on the left. The path was very well marked; I couldn't have missed it the day I had escaped, had I not been on the other side of the road, and jogging to escape my pursuers. I parked the car nearby, and told Laurie to come with me. Regardless of the advantages of having her in the car at all times, I didn't want her to be alone out of my sight—and I guess I didn't want to be alone, either. I hadn't expected to encounter anyone at the other house. Now I definitely did expect to see someone, and again, while my rational brain had figured out he was harmless, lower neural structures begged to differ.

The path looked like any ordinary hiking trail, with hard-packed dirt that took the route of least resistance around trees, logs, rocks and other forest obstacles. The deeper we went into the woods, the greater my feeling of vulnerability. Laurie, undoubtedly feeling the same thing, clutched my hand tightly. I reminded myself that the owner had told Burris that hikers frequently used these woods, so there was nothing unusual about our being there.

After about half a mile, we saw a house through the trees. It was a cottage, really, a one-story structure much smaller than the other house down the road. And there was a man standing in the small clearing in front of it, chopping wood. The mere sight of the ax in his hands sent shivers up my spine. If he expressed any hostile intent towards us, we didn't stand a chance.

We didn't have to hail him. He saw us seconds after we saw him, and immediately stopped chopping, resting the ax head on the ground and leaning on the handle. Up close, he did not appear threatening. I guessed he was about 5'9", though a little on the heavy side. He had thinning sandy brown hair, and sharp features softened by large hazel eyes that bulged out ever so slightly from his face. He was wearing jeans and a flannel shirt.

"Hello," I said, mustering as friendly a tone as I could manage.

"Morning," he replied. I guessed he was used to people hiking in this area, because he gave no indication that we were trespassing, or unwelcome. I swallowed my fears, and took the plunge.

"Are you the owner of that house down the road?" I said, gesturing vaguely in that direction.

He looked at me suspiciously. "Yeah, why?"

I glanced at Laurie. We had already planned what to do when this moment came. She would stand a little apart from me, ready to dial 911 and run like hell back to the car, if it came to that. When we were discussing this beforehand, the notion seemed silly and melodramatic, but at this moment, it gave me a little assurance.

I offered my hand. "My name's Alan Rupert," I said. "I'm the guy who was locked inside that house."

The man reacted very strongly to that, standing stock still for a moment.

"Whoa," he said finally. "The guy who locked me in my own basement."

A few minutes later, we were sitting inside his cottage, drinking iced tea. The place consisted mainly of a single large room, with a bed that doubled as a sofa on one side, and a table with chairs in the middle. Part of the large room was made over into a kitchenette, with a hotplate and a small refrigerator, and there were several smaller rooms or spaces attached, one of them a bathroom, the others apparently closets or storage space of some kind. Sitting at the table with Laurie and the man, who introduced himself as Wilson Travers, I looked around the place and wondered why he would live in such cramped quarters when he had a much larger place down the road. Maybe he needed the rental income, though apparently he wasn't getting any now. And if what I suspected was true, he wouldn't want anyone else living in that house.

He did not need too much prompting to tell his story. He said he had felt guilty when the police told him what had happened to me. He had wanted to make amends, and was actually glad that I had showed up.

"About two months ago," he began--"this would be early May — a man called me about renting my house. He said he had been looking for a place in this area, had done a lot of driving around on back roads, and really liked the place. He told me he wasn't sure

134

how long he would want to stay, but was willing to pay me three months rent upfront, paying month-to-month after that."

So the bastards were planning to hold me there for several months, I thought. That supported the theory that the purpose of the kidnapping was to keep me out of circulation for an extended period of time, rather than to extract information from me. Or maybe both?

"The one peculiar thing about this guy was that he never asked me what the rent was, how much I wanted. He simply made an offer that was generous, to say the least. More than twice what I wanted or expected."

He paused to take a sip of his iced tea. There was also a plate of sugar cookies, and I nibbled on one.

"He said he knew that was a lot for the rent, probably more than the going rate around there, but he really liked the place, and was willing to pay that much under one condition. That I leave him absolutely alone. He didn't want me or anyone else coming over to the house to bother him."

Of course, I thought. That had to be part of the deal.

Travers heaved a long sigh, and set his glass of tea down on the table.

"Well, I wasn't born yesterday. I smelled trouble. All my instincts told me he was planning to do something illegal. I was very blunt with him about that. I said I could not have any problems with the law, because as owner of the house I was liable for anything that happened there."

Travers paused, turned, and spat through the open door, about six feet away. An occasional fly meandered in and buzzed around the cottage, but otherwise the direct fresh air of the woods was cool, moist, and welcome.

"At this point," Travers went on, "the guy became very thoughtful, like he was considering something carefully. Finally, he said, 'OK, I'll come clean. My mother is institutionalized. She has Alzheimer's disease, or something like that. She is definitely suffering from some advanced form of dementia. I don't like to see her in one of these damned rest homes, you know, they don't really care about their patients at all at these places, sometimes they even abuse them. Not really safe. This is my mother we're talking about. I just couldn't do this to her. I thought if I could bring her up here, in the north woods, away from the city, she would be better off.'"

I wanted to turn and smile at Laurie, but I knew it was imperative that I act like I was buying this whole story. I only hoped she understood that, too.

"The guy continues, 'But she really can't handle other people. She still recognizes me, sort of, at least she accepts me, but she can't deal with anyone else. They're all strangers to her. No matter how many times she meets someone else, that person is always a complete stranger to her the next time. And not just a harmless stranger. She become paranoid, certain that everyone else is an enemy. And when she gets paranoid, she can get violent. That's really the reason I want to get her out of that place. Half the time they have my poor Mom in a straightjacket.'"

Clever, I thought, very clever.

"Well," Travers continued, "it was a strange story, but to me a believable one. I know those institutions are very expensive. Even at the price he was paying to rent my house, it was a bargain, plus he got to be with his mother. I didn't like it, I didn't like it at all, but I felt sorry for his situation, and really wanted to help him. So we talked back and forth, and eventually we came up with this very strange agreement."

"You were to leave them alone," I said.

"Exactly. I was not to enter the house, ever. But to assure me that everything was all right inside, he agreed to make periodic videos of the place. You know, like those virtual tours that all the real estate agents have these days? You log on to some internet site, pick some house you're thinking of buying, and you can actually move through it, room by room. You see all the details, it's almost as good as being in the house for real. He said he would include in these videos some way to guarantee the date, like some newspaper headline. So I could see for myself that the house was fine. Then he would post these on an internet site which I could access."

"Neat!" commented Laurie, who was either very naïve, or acting very well. "Whose idea was that, yours or his?"

Travers spat again, then rubbed his mouth with the back of one hand.

"Well, both of ours, I guess. We were looking for some sort of way both of our interests could be protected, and that's what we came up with."

"So you never met his mother?" she asked him.

"No. In fact, I never met him, neither, as it turned out. I FAXed him the contract, which he signed, and he sent me a money order. I told him I would leave the key under the front porch. Hell, I could have left the front door unlocked, there's nobody around here to know, anyway, but a few harmless hikers."

These guys really covered their asses, I thought.

"But I was never entirely comfortable with the arrangement. The virtual tours—he posted one regularly every week for three weeks—could assure me that the house was being kept up properly, but that of course didn't mean that anything illegal wasn't going on there. He could always do his thing, whatever that was, then afterwards fix up the house nice and pretty for the video. This gnawed at me for a while, until finally one day I couldn't stand it any more. I had to see the place in the real. At least from the outside, maybe look through some of the windows."

He got up for a moment, and went over to the kitchenette. He stood there for a moment, his back to us, snorting and spitting in the sink. I took the opportunity to look carefully around the room. The moment we had entered the cottage, I had spotted what I was looking for, several large boxes stacked against the wall. Studying them now, I thought they were about the same size and shape as those that had been stacked to virtually the rafters in the basement of the other house that day. What was in them? I wondered. That was what I had come to find out.

"I called him first, of course," Travers said, still with his back to us. "A landlord can't just go barging into his tenant's property without permission. But he didn't answer. I tried many times to call him, many, many times, using the cell phone number that was the only one he had I knew about. But he never answered. Then, not long after that, the virtual tours ended. There was no new tour on the site at the appointed time."

Now he returned to the table, still talking.

"At that point, the situation had changed. For sure. I knew my rights as a landlord. If I couldn't reach him by phone, I had every right to go to the house. If it turned out he was there, and still didn't want me to enter, maybe I could accept that. But of course I had to have some kind of communication with him. So I walked over to the place. I guess now you know that this place here is about a mile and a half from the house. I take that path you just came up on to the road, then follow the road to the house."

"And that's when we met," I said.

He shook his head.

"No. This was before that, around the end of May. I went up to the house, peered through the front window. The front room was absolutely bare, devoid of furnishings. So I knocked. No answer. Finally I unlocked the door and went inside."

"And the place was bare," I said. "Completely empty."

"You betcha. Not a sign of anyone there. So at that point I figured the guy was gone. Maybe it hadn't worked out with his mother, he had taken her back to wherever she had been before. But he was still legally the tenant. He had paid up for the next two months, more or less. So there was nothing to do but leave the house as it was. Legally I had no right to try to rent it out to someone else, and since I had all that money — three months rent at more than double what I had wanted--I had no problem letting sitting dogs lie."

He turned towards the door, snorted as if to spit again, but didn't.

"So I left the house, locked it up again. But after that I came by often, though I didn't always go in. I would knock on the door, and hearing no answer, figure nothing had changed, and leave."

I finished the cookie I was eating. "OK," I said. "Now tell your story about the day you found me there."

"Right." He gave a sort of half grin at the recollection. It was a very disarming gesture, and for the first time since I had met him made me feel fully relaxed in his presence. This guy was as crooked as the path we took to get to this place, I had no illusions about that, but friendly and gentle nonetheless. I really harbored him no ill will. "I came over on one of my periodic visits. As I was leaving the path through the woods, and walking onto the road for the final stretch, a car came by, passing me and heading, obviously, towards the house. That was all there was to go to. The road ends there."

I had waited patiently through his story to get to this point. I was all ears now.

"Did you recognize the car or the people in it?"

"No. Remember, I never met this guy. As for the driver or passengers, I really didn't get much of a look at them. I was on the side of the road, I just glanced back to make sure the car had room to pass me. The only thing I'm fairly certain of is that there were two people in the car, the driver and someone in the front passenger seat."

I nodded. "That checks."

"It was still a little ways to the house from that point," Travers continued. "By the time I arrived, the car was parked on the side of the road."

"In front of the house, but not next to it, on the far side of the road," I said, clearly recalling that day.

"Exactly."

"And you didn't see anyone, either in the car or around the house?" I asked.

"No. And that didn't surprise me terribly. As I told the police before, people occasionally drive down one of these roads, park their car, and hike into the woods. I figured that was the case here."

This did surprise me, but I didn't want to interrupt his story at this point. So I nodded, and said, "Go on."

"Well, this is where you come in," he said, referring to me. "I went into the house, and everything looked the same as before.

Except not quite the same. It hadn't been thoroughly cleaned at the time I originally rented it out, and on all my visits to it since, there was a layer of dust covering, you know, the floors, the window sills, any flat surface. That dust was still there this time, but I could see disturbances in it, places where it was pretty clear someone had been walking. I guess I just sort of noticed this in the back of my mind, I wasn't really registering it. Then I opened the door to the cellar. And you know the rest."

"Too well," I said, "too well."

We didn't talk much longer. Just before we left, Travers got up to go to the bathroom. Motioning Laurie to be quiet, I immediately got up also, and went over to investigate the boxes I had noticed earlier. They were sealed, and unmarked on the outside. I felt that I had to see their contents.

It was a tricky situation. Travers could emerge from the bathroom at any moment, and when he did, I would be in his view almost instantly. I had to act very fast. I had no knife. The only tool I had on me to slice through the cardboard was the car key. As surreptitiously as possible, I slid it down next to a side of one of the boxes that was facing the wall, out of sight. By pressing hard, I was able to cut it open, though I thought I made enough noise to easily alert Travers. When I heard the toilet flush, I reached into the slit I had made and quickly explored the inside of the box with my hand. I felt something wrapped in cellophane. I had no time to do anything more.

I stood up and moved away from the boxes just as Travers emerged from the bathroom. I pretended to be stretching myself, walking around the room. Laurie, playing along, also got up, making ready to leave.

"One thing I don't understand, though," I said to him, "is why you never told this story to the police. I mean about renting the house out to this guy. What were you afraid of?"

I held my breath at this point, because I was pretty sure I knew the answer to that question, and also pretty sure it was not something Travers would admit to.

Travers shrugged. "The rental agreement. It's not really legal. I mean, as a landlord, I can pretty much agree to anything that I want, but if I waive my rights and responsibility for periodically checking on the house, then I suppose I could be held liable for what happened to you."

"Well, I don't blame you for anything of this, believe me."

Travers smiled thinly. "That's very generous of you. But the fact remains that it was just chance that I came when I did. I might not have come over to the house for several days, a week or more — and you might not have escaped. You could have been imprisoned in that room indefinitely, killed for all I know. A landlord that lets things like that go on could be considered criminally negligent. If I had simply refused the guy's offer in the first place, maybe none of this would have happened."

"Oh, I'm sure," said Laurie, "that these thugs would have found another place."

"Maybe," said Travers, "but that doesn't absolve me. I'm so glad you gave me a chance to unburden myself."

"So you won't go to the police?" I suggested. "You could at least tell them the name of the guy who rented the house. That would be very helpful."

Travers actually flushed a little.

"Actually, he never signed his name on the contract. He just wrote an "X" on it."

Laurie appeared incredulous at that, but I nudged her and we left.

"What were you *doing* there, Alan?" Laurie asked me, as soon as we were out of earshot, walking on the path back to the car.

"Remember I told you that the cellar of that house I was locked in was full of boxes? Those were more of the same boxes, I'm pretty sure. I wanted to see what was in them."

"And? Could you tell?"

"I think so, yes. Cigarettes."

"*Cigarettes*? Why would he store boxes of cigarettes in his basement?"

She had stopped to face me, but I grabbed her hand and pulled her roughly forward. I doubted Travers would notice that little slash in the box very soon, and even if he did, he probably wouldn't connect it to me. But still, I was uncomfortable hanging around this area. After all, I now had real evidence of illegal activity. I was a threat to him. Best to get right back to the car without delay.

"I think he's smuggling them," I said. "I think that's what he uses that house for. To store them as they come over the Canadian border. It's the perfect setup for that."

After we reached the car, we drove back to the highway and turned south. Though we were on the way back to Minneapolis, we had planned beforehand to stop somewhere along the way for a picnic. While we searched for a good spot, I explained to her what I had worked out.

"When I had that second interview with Officer Burris, the one in which he told me Travers' version of the events the day I escaped from the house, a couple of things really puzzled me. One was that Travers thought I was a burglar. What was in the house to steal? It could have just been a story, to cover up the kidnapping, but as I told you before, I had no reason to believe he knew anything about the kidnapping. That being the case, burglary would be about the only possible explanation for finding a stranger in your house."

"He could have thought you were some homeless person crashing there," Laurie pointed out.

"A bum who had been living up here in the north woods? Highly unlikely, I'd say. Anyway, why would I go into the basement? Indeed, how could I get *into* the basement? When Travers entered the basement that day, he had to unlock it. That means any stranger who managed to get into the house would not be able to get into the basement at all—except by the way I did, involving so much time and effort that it couldn't possibly be worth it unless the intruder thought there was something of value in the basement. If Travers really thought I was a burglar, he must have known there was something of value in the basement."

"The cigarettes."

"Yes, though I obviously didn't know at the time—when I was talking to Burris--what might be in those boxes, I figured it had to be valuable. And since Burris never mentioned any boxes in his report to me, I guessed the owner of the house must have moved them. Ergo, they contained something he preferred the police not see."

"OK, I see that."

"A second thing Travers told the police that made no sense to me was that the door to the room I had been locked in was open. Yet it was locked when he entered the house that day and found me in the basement. Why would he lie about that?"

Laurie was silent for a moment, thinking this through.

"When the police confronted him with your story of being held there," she said finally, "Travers must have felt the heat. After all, he was the owner of the house, and liable for what happened there. It had to look highly unlikely to the police that a kidnap victim could be held in someone's house without the owner knowing about it. Travers might have felt that the police wouldn't believe his innocent man story unless he embellished it with a few supporting details."

"Possibly, yes. But there's a third issue here. The day I escaped, I was pursued by not one but two cars. Two pairs of men were chasing me. One pair must have been the guys who kidnapped me the night before. But who were the other two guys?"

Laurie of course had no answer to that, and I continued.

"Now let's return to Travers' story. He says that when he went to the house that day, someone in a car passes him and parks in front of the house, getting there before he does. According to Travers, these are just hikers. But when I escaped from the house, the men in that car chased me."

"Because they were the kidnappers. Travis said he had never met them. If he was telling the truth, he wouldn't recognize them, and they wouldn't recognize him."

I nodded.

"I think we can conclude that he was telling the truth about that--he never met the kidnappers. Obviously, it's in his interest to make that claim, to deny any interaction with people who committed a crime. But I still believe him, because if he and the kidnappers had met previously, that scene on the road would have played out differently."

"What do you mean?"

"Think about it. If the kidnappers recognized Travers as the owner of that house, there's no way they would have allowed him to enter it that day alone. If Travers was in on the kidnapping, they would have entered with him, or welcomed him after they had entered. If he wasn't, they surely would have exercised their rights as tenants to bar his immediate access. Even by the ordinary rules of tenancy, the landlord is supposed to make an appointment ahead of time to see the premises. According to Travers, he, the owner, wasn't supposed to enter the house under any circumstances. Surely the kidnappers could have and would have enforced that rule. They got to the house before Travers did. One of them could have gone in and checked on me, while the other stood outside, making sure that Travers didn't enter."

Laurie was silent for a moment, studying the map, looking for an interesting place to stop. I vividly remembered the last time I rode on this stretch of the highway, picked up as a hitch-hiker and thinking I was finally safe.

"So you buy Travers' entire story? That he rented the house to the kidnappers, never having met them?"

I shook my head. "I just can't believe he would really rent his house to someone he had never met, someone who, according to him, never even put a real signature on the lease.. Also, it doesn't explain the other two men who were trying to pick me up that day."

"So who were they?"

"Here's what I think happened. Travers rented the house to *another* pair of men. Who? A couple of bootleggers, guys who are smuggling cigarettes. Or maybe he gave them free use of his house in return for a cut of the profits, but the essential point is, there are a couple of guys using the house with Travers' knowledge and approval to store these cigarettes. The cigarettes are smuggled over the border from Canada, where the taxes on them are much higher, then imported back into Canada, masquerading as lower-taxed American cigarettes. This is a big business at the American-Canadian border. In fact, I understand that some of the large tobacco companies actually condone it. It's illegal, of course, so Travers doesn't tell the police anything about it. Nor me."

"OK, then where do the kidnappers enter the picture?"

"These two smugglers, who are renting or otherwise using the house, turn around and sublet it to the kidnappers. Without Travers' knowledge, I think."

"*Sublet* it? Are you serious?"

"Very. I'm not saying they knew that the guys they rented it to planned to use it to hold a kidnap victim. They just knew that these guys were willing to give them a lot of money for the use of the house. The kind of money that makes you not ask any questions."

I glanced over briefly at the map.

"The smugglers don't live in the house," I pointed out. "They don't even use it, except for the basement, which apparently is locked. So why not rent it out to someone else? Kidnappers, as Travers implied, would pay a king's ransom for a place like that. I'm guessing that the story about the mother with Alzheimer's was actually told by the kidnappers to the smugglers. The latter may or may not have believed it, but they didn't really care. They told them they wouldn't be using the house, and they didn't expect Travers would, either. It would seem to be a great deal for everyone."

Laurie stared in silence out the window for a moment, absorbing the scenery, or maybe checking our bearings with the map.

"This sounds so complicated, Alan."

"I know, but it's the only story that fits all the facts, as far as I can tell. It explains, as I just pointed out, why the kidnappers didn't enter the house that day. As they approached the house, they passed a man walking towards it on the road. They presumably didn't know it was Travers, the landlord, but anyone's presence in that area would be unwelcome. They didn't want any witnesses who might later connect them with this house."

"OK."

"So they parked the car and moved into the woods, pretending to be hikers. They must have been very unpleasantly surprised when they saw Travers go into the house. What to do now? They must guess he's the owner, at least someone who knows the smugglers, since he has a key; but whoever he is, he complicates the situation. Does he know about the kidnapping? If he does, no problem. But if he doesn't, they will almost certainly have to use violence on him. This is more than they bargained for; they decide to wait and see what happens."

"Then you come barreling out the door."

"From which they conclude that Travers unlocked the door to the bedroom, and I, perhaps thinking he was one of them, overpowered him and made my escape. From the way I was running, it certainly doesn't look like I trusted Travers and sought his help; and it also appears quite certain that Travers didn't know anything about the kidnapping. So they rush out of the woods where they were hiding, hop in the car, and follow me."

By now, Laurie was into the scenario. She began to fill out the rest of it.

"Then Travers calls the two smugglers, briefly explains what happened, and asks them to come unlock the door to the cellar."

"Right. They may guess that my presence in the house had something to do with the two guys they rented the house to. They might in fact know I was a kidnap victim. But even if they don't, while they head for the house, they call the kidnappers to inform them of what happened. The kidnappers, of course, are very angry. They thought they had a deal that no one would enter the house during a certain period of time. I'm not sure exactly what they tell the smugglers, but they ask them to help try to catch me—maybe even for a cut of the money the kidnappers are getting paid for the job. The smugglers agree, but first they go to the house. They do this not just to let out Travers, but to remove the evidence of kidnapping. In other words, before they let Travers out of the cellar, they unlock the bedroom door. The kidnappers would have told them to do this, and maybe the smugglers think up the story that I broke into the cellar to steal the cigarettes."

Laurie nodded.

"Do you think Travers knows all this?"

"Oh, of course. When the police began investigating, he must have figured it out. He then goes to his two confederates, the bootleggers, who confess, insisting that they had no idea that these two guys were kidnappers. In other words, they give Travers basically the same story that he just passed on to me. And he sticks to this story — which could be entirely true, except I think it was the smugglers, rather than Travers himself, who rented the house to the kidnappers. Travers is keeping that detail from me, because he doesn't want me or the police to know about the smuggling. And of course, he also doesn't what the police to know he has any connection with someone who could actually identify the kidnappers."

"Neat," commented Laurie. "So what's next? Where do you go from here on this case?"

I sighed. "Travers is a nice guy in some ways. Obviously I have no use for cigarettes, but still I hate to rat on him. But someone he knows has met my kidnappers, and the only way we're going to get that information is to put the squeeze on him."

"The cigarettes."

"Of course. I figure Burris can offer Travers a nice little deal. That information in return for a light sentence for smuggling."

We pulled up next to a little jewel of a lake nestled in the woods. Being Sunday afternoon, there were other people around, but we walked along one side of the lake till we found a fairly secluded spot. We spread a blanket down on the ground near the shore, ignoring the knobby roots of a couple of trees, and feasted on sandwiches, pickles, potato salad, and a little beer. Later we lay next to each other on our backs, staring up at the forest canopy overhead. I felt very peaceful now, still thinking about the kidnapping, but more annoyed than scared.

"You know what upsets me most about the kidnapping?"

Laurie turned on her side to study my face. "All the extra work you're having to do to investigate. All the time spent away from the lab."

I smiled. All the extra time in the lab, too, I thought. "Well, yeah, that. But it ruined the most beautiful night of my life." I tried, inadequately, to describe the experience I had had in the lab that night. It was the first time I had mentioned it to anyone else. Indeed, it was the first time I had really gone over it in my own mind since it had happened.

"I'd give anything to have that feeling again," I concluded simply. "Not even a feeling. Just an experience."

She leaned close and kissed me. "I'm sure you will. The next time you make a great discovery."

This response seemed totally unsatisfactory to me. I rolled my head to one side to look at her.

"*That* was the discovery I made that night, Laurie. Just the experience itself. Learning something fundamentally new about cancer was incidental."

"What do you mean?"

I sighed and looked back up at the sky through the trees, trying to understand what I did mean.

"As scientists, we spend our entire careers trying to observe the world, but there's one part of the world we never observe, right?"

"What's that?"

"The observer! Ourselves. Science carves up the world into two parts—the scientist, and everything else."

"What's wrong with that?"

"But what science itself teaches us is that we're just as much a part of the world as everything else. The observer is not some supernatural force independent of the observed. It's a brain just as much subject to cause-and-effect as the rest of the world."

"So? We study the brain, too."

"But don't you see how paradoxical that is? It's like a cat chasing its tail. How can we study the thing we use to study everything else? How can we observe the observer?"

I rolled over on my side, looking at her.

"Well, that night, I crossed the line between the observer and the observed. I mean, I obliterated it. I mean, there was no line."

12. INSUFFICIENT EVIDENCE

The following day began with another meeting with Mitch. He was on the phone when I arrived. His door was open, as it almost always was. He didn't seem to mind that people—especially Dick and Candy, but students as well--wandered in freely, even when he wasn't around. In the past—before the divorce—I would have walked in and just sat there waiting for him to finish. Now, more out of respect than from any command of his, I loitered outside, knowing he might be talking with his lawyer about personal details of his life. And indeed, when I heard him put the phone down and entered the office, I could see from his weary expression that it had been another one of those calls.

"How's it going?" I said. I just blurted that out. Normally, I would avoid referring to the divorce in any way. I would begin talking science as soon as he put the phone down. That's what I would have wanted someone to do if I had been in Mitch's situation, and I was pretty sure that was what he wanted.

His shoulders slumped a little. "Awful," he said. He looked away from me, as if talking to someone else. "You work so hard for something, so long, and then just watch it disappear."

I wasn't sure if he was referring to his marriage or his money.

"How's Lizzie?" I said, referring to his pre-adolescent daughter, whom I had met once or twice when Mitch brought her to the lab.

Mitch frowned. "I think she blames me for this."

I stood there awkwardly, my curiosity finally getting the better of me.

"Why?"

To my surprise, Mitch actually blushed a little. I couldn't recall ever having seen him do that before. "Oh...well, she thinks I, er, started all this."

He was so obviously uncomfortable and vulnerable that I would have felt pursuing this topic any further would have been to take unfair advantage of him.

"When will it be...well, final, or settled?"

That thought seemed to bring him a little cheer. "Very soon now." He suddenly looked down at the top of his desk, as if checking to make sure all his papers were there, as if he expected his wife might try to steal them. "It will be so nice to have a normal life again."

I didn't say anything in response, but sat down and opened my notebook, indicating I was ready to get back to business. Mitch was only too happy to comply.

"OK, now what have you got for me?"

I was already answering him as I leafed through the pages, but I stopped abruptly.

"Oh, *shit!*" I ejaculated.

"What's the matter?" asked Mitch.

I held up the notebook, open. "Several pages are missing. They've been torn out."

Under ordinary circumstances this would have been a major annoyance. Under the current circumstances, it was a little scary. I didn't have to tell Mitch that. He took the notebook from me briefly to look at it, then handed it back to me.

"Anything vital? Anything we don't want to get out of this laboratory?" Even if my claim on the genes was safe, we didn't want other groups knowing exactly what we were doing from day to day. And of course, now that I understood the importance of my notebooks in claiming priority for any discovery, I had another reason to worry. At least this notebook was not the one in which I had recorded my original discoveries.

I was studying the pages immediately proceeding and following, trying to place the context of the missing ones, to understand what I had written on them, what experiments were carried out on those days.

"I'm not sure," I said. "It may take me a while to figure this all out."

Abruptly I got up from my chair.

"Where are you going?" said Mitch.

"To my desk. I better check all my other notebooks now. And my computer files, too."

Mitch held up a hand to detain me. "Just a second, Alan. When did this happen? When was the last time you remember using this notebook?"

I thought a moment.

"Last week sometime."

"So it probably happened over the weekend."

"Most likely, since I wasn't here yesterday."

But why, I thought as I returned to my desk, didn't the thief just photocopy the pages? Surely anyone intent on stealing data would be sophisticated enough to know that these particular pages, whatever their value, did not establish patent priority. That would be the only justification for removing them rather than copying them. So why remove them? Why call attention to the theft in such a blatant manner? Was the perp not interested, or not only interested, in stealing my data, but in sabotaging my research, slowing it down so that it would take me longer to complete it? Giving him, whoever it was, a chance to make some new discovery first?

Or could it possibly be a message? What kind of message? Maybe: I've been through your notebooks, I know what's there. In other words, the thief not only had found the information he or she wanted, but for some reason wanted me to know that.

I sat down at my desk and went through all my notebooks, one by one, checking each and every page. Most of them, the ones I wasn't currently using, I kept locked in one of my desk drawers, and there was no sign at all that the lock had been tampered with. I went first to the notebook where I had first recorded the identity of the three genes. That was intact, no pages missing. I then went through the others I had, about half a dozen of them. They were fine, too.

I next started going through my computer files. A relatively unsophisticated user would leave tracks. If any files had been opened, that would be easy to confirm. They hadn't been. I also had some software that was supposed to warn me of any access of my computer by any unauthorized users, including those who would know how to avoid leaving the most obvious kinds of tracks. No records of that happening, either. And definitely no files missing.

Like everyone else in our group, I was connected to a network, but no one could access my files without a password, which would require my knowledge. The system administrator, of course, would have access to everything, and it occurred to me I ought to ask him if he had any evidence of tampering with my files. But everything looked fine.

Having satisfied myself to that extent, I turned my attention back to the one notebook with the missing pages. I needed to understand exactly what was missing, and how important that information might be. Since I had dated all the entries, I was able to pinpoint which day's work had been removed, and by studying carefully the preceding and following entries, come up with at least a rough idea of what was missing. As far as I could see, it wasn't anything too critical. For example, no values from some experiment that would have to be repeated to generate new values. Mostly a description of what I had done during that period. I could live with that.

I put my hands behind my head and sat back in my chair, gently rocking it back and forth. So, again, why had the perp not just photocopied the notes? Another idea occurred to me. Perhaps the thief had been caught in the act. He had heard someone coming just as he was picking up the notebook. If he was not a member of the lab, his presence would have attracted suspicion, so he had to leave, immediately. He might have had trouble getting the entire notebook out of the building without being caught, but a few pages, folded and stuffed in the back of his pocket, would have been no problem. He didn't have time to see what information he was actually taking. This explanation seemed unlikely to me, but I had to check out all leads.

Later that morning I met again with Bill Tye. To my pleasant surprise, Bill himself had asked for the meeting. He had some data to show to me. He even brought it to my desk.

"This is just small cell lung cancer," he explained to me. "I will be doing the non-small cell group next."

I looked over his data. Rows and rows of numbers that only a scientist could love, the product of a software program that had taken the raw data from the microarray and transformed it into a level of expression, or activity, for thousands of genes. Bill had also created a heat map, in which the expression levels are represented by colors, with the lowest values in green shading into black and finally bright red for the highest values. Each map was a rectangle consisting of a number of vertical strips in different colors, each strip depicting hundreds of genes under some particular experimental condition.

But I'm more a numbers man than a colors man. I buried myself in the table like a kid in a comic book, searching for old familiar faces.

"Ethanolamine kinase...ah, a voltage-gated potassium channel!..glucosidase...a homeobox..."

I was looking at these names and numbers as filtered through several different criteria. Which were known to be involved in other types of cancer? Which were known to carry out some essential function in the lung? Which had been previously correlated with other disorders of the lung? What we wanted were genes that signaled lung cancer specifically.

Bill was silent for a moment, letting me have my way. I was sure he had his own ideas about which genes to choose. I kept waiting for him to throw out some names, to assert his authority, but when he finally spoke, it was to provide another, very different kind of challenge.

"By the way, did you ever find out who sent you that text that night? Before you were kidnapped?"

All the numbers instantly went blurry. I hardly knew I was at my desk. When I finally recovered, I blurted out, "What text? How did you know someone sent me a text that night?" I was surprised at how easily and naturally I was able to hide the fact that I knew exactly what he was talking about. What I guessed I wasn't hiding so well was my astonishment that he knew something.

"Someone must have. You texted me about a freezer problem at the Ice Palace. But Bernie didn't text you about that. He texted Marissa."

"How do you know Bernie texted Marissa?" I was still holding the printout in front of me, my eyes still focused in its general direction, but none of its information was getting beyond my retinal ganglion cells.

"He told me. When I went down there that morning, he mentioned that Marissa must have told me about the problem. I said no, Alan did, and Bernie said, oh, I guess Marissa told Alan." He paused, then passed from observation to interpretation. "But Marissa didn't text you that night, did she?"

Still I resisted turning around, clinging to the pretense that I was primarily attending to the data.

"How do you know that?"

"I asked her."

I felt a stab of pain. Now we were talking about possible acts of both love and war, as if one of them alone wasn't bad enough.

"Why would you ask her?" Because the two of you are lovers? I wondered. You're in bed together, comparing notes, and realize that each of you has a piece of the puzzle. Or maybe the two of you *created* this puzzle...But then why are you telling me this?

I finally turned around. Bill's expression made it clear that the microarray data, for the time being, were just as irrelevant to him as they now were to me.

"I'm sorry, man, I'm just trying to help here. Some weird shit happened that night—I mean, even before you were kidnapped. There was a freezer problem. Bernie texted Marissa about it. Unless Marissa is lying, someone else received that text on her phone, then texted you. You said you couldn't go, right?"

"How do you know that?" I was still on automatic pilot. I wasn't thinking what I was saying, I was just programmed to provide the minimal amount of information that allowed me to pass to the next question.

"Because you *didn't* go! C'mon, man, I'm trying to help you. You didn't go, and you texted me that I should go. But that doesn't make sense."

"Why not?"

"Because of the times of the texts. Bernie told me he texted Marissa about 8:30. But you didn't text me until more than four hours later. Why?"

I set the printout down. Should I tell Bill everything I knew or had deduced? It seemed as though he had figured out most of it already, anyway. Maybe he was fishing for something he didn't know, and maybe I should worry about why, but what did I know that could be used against me at this point? I took a deep breath.

"Here are the facts as I understand them. I received a text from Marissa's cell around 8:30, informing me about the freezer problem. I texted back that I couldn't go down to the Ice Palace at that time. I then received another text from the same phone saying never mind, I will take care of it."

Bill nodded. "That's what I thought. Only that person did not take care of it. Not unless he or she spent the next four hours calling or texting everyone in the lab, asking them if they could go down there."

I turned back and glanced briefly at the printout. I wasn't trying to escape the new subject at this point, just ground myself a little. Remind myself that I was still in the lab, that I still had a life here.

"So you didn't text me that night, did you?" continued Bill. "If you had, you would have done so earlier."

"That's right," I said slowly.

"So whoever texted me from your cell phone was definitely involved in the kidnapping. And probably whoever used Marissa's phone, too." He paused. "You do understand that, don't you?"

"Of course I understand that!" I snapped, my frustration spilling over.

"Do you have any idea who it was?"

"As far as I can tell, it could have been anyone—well, a lot of people. Anyone who was in the lab at that time." I paused, then thought, well, hell, since you're being so blunt with me, I'll be blunt with you.

"Were you in the lab at that time?"

"Yeah, I was, which is another reason why I know whoever texted me was involved in your kidnapping. Because when you texted back that you couldn't go to the Ice Palace, this person could have texted me immediately. Instead, he or she waits for four hours."

So Bill admits he was around then. That gave me another idea.

"Your cubicle is right next to Marissa's. If anyone used her cell phone that night, you would be the most likely person to have seen them."

Bill shook his head. "I didn't see anyone." He paused, and added carefully, "I don't think her cell was at her desk then."

"Why not?

He leaned closer to me and lowered his voice. "A little earlier that evening, I opened the drawer where she keeps it. I was looking for an article that she had borrowed from me. I didn't see the phone. I know that she keeps it in that drawer. I've seen it there before."

I mulled over all the information in that statement.

"So she was carrying it with her? Are you saying you think she sent that text?'

Bill shook his head. "Have you ever seen her carry that cell phone with her around the lab? I never have."

"So where was it then?"

Bill shook his head. "Beats me. I didn't ask Marissa, because…well, at the time it didn't' seem important. But now that I know the significance of that cell phone, I think you should ask her, Alan. See what she says."

Yes, indeed, I thought. Hadn't Burris told me the same thing?

I found her in the cell culture room, a glass-sided enclosure kept at 37º C. We grew the cells in large, rectangular-shaped clear plastic flasks that contained a bright pink solution. It looked like one of those sports drinks, the color resulting from a pH indicator. As the cells multiplied and consumed nutrients in the medium, the latter became more acidic, and gradually turned yellow, telling the experimenter it was time to put in fresh medium.

She looked up as I entered the room. Her hair was tied back by a bright blue scarf, and there was a trace of rouge on her cheeks. She looked, as always, luscious to me.

"It's that cell phone text again," I said. "I didn't explain to you before why it's so important, so I will now." And I did. She didn't stop working while I talked, but continued sucking out stale yellow solution with a vacuum pump. I had to speak over the hissing sound the vacuum made, which I found myself resenting. Like, she couldn't have stopped for a minute or two while I had my say.

"So you think whoever sent that text on my cell phone that night was involved in the kidnapping?"

"It sure looks that way." To make sure she got the message, I reiterated the key point. "After receiving my text that I couldn't come to the Ice Palace, they did nothing. No further texts to anyone else in the lab, as far as I can tell. If the text to me was really about the freezer problem, why didn't they pursue that?"

She was silent for a moment, still concentrating on her work. If what I was saying ruffled her in the slightest, she sure didn't show it.

"Maybe the best thing for me to do, Alan, is check my account. I can see if any other texts were sent that night."

"Go ahead, that's fine, but it won't answer the key question. Who used your cell phone that night? I understand that you don't know, but you should at least know where it was. That would hopefully provide a major clue about who might have used it."

"I told you before, Alan. I keep it in my desk drawer. I showed you where."

"Bill Tye told me it wasn't there that night."

That definitely got a reaction from her. It was, in fact, about the first time anything I had ever said to her provided any evidence of a disturbance. She turned off the vacuum pump, set the flask down on the little table where she was working, and turned towards me. She was actually glaring at me. I had to admit that it was a very sexy glare, it definitely turned me on. I guess I kind of enjoyed provoking some kind of emotion in her. It made her look so human.

"What was Bill Tye doing going through my desk drawers?" she demanded.

Well, I thought, unless she's a really good actress, I can rule out any collaboration between the two of them.

"He told me he was just trying to find an article he loaned you." It's funny how someone tells you something which seems perfectly credible, until you repeat it to someone else. Somehow, by saying it out loud, you see it in a different light. Why would Bill loan her an article? I now wondered. She could just photocopy her own. But maybe she hadn't gotten around to it.

In any case, to my surprise, Marissa didn't challenge Bill's rationale. Nor his observation.

"Then someone must have taken it. I was away from my desk in the lab for a long time, and when I went home, I did not take the cell phone with me. I never do. I have another cell phone I use outside the lab."

"And you have no idea who could have taken it?"

She was silent for a moment, thinking. "I'll ask around the lab later, Alan."

"Yeah, please do."

If it were my phone, I thought as I left the cell culture room, I sure as hell would want to know.

Later in the afternoon, I visited Officer Burris again. I wanted to tell him all about my visit to Wilson Travers, and of course enlist the police's help in getting him to talk further. I thought Burris might be a little upset that I had taken matters in my own hands in this way. On the other hand, Burris was the one who had told me that Travers had denied any involvement in my kidnapping. So I tried to present my trip north as a sort of social visit that had happened purely by chance to yield some very interesting information.

"Cigarettes, huh?" said Burris. I could tell by the expression on his face that he knew very well why I had gone to see Travers, and that I had probably suspected there was something important about those boxes all the time. If he was resentful or worried that I was doing his job, though, he didn't say anything.

"Yeah. I told you the first time I talked to you that the cellar was jammed with these boxes. Didn't the police notice them when they went to talk to Travers?"

Burris shook his head. "No. The cellar was empty. The officer who visited the house did not know at the time about your statement that there were boxes in there. Later, when we realized Travers must have moved them, I thought that was reasonable. For all we knew, he could have had valuable antiques down there."

"So what are you going to do?" I demanded. "He must be storing those boxes somewhere. There were only a couple in the cottage that I could see, but he had a couple of closets there he could have used. Or maybe he's moved them all back to the basement of the other house again. After all, at this point, he has no reason to believe the police will be visiting him again."

Burris pondered this. "I don't know if we can get a search warrant for this. You didn't bring me back any physical evidence of the cigarettes, if I understand you correctly, you didn't even see them. You're just guessing that's what they are."

"I could feel the individual packs in the carton," I protested. "I could feel the cigarettes in the packs."

"Maybe, but there's nothing illegal about having a box or two of cigarettes. What we have to prove is that large quantities of cigarettes were purchased in Canada, smuggled across the border into the U.S., then imported back into Canada masquerading as low-tax U.S. brands."

I was upset by this answer, but I had to admit that it was a reasonable one.

"So there's nothing you can do about this?"

Burris moved his head back and forth from side to side. "We can do *something*. We can keep an eye on Travers. Certainly we can tell border officials about him. But if you're right about this, Travers himself is not doing the bootlegging. He's just making his house available for temporary storage."

"But don't you agree with me that Travers knows people who have actually met the kidnappers, who rented the house to them?"

Burris nodded. "Of course. Obviously, the kidnappers had to deal with someone who had a key to that house. That was clear from the beginning. And we always suspected that Travers knew more than he was saying. But again, we can't force him to talk."

13. ID'D AT THE BAR

Since Burris and the police seemed unable or unwilling to do anything further, I decided to take another trip north. It was not that I thought I could get any additional useful information out of talking with Travers. I was quite sure he had not met the kidnappers himself, that his only connection with them was through his confederates, the bootleggers. I couldn't ask him to ask them, though, without revealing that I knew about the cigarette smuggling. Not to mention that if, as I guessed, the smugglers were now in league with the kidnappers, they were a big part of the problem, not the solution.

My only option seemed to be to get better evidence of the smuggling operation, which I could take to the police. Where were the stacks of cigarette cases being stored now? Assuming Travers had not moved them back to the house, which was quite possible, I thought there was a good chance they were somewhere in the vicinity of his cottage. There clearly wasn't room inside the little bungalow for all of the boxes that I had seen in the cellar that day, and I had already confirmed that most of the available space was not being used in that way. It seemed to me that Travers might have hidden most of them in the nearby woods. It would be simple enough to stack them on some structure that kept them off the ground, and cover them with a tarp to keep off the frequent summer rains. Maybe add some branches to camouflage them from the occasional hiker in the area.

Laurie accompanied me again. On the drive north, I filled her in on my progress on the second kidnapping case.

"I got the guy's DNA fingerprint, but Iris—that's the cop working on my case out there in California—says there's no match. That's no big surprise, there's only a few million DNA fingerprints on file, and she told me they're mostly sex offenders."

"Would it be worthwhile to look for SNPs?" she replied. "Do you have enough DNA to do that?"

SNPs, or single nucleotide polymorphisms, are the source of

most genetic variation between individual human beings. As members of a common species, we all share the same set of genes, but many of these genes come in several mutant or variant versions. Alone or in combination, these variations are the basis of such individual differences as our height, eye and hair color, physical abilities and to a great extent mental and emotional characteristics as well. Of particular interest to researchers now — and to individuals who pay several thousand dollars to get a scan of their genomes — certain SNPs also predict the likelihood that we will develop many diseases, including cancer. The keratin mutation I had detected in the paper bag sample was an SNP. Hundreds of SNPs have been identified in the human genome, and they probably only scratch the surface of what's there.

"I've already started. I was hoping it might help in getting more of a description of the guy. He was wearing a mask, and I really didn't see him very well. But now I have a better lead."

"Really? What?"

I told her about Ed Cole, the science teacher who had approached me at Mitch's party.

"I managed to find him on the internet, and I emailed him. I was mostly just trying to confirm he was who he said he was. Anyway, look at his response."

I handed her a folded sheet of paper, a printout of the email Cole had sent me:

Dear Alan:

So nice to hear from you again, and thank you again for taking the time to talk to me about your work. I feel very lucky that I got a chance to meet you at all. I didn't know about that party, and it was pure chance that someone came up to me in the lobby of my hotel, not long after I arrived in San Francisco, and told me about it. He not only accompanied me there, but gave me your name and told me I should try to meet you, as your work was particularly exciting.

Keep up the good work!

You are appreciated,

Ed

Laurie gave a low whistle. "Wow...It sounds like this guy Cole was used as a stalking horse." She handed the email back to me.

"Yeah. My theory is that the kidnapper didn't know what I looked like, or where I was staying. He didn't want me to notice him, so he had Cole find me at the party."

Laurie saw the problem immediately. "But if this was one of the guys who kidnapped you before, wouldn't he know what you looked like?"

In response, I now provided her with another piece of the puzzle. I told her for the first time about the keratin analysis I had done on the paper bag discarded by the two Minnesota kidnappers.

"So I've checked the keratin sequence of the DNA from the San Francisco kidnapper, and guess what? It's different from either of the two Minnesota guys."

"So the San Francisco kidnapper is *definitely* not one of the guys who took you to that house."

I nodded. "It's even worse than that, though. Suppose whoever is behind the kidnapping hired someone else for the San Francisco job. Maybe that seemed easier than having the Minnesota kidnappers flown across the country. But even in that case, the kidnapper would know where I was staying. Anyone in our group could easily find out what hotel I was registered in, and what the general schedule was. Hell, as you know, most of us were in the same hotel."

"What about Dick or Candy?"

"I wondered about that at first, but I think they could find out fairly easily. In Dick's case, he would have to know, because the hotel bills of course were charged to the grant."

Laurie looked at me in wonder. "Is it really possible two different people are trying to kidnap you, Alan?"

I shook my head. "I refuse to believe that. These kidnappings have to be related. I just don't understand how."

"Well, at least now the police have a description to go on. You can ask Ed Cole what this guy looked like.'

I thought of the trouble I was having getting Burris to accept any of my evidence.

"Well, the fact that some guy told Ed Cole to approach me at a party doesn't really prove much. Unless he's got blue eyes."

"Blue eyes? You know that? I thought it was dark and the guy was wearing a mask."

I smiled. "Preliminary SNP analysis."

We parked the car a little ways down the road from the trailhead, so that it would not be obvious to anyone who might come by that someone was visiting Travers. We walked along the trail quickly. Before we reached the cottage, we split up, according to our pre-conceived plan. Laurie was to leave the path and make a wide circle around the cottage, searching for the tobacco stash in the forest behind it. I remained on the path, intending to approach the cottage, and if possible, look around its vicinity. I was not too worried about encountering Travers. In that case, I would just say that I was hiking in the area. I would keep his attention occupied so that Laurie could search the forest behind his cottage without being spotted.

I soon saw the cottage through the trees, and was just entering the little clearing surrounding it, when I heard voices, coming from behind the cottage. I froze. Travers obviously had some guests. Who? Could it be the bootleggers?

My first thought was to retreat back on the path, out of sight of the cottage. But my curiosity to hear what was being said overcame my fear. Scanning the area quickly, I noticed an old rowboat lying upside down at one side of the cottage. It appeared as though it hadn't been used in a very long time, indeed, as I approached it, I saw that some of the wood was rotting. I knelt down, carefully lifted up one side of it, and crawled underneath.

I immediately texted Laurie, apprising her of my situation. I asked her to try to get a look at who Travers was with if possible, but that under no circumstances was she to allow them to see her.

I strained to hear the conversation. For at least fifteen or twenty minutes, they discussed hunting, fishing, sports and women—typical male talk. I heard an occasional clinking sound, and that, along with occasional loud, raucous outbursts by one of the men, suggested to me they were doing some serious drinking. Laurie and I kept each other regularly informed. She told me there were three men sitting at a table behind the cottage, but couldn't get close enough to see any of them clearly.

"...over the border next week..."

"You sure it's safe?"

"You keep asking that, Will. Nobody's watching the house. It's not a big deal. Relax. Nobody really cares that much."

"Maybe we should just lay low for a few weeks."

"Can't afford to, now, can we?"

"What do you mean by that?"

"We owe them money."

"*You* owe them money, not me. It's not my problem."

"It's all of our problem."

"It's not my problem! This was all your idea. You never told me you were doing this."

"Yeah, well they're really pissed off now. They're saying if they don't pull this off, they're holding us responsible."

"Pete, I told you before, I don't have twenty-five grand. And if I did, I wouldn't give it to them. This is not my problem. I never asked for this."

"Well, like we keep telling you, Will, if we help them, then we won't owe them nothing."

"Help them, hell. We're going into business for ourselves."

"Shut up, Jack!"

There was a pause, punctuated by the sound of the bottles.

"Why do they want to kidnap him, anyway? Is it for ransom?"

"Uh-uh. They just have orders to keep him there for a while."

"What do you mean, a while? How long?"

"A few weeks. Till the end of July, I think."

"And then what? They let him go?"

"Yeah, that's what they told me."

Hearing that, I naturally felt a surge of relief. I had already guessed that they did not intend to kill me, but there's nothing sweeter than those words, "you're not going to die".

"But why? What's it all about? They hold him, then let him go, no ransom involved? I don't get it."

"I don't know what it's all about, Will. *They* don't know. But they say they're under a lot of pressure to do this. Like if it doesn't happen very soon, it will be too late."

"What do you mean, too late?"

There was no response to this.

"Pete, who's paying these guys? Who's behind this?"

"You keep asking me that, and I keep telling you! I don't know."

There was another long pause, punctuated again by the sound of drinking. One of the men loudly belched.

"It don't make sense to me. He's a young man, a doctor, is what the police told me. I don't understand why anyone would want to do this to him."

"He knows something."

"What does he know?"

"Something we want to know."

"Shut up, Jack!"

"What do you mean, something you want to know?"

"He's drunk, he don't know what he's talking about!"

"Pete, this young man knows something that's worth twenty-five grand?"

"A lot more than that!"

"Shut up, Jack!"

"The boyfriend, too."

"Shut the fuck up, Jack!"

The three men continued to talk for a while, but the conversation shifted to other subjects. Deciding there was nothing more to be gained by staying there, I crawled out from under the rowboat, and started to walk away from the cottage. I had just reached the path, and was about to turn to head back to my car, when one of the men walked around the other side of the cottage. I heard Laurie's text arrive too late. I stopped dead in my tracks.

"Ho!" he cried. "Can I help you?"

The man had short red hair and glasses, and a sizeable belly that made him look a little like a penguin. He was wearing jeans and a T-shirt, and holding a bottle of beer in his hand. He didn't look a lot older than I.

"Nope," I replied, trying to project a matter-of-factness I definitely did not feel. "Just hiking a little." I was wearing a broad-brimmed hat and sunglasses, partly to make it harder for anyone to recognize me, and now I pulled the brim of the hat down further over my face. I knew this had to be one of the men who had tried to pick me up when I was hitch-hiking that day, but so far he showed no sign of recognizing me.

I wanted to text Laurie, but was afraid it might look suspicious. So I took another step in the direction of the road and safety, but then Travers and the third man came around the cottage and joined the first man. At that point, I wanted to bolt like a deer, but I stopped, unable to move.

Travers seemed equally paralyzed. For what seemed like an eternity, he stood stock still, next to his two buddies, staring at me. Finally he spoke, slowly and quietly, still not moving any closer to me.

"Not a good idea to go hiking around here. There are hunters roaming this woods, shoot at anything that moves."

"C'mon, Will, it's safe! Nothin's in season now," protested one of his buddies.

But I was already on the move again, walking fast and not looking back.

Back in the car, with the doors locked, I waited for Laurie. I had gotten a good look at both of Travers' buddies, and took a couple of minutes to write down a physical description of each. I couldn't prove either one had a connection to the kidnapping, of course. I wouldn't have sworn either man was in that car that day, and even if they had been, they had done nothing at that time that established they were trying to kidnap me. The best evidence of the connection was the conversation I had just heard, but I hadn't thought to bring recording equipment. I wondered how much Laurie had heard, whether she could corroborate my testimony.

Beyond that, I seemed to have done all I could. Laurie's texts indicated she had seen no sign of the cigarettes, and at this point, I felt the stakes were not worth the risk. Maybe they were hidden somewhere in the woods, maybe not. If there were a stash out there, maybe I could get the police to check it out, maybe not. But even if I had the opportunity to put the squeeze on Travers, and was willing to do so, I didn't think he would help much. Clearly, he was willing to lie to protect his buddies.

What was taking her so long? I texted her again. Her reply relieved me. She said the three men had left the cottage, heading in the direction of the road. She was following at a safe distance.

A few minutes later, I saw the three of them emerge onto the road and turn in the direction of the house. Probably going to check on the cigarettes, I thought. I wondered if Travers suspected why I had been there; if he did, he would have to move them again. Laurie came soon after. She walked slowly down the road, as if he she were just another carefree hiker, not revealing any worry about the men. This irritated the hell out of me.

"What were you waiting for?" I asked her as I opened the door, and practically dragged her into the passenger seat. "Don't you realize that those two guys tried to kidnap me?"

Laurie took off the backpack she had been carrying, and as she did, I could hear something rattling around inside.

"Beer bottles?'

"Why not? Might as well get some more DNA samples."

I laughed, welcoming this relief from all the tension I had just experienced.

"What will Travers think when he finds those missing?"

"He won't. There were more than a dozen on the table, and I just took one in front of each chair."

I reached over and yanked her hair. "You're good," I said. "You're really good, Inspector Godefrut."

We agreed to skip the picnic and drive straight back to Minneapolis, so that we could begin isolation and analysis of the DNA. I told her what I had overheard while hiding under the rowboat.

"So they just want to hold you for a few weeks?"

"Yeah. That's right around the time the provisional patent expires."

"The idea being you won't be able to apply for the full patent."

I nodded. "But I don't get it. Mitch can still apply."

"With you out of the way."

I looked over at her.

"Laurie, do you really think Mitch would have me kidnapped? Just to have a greater share of the patent? And wouldn't it be kind of awkward if I were released right after he applied for the full patent? What's he going to say, oh, sorry, Alan, guess you just missed."

"If you disappeared, could Mitch apply on your behalf?"

"Sure. As long as there was no evidence I was dead. And I'm

sure he would do that, too."

"Then what's the alternative? Why get you out of the way temporarily?"

I told her about my conflicts with the board of OS.

"At this point, I don't think anyone there could possibly be behind this. They voted unanimously to keep me. But if I were not around, Mitch would want to have another scientist on the board."

"Who do you think he would pick?"

"Either Bill Tye or Alex Pignatti. Either one would be well qualified to take my place." And replace me on the patent, I thought.

We stopped at the same gas station where I had had another encounter with my kidnappers that day, not to fill up, but to get some ice to keep the beer bottles cold.

"I don't suppose you know who's who here," I said to Laurie, as we set them carefully into a cheap Styrofoam chest that we bought to put the ice in. We were careful not to touch the bottles anywhere near the mouth.

"Of course I do," she replied, pointing to some markings on the labels. Pointing to one, she said, "that's the guy who got up first, who went around the house and ran into you. This one is the guy with the red shirt—that was Travers, wasn't it?"

Back in the car, I continued to report to her what I had overheard.

"One of them said something about kidnapping me before it was too late."

"You mean, before the end of July deadline?"

"That's what I thought at first. But thinking it over, I think what he meant was that if I weren't kidnapped soon, I would know who was behind it. Then it would be too late." Laurie was driving now. I turned towards her. "So whoever the perp is must think I'm very close to identifying him or her. Which I'm not, of course. But I must have done or said something that scared the perp into thinking that I am."

"That also means you're in more danger, Alan."

"Yes, maybe. And not just because of that. These two guys, Pete and Jack, are clearly in this game, too. Remember I told you that they must have been the guys in that other car that day, the ones who tried to pick me up when I was hitch-hiking? They made it clear that they're still willing to try."

While I was talking, I was busy scribbling down everything I could remember. Already, much of what I had heard was fuzzy in my mind. I wished I had brought some recording equipment, though I had never imagined I would have such an opportunity.

"Anyway, at least I know how much I'm worth now, to someone. Twenty-five thousand dollars."

Laurie half laughed, half snorted. "Twenty-five thousand dollars!? Is that what they said your kidnappers have been offered?" She reached over and squeezed my hand. "You're worth a lot more than that, Alan."

The gallows humor seemed appropriate at the time.

"Yeah, they seemed to understand that themselves."

14. THE ENEMY OF MY ENEMY

The following day we held a mini-group meeting. In addition to myself and Mitch, also present were Marissa, Bill Tye, and Alex. The purpose of the meeting was to consider our strategy in identifying genes associated with ovarian cancer. Everyone in attendance was a major player in that effort. Including Alex, who had been invited as part of our ongoing attempts at collaboration.

This was the first time I had seen Alex since the conference at San Francisco, and I made a point of talking to him just before the meeting started. I told him Mitch and I were willing to take him on as a partner when we applied for the full patent. I added, though, that I was a little upset to learn that the federal government was claiming ownership of one of my three genes—the one Alex had also discovered, but had failed to inform the government about.

He nodded morosely.

"This never should have happened, Alan. When I wrote that grant, I was careful to make certain the funds would be there to cover all the planned studies. I don't know how I ran out early."

"Did you add some new studies after the grant was awarded?"

"Yes," he admitted. "But there still should have been enough funding for them." He threw his hands up in disgust. "Somehow, we outspent what we planned for, and I don't understand it. I was watching all the expenses very carefully."

"Never mind," I said, as we walked into the conference room together. "The government needs us more than we need them."

Marissa, whose graduate thesis was devoted to ovarian cancer, was the star of this meeting. Since she was the only one in our group, up to now, investigating this type of cancer, she was to tell us about her work, providing a background that would guide the rest of us in setting up our own studies.

She began with a brief description of the disease, pointing out that much like lung cancer, ovarian cancer is difficult to detect, and that most women who are diagnosed already have an advanced form of the disease, one difficult to treat.

"Our initial goal is to identify genes that are more active in particular forms or subtypes of this cancer. If we can do that, then we can use these genes as markers to predict how aggressive the cancer will be, how long the patient will survive, and hopefully, which types of treatments will be most effective. For example, we want to profile women so that we know the best types of drugs to use, or how successful alternative treatments like radiation and surgery are likely to be."

Most of us were already familiar with this general approach. Her opening remarks were really intended mostly for Bill, who was not supposed to be very familiar with ovarian cancer. Thus I was quite surprised when he spoke up with surprising authority. Apparently he had been doing some reading on his own.

"There are several blood tests for ovarian cancer," he pointed out. "Several protein markers have been identified that strongly correlate with the disease. What exactly do you expect to do that hasn't already been done?"

Challenge and conflict are essential to science. Individuals who are the best of friends outside the lab may frequently come to verbal blows within it. Yet somehow, listening to Bill, I sensed an undertone of anger towards Marissa. I wondered if she had had it out with him for looking into her desk drawer that night.

Marissa, however, was her usual cool self.

"None of these protein markers has been through large-scale clinical trials. And even if they are successful, there's good reason to doubt that any marker can identify all the variations of the disease. I'm hoping I can find some new and better ones."

She then began to discuss her current results. Like others in our group, she was using microarrays to identify those genes that appeared to be most active in the cancer. She then zeroed in one some of these genes, using PCR, a more sensitive assay. She had analyzed tumor samples from several dozen women with this disease, made available to her through collaboration with surgeons at the university. She put up a slide on the screen at the front of the room to illustrate some of her results.

Bill Tye went on the attack again, this time not even dignifying it by speaking to Marissa. Instead, his remarks were directed to Mitch.

"Why is she continuing to use these out-of-date techniques? My microarrays are far more sensitive to some of these genes. I've told her several times that it's time to switch over."

Now Marissa did look flustered. She deferred to Mitch.

"We will be phasing over soon, Bill," he explained. "Remember, this work was begun before you got here. I wanted her to continue using the same system she began with."

One person in the room who thought her techniques were just fine was Alex.

"Your work is so beautiful," he crooned to her. "I have rarely seen such clear-cut results. The figure, it is perfect. So well done."

Marissa beamed, no doubt glad to have this unexpected support. "Thanks."

Alex was referring to more than one kind of figure, of course. But the compliment, unlike the complimentor, was not full of BS. Marissa was an excellent bench worker, and the grad students and technicians often came to her for advice on how to get an experiment to work. The question was whether she had any originality, the ability to develop a project on her own. Granted that she was just a third year student, as far as I could see she was just following Mitch's orders.

She pressed a button on the remote and put up another slide. "These are the genes I'm concentrating on now. They seem to be changed the most."

"Oh, yes, those are very big changes," said Alex encouragingly. "Those genes stick out. Very good data."

I asked her how my three colon cancer genes had turned out. Whether their activity was dramatically altered in ovarian cancer.

"Basically unchanged," she replied.

Disappointing, but not very surprising. One just didn't expect that genes related to one kind of cancer would also be related to another. Unless, of course, they were involved in really fundamental processes, ones found in all or most cancers. There were a few such genes known, and we were always on the lookout for more.

"What about Alex's genes?" I continued.

Marissa shrugged, appealing for help here. "I'm afraid I don't know what those are...?"

In response, Alex bolted out of his seat, and strode up to the front of the room. It was all an act, of course. It didn't matter how close he got to the screen, he wasn't going to find his genes among the thousands represented on that slide. But of course, it gave him a chance to snuggle up to Marissa. He played the moment for everything it was worth. Instead of just naming the genes to everyone in the room, he bent over and whispered them into Marissa's ear. With one arm around her to make sure that ear was close enough, of course.

If Marissa felt this was all a bit too much, she didn't show it. Though she withdrew from Alex as soon as she heard the names, she did so slowly and gracefully. Then she consulted a list she was holding in front of her.

"I can't find them right now," she said finally. "But they weren't anywhere near the best genes, I'm sure of that."

The meeting broke up a little before lunch. Mitch summed up the progress Marissa had made so far, and praised her work in the most extravagant terms. Made it sound like she would be winning the Nobel Prize in a couple of years. It was all a bit much, I thought. A glorified technician, is what she was. But very glorified, indeed. I was unable to take my eyes off her butt as she walked out of the room, talking to Mitch. Alex's eyes, of course, were riveted to the same spot.

I was so entranced with her that I almost forgot that she still had not told me if she had learned who had used her cell phone to text me, the night of the kidnapping. I didn't want to discuss any details about it in public, because I didn't want others to know about the link between her cell phone and my kidnapping. On the other hand, I wanted to remind her that I was waiting to hear from her. So I caught up to her as she and Mitch were walking down the hall towards the labs.

"Hey, Marissa, have you found out anything about your cell phone?"

The question had an extraordinary effect, not just on Marissa, but on Mitch, too. The two of them stopped dead in their tracks, and I noticed Marissa was blushing to her roots. Mitch was staring at her with a questioning look in his eyes.

"No, not yet, Alan," she replied. "I'll let you know. Then she grabbed Mitch's arm, and literally pulled him down the hall with her.

I stood still for a moment, trying to decide whether to follow her to her cubicle now, so that I could talk with her alone, or to wait for a while, when I felt a restraining hand on my arm. It was Bill Tye.

"Let it go, man," he said. "She doesn't know anything."

I turned around and stared at him in astonishment.

"You were the one who told me to ask her," I pointed out. Lowering my voice, I added, "You were the one who said her cell phone was missing from her drawer that night."

Bill glanced around to make sure that no one was within earshot, then said quietly, "I think I know who it was, Alan."

"You know who used her cell phone? Who?"

Bill lowered his voice another couple of notches, so he was barely whispering.

"Who had you kidnapped."

"Are you serious?!?" I hissed. "You really know who?"

But he shook his head. "I'm not going to say any more until I'm positive. I don't want to falsely implicate anyone." He started to move away from me. "I'm not even at the 5% confidence level yet. But I have found a very suggestive correlation."

In the afternoon I got together with Andrea and Laurie, to see how their project was going. When I had begun sleeping with Laurie, I worried about how that would affect our relationship in the lab. I had been to bed with other women in my profession before, but never with someone in my own laboratory, someone I saw day to day on a routine basis. I was feeling my way along, trying to balance what at the least was my affection for her with my desire to treat her no differently from any other student, certainly no differently from Andrea.

I recalled a former graduate student in the lab, a guy who had finished his Ph.D. and left last year to do a postdoc with another group. James was a classic sex addict—never saw a pussy he didn't like. I once asked him about it, and he confessed that part of the reason he got involved with so many women was that once he had been to bed with someone, he felt he could get along with her better in the lab. It broke the tension. He was definitely deluding himself a little; he left a trail of broken hearts behind him. But I could understand his reasoning. If I had had to work right alongside Marissa Cheng all day, I doubted I would have discovered those three genes.

Anyway, I was surprised at how smoothly Laurie and I got back into the mentor/student groove. Not she would have cared, anyway, but Andrea, I felt certain, could not tell that there was anything going on between Laurie and myself but business. Truth be told, I couldn't tell. I felt at this time none of the lust I had felt for her in bed, not because she looked unattractive again in the light, but just because we were engaging at another level. It made me wonder how many other relationships were going on in the lab, ones that neither I nor anyone else other than the involved parties knew anything about.

"How do they look?" I said, holding up a Petri dish and examining it closely. I took it over to the microscope.

"Whee!" exclaimed Andrea. "They're growing! They're growing! Whee!"

We were in the cell culture room. She began to do a little dance, then segued into some basketball moves, dodging this way and that. Whenever she was in a good mood, she would do that, pretend she was on the court, dribbling an invisible ball, dodging wastebaskets and other stand-ins for opposing players.

This was the first time she had ever worked with isolated cells. She and Laurie had just managed to insert into these cells one of my three colon cancer genes. The purpose of the study was to see what the gene did, how it changed the morphology and physiology of the cell. Actually, some more experiments would have to be done to confirm that the gene really was in there, but I didn't want to spoil her moment. The cells were alive and looked very healthy, which was half the game. Along with the cancer gene, we had inserted a gene that provided resistance to a certain antibiotic. The cells were then grown in a medium containing this antibiotic, so any cells that survived under these conditions had to have that resistance gene, and therefore also the cancer gene.

Laurie was much calmer; she had done stuff like this before. While I studied the cells under the microscope, she was already asking me about details in setting up the confirming experiments that we would have to do next. I could feel her attraction to me in every word she said, yet somehow it was not something that was easily visible to anyone else. I was very relieved about that.

"What if the copy number is low?" she said, referring to the amount of the gene transferred into the cells.

"No problem. I want several cell lines, with different copy numbers. That way, we can correlate the magnitude of the effect with the amount of gene."

"But more gene doesn't necessarily mean more product, does it?"

"Good question!" I had to bite my tongue from adding, "babe". "That's why we have to measure protein levels, too."

"Can we do antibody studies to see where the protein is localized?"

"Eventually, yeah, we'll get to it."

The two of them made an odd couple in the lab, I thought. Andrea, nearly six feet tall, full of energy and enthusiasm, Laurie, barely five-two, quieter, more thoughtful. Yet they got along splendidly. Andrea, grateful to have Laurie's experience and technical savvy, had nicknamed her "my little point guard".

"Let me see that control plate."

I removed the Petri dish I had been looking at from under the microscope, and Andrea handed me another Petri dish. "Yep, that looks good. Take a look." I got up from the chair and let Andrea look. These were cells that had not been transfected with the colon cancer gene nor with the accompanying gene that conferred antibiotic resistance.

"I thought it was supposed to be like totally blank," she said. "Why are there still a few cells growing?"

"Maybe the antibiotic wasn't one hundred percent effective in killing them. Or maybe a little contamination...?" That last point implied that maybe one of them had been a little sloppy in their experiment.

"Let me see," said Laurie, pushing Andrea out of they way. "Oh, that's beautiful, Drey, what are you talking about?'

"Don't you see those cells?"

"Hardly any! Even I might score one basket playing one-on-one with you."

"No way."

I handed the plate back to her. "Looks good. OK, ladies, time to run some gels."

"Yippee!" said Andrea.

Laurie grabbed my crotch and gave it a gentle squeeze. I flushed beet red, and glanced quickly through the window of the room to the main lab to see if anyone out there had noticed.

Later in the afternoon I went to see Dick Johnstone in his office. My ostensible purpose was to hand him the budget portion of the grant, which I had finally finished to my satisfaction. But again, I found myself going in there with an ulterior motive.

Ever since I had suggested to Dick and to Candy the possibility that someone in the lab might be selling, or trying to sell, information about my three genes, I had done a lot of thinking about their responses. And the more I thought about that, the more convinced I became that my entire approach had been wrong. Though I had been trying to be subtle, and certainly not give either one a reason to believe I suspected them, I had simply come on too directly.

Science is all about asking the right question, and frequently that requires approaching a problem indirectly. You can't always ask the question you really want answered. You can't, for example, ask whether a certain gene causes cancer. The gene doesn't know how to respond to a direct question like that. You have to ask it a more indirect question. For example, is it more active in people with cancer? Does its activity progressively increase as the cancer progressively worsens? Are other genes, known to be associated with the gene of interest, also affected by cancer? What happens to individual cancer cells, removed from the patient's body and grown in culture, if the gene is manipulated in certain ways?

So I had come up with a different approach. Let's suppose, I thought, someone in the lab really was selling information to someone in another lab. Dick and Candy were in a unique position, in that both of them had access to certain kinds of information about not simply my work, but the work of other laboratories in our building. Candy helped with the grants from these other groups, while Dick's financial duties likewise extended to them.

So what would happen, I asked myself, if I came to one of them and suggested, ever so subtly, that I was interested in someone else's information? What would their response be? If they were selling information about my work to someone else, why wouldn't they sell information about someone else's work to me? Why would they care who was the buyer and whose information was being sold? It was all just business to them. So if they were willing to sell to me, then they had as good as admitted that at the very least, they would be willing to sell my information to someone else. It wouldn't be an actual confession, but it would be damned close. Yet—and this, it seemed to me, was the beauty of the approach-- nowhere in such a discussion would I provide any clue that I thought they were actually selling my work.

It was too late to try this tactic on Candy, I knew. I had told her too much already. I had told her that I suspected someone was selling my data, and she had already categorically denied that she was the one, so of course it would make no sense at all for me to suggest that she sell someone else's data to me. At the very least, she would think I was guilty of major hypocrisy, and most likely, she would see right through my little scheme.

But it was still possible to play this game with Dick. I hadn't mentioned anything at all to him about financial information. In fact, I hadn't even raised the issue of selling. All I had said to him was that I thought someone was trying to steal my data.

So after our regular business was concluded, I said to him, sort of wistfully, "I wish I could see some invoices from another lab."

I had really hoped that Dick would respond to this encouragingly, perhaps ask me which ones I might be interested in, was I really *very* interested in these, and so on. But again, my little experiment turned out very differently from the way I had anticipated it might. Dick in fact reacted in just the opposite way. His face darkened into a scowl, and he became very protective.

"Why on earth would you want to do that, lover boy?"

"Just to compare my grant with theirs. Just to get some insight into how someone else does it."

Dick looked scandalized. With exaggerated emphasis, he put a finger to his lips.

"Alan, any kind of financial information from other laboratories is *confidential*. I can't show it to you."

"I was just curious," I said quietly. "I mean, what's the big deal about a few invoices?"

Dick glared at me in silence for a moment, then looked down to brush some invisible piece of lint off his shirt. He looked almost hurt, as though he were waiting for an apology from me.

"Alan, I work on this crap all day, and I can tell you that 90% of finance is boring as shit. Most of the information has *no* value or interest to *anyone* except me." He ran his fingers slowly through his hair. "But some of it *is* important, and because it is, all of it *must* be confidential. Rules are rules."

182

"Not even just a few?"

"No," replied Dick firmly. "No, no, no, no." He waggled a finger at me. "Mustn't, mustn't, mustn't. Bad dog, bad dog. Stay, stay."

Still later in the day, it was almost six, I had another meeting with Officer Burris at the campus police office. I told him about my latest visit to Travers' cottage, and the conversation I heard. I gave him a description of Travers's two confederates, the tobacco bootleggers.

"You're likely to get yourself kidnapped again if you keep prowling around there," he growled at me.

"Then you agree with me that these guys know the kidnappers, and are probably trying to help them capture me?"

Burris moved his head back and forth. "On the basis of your story, it sounds that way, yes. But you understand that it's your word against theirs."

"Not any more it isn't." I now revealed my trump card. I removed from a large envelope I had brought a series of DNA fingerprints. Burris, to his credit, knew or guessed what they were.

"This one is from the guy who kidnapped me in San Francisco," I explained, as I laid it down on the table in front of Burris. I added that I was also able to conclude, from analysis of the keratin genes, that the San Francisco kidnapper was distinct from either of the Minnesota kidnappers. It was a third man.

"Interesting," said Burris. "So you think a different man was hired for the San Francisco kidnapping?"

"Definitely. But there's more." Now I lay down on the table three other DNA fingerprints.

"These are of Travers and his two friends. I got them from the beer bottles they were drinking out of."

Burris studied the fingerprints. They were patterns of DNA fragments run on a gel, ladder-like rows of dark black lines on a clear plastic sheet of photographic film.

"Any matches...?"

"No, not exactly," I said. "But look at these two. This one is the San Francisco kidnapper. And this is one of the Travers's friends. See how similar they are? What that means is that they are closely related. In other words, they are probably brothers, or possibly cousins."

Burris raised his eyebrows. "Really? Yes, I see the similarity. In fact, at first glance I thought they were the same. But you're right, not quite." He looked up at me. "Are any of these on file with the FBI? Do you know that yet?"

I shook my head. "The San Francisco guy isn't. Iris Hamilton checked for me. I haven't had the chance to see about the others. I kind of doubt that they are, but I'll leave that up to you."

Burris nodded, and began walking around the room, lost in thought.

"So you think one of the guys in Minnesota calls his brother, let's say it is, in San Francisco, gives him a description of you, and has him kidnap you."

I shook my head. "There's more to it." I explained what I had learned from Ed Cole.

"Do you see what this means?" I continued. "The kidnapper in San Francisco didn't know what I looked like, or where I was staying. If his brother in Minnesota was working with the kidnappers, he would have had that information."

"I thought these two friends of Travers tried to pick you up when you were hitch-hiking that day you escaped. So you say."

"Yes, they had a general description of me, but not a detailed one, which the original kidnappers probably would have. When they tried to pick me up that day, they were probably just told to look for anyone about my age and general appearance hitch-hiking on a certain stretch of road. Hell, they knew what clothes I was wearing."

Burris nodded. "Yes, I see what you mean."

"This suggests to me that Travers' buddies are working on their own. They had the brother kidnap me without the knowledge or permission of the original Minnesota kidnappers." I added, as further evidence for this, one of the remarks that one of the bootleggers had made, that they were "in business on their own".

Burris digested this quickly.

"Then how would they even know you were in San Francisco?"

I threw the question back at Burris. "What did the police tell Travers when they questioned him? They must have given him my name. I had filed a complaint involving his house. After Travers was questioned, I know he went to his friends, asking them what the hell some kidnap victim was doing in his house, and he would have told them everything the police told him. With that name, and the knowledge that I lived in Minneapolis, they probably could have traced me to the lab." I hesitated a moment, recalling the conversation I had overheard at Travers' place. "Travers in fact knew I was a doctor."

"OK," replied Burris, "but what would be the point of kidnapping you without the help and permission of the person paying for the job?"

Yes, I had wondered about that, too. And I thought I had finally come up with an answer. I got up from the table and faced him.

"How about blackmail?"

"Blackmail?"

"Sure. Let's say the brother successfully kidnaps me and holds me somewhere in northern California. He, and his brother back in Minnesota, don't know who originally ordered the kidnapping. They said as much when I was listening in on them, and I wouldn't expect the original kidnappers to tell them. So the California kidnapper sends word, through his brother in Minnesota, to the original, Minnesota kidnappers that he wants the name of the person who hired them. If they comply with this request, he will just hold me where I am, and let the Minnesota guys take the credit — and the money, of course. These guys will almost certainly accept this deal, because they have nothing to lose. As long as they get the credit for the kidnapping, what is it to them if someone knows the name of the person who hired them? They're already known to this guy in California."

"Hold it. If they know the name of the perp hiring the Minnesota kidnappers, they can just deal with him."

"No, the deal is California doesn't learn who it is until he hands me over to Minnesota. Then California waits until I'm released by Minnesota, or maybe even before that, at which point he threatens to expose the person behind my kidnapping. He not only knows the identity of this person, but also the identity of the Minnesota kidnappers — from his brother in Minnesota."

"The man in California doesn't really have any evidence," countered Burris. "He will have difficulty proving that the perp even knew the kidnappers, since they obviously aren't going to testify against him in court, and he certainly won't be able to prove that the perp paid them. I think if I were the perp in this situation, I would call the guy's bluff."

"But the guy in California could get evidence," I persisted.

"How?"

"From me. Suppose while he's holding me, he asks me who I think is behind the kidnapping. I don't know, but I name all the suspects for him, and tell him what each of them might have to gain."

Burris moved his head from side to side. "That's still not enough evidence."

"Maybe not to convict the perp, but certainly to put the heat on him. In that situation, it might be easier to pay up then to have this guy making life miserable. Suppose he contacts him and tells him what he knows?"

Burris almost laughed, the first time I could recall seeing humor in him.

"You make it sound like this guy in California is almost on your side."

"Yeah, that's the American way, isn't it? Fight evil and help the oppressed, as long as you can make a profit while you're doing it."

186

15. SOUL TALK

Burris didn't accept my theory of blackmail without reservations, but that wasn't really important, anyway. What did count was that I had positive evidence that one of Travers' bootlegging buddies was related to the man who had kidnapped me in California. Regardless of what accounted for the connection, I thought that the DNA evidence would be sufficient for the police to bring the two bootleggers, Jack and Pete, in for questioning.

"Can't we force him, whichever one it is, to tell us who the relative in California is?"

Burris was walking back and forth alongside the table, hands behind his back.

"There are some really sticky legal issues here, Alan. In the first place, he—whichever the two of them it is--could argue that the DNA evidence was illegally obtained. Obviously, he didn't give his consent, nor could we order him to provide an official DNA sample, since on the basis of our current evidence, he can't be considered a suspect in the crime."

"Despite what I overheard?"

"It's your word against theirs, since Ms., ah, Godefrut you said did not hear it." He shot this out without breaking stride. "In the second place, given the manner in which the DNA was obtained, from several beer bottles, each of these guys could argue that it isn't his, further complicating the issue."

"We know which DNA sample corresponds with each guy," I said, explaining to him how Laurie had collected the bottles. "I don't know which guy has which name, but if I saw them again, I could tell you which DNA sample belonged to who."

Burris shook his head.

"Not good enough. They could argue that the beer bottles were moved around so much that it would be impossible for Ms. Godefrut to know which ones she was picking up when she finally approached the table. To sort it out, each of the men, including Travers, would have to provide another DNA sample, and at this point I'm not sure they could be compelled to do that."

He paused, thinking that over, then continued pacing.

"And finally, whichever one it is, he could have a lot of relatives who would have a similar DNA profile to his own, and he might deny that he knows which one it could be. If he is really involved in this himself, of course he will do just that."

"Couldn't we have all the relatives tested, to see which one matches the DNA profile?"

"Possibly. But it depends on the cooperation of this Minnesota guy just to track down these relatives, just to find out who they are and where they are, and it sounds to me like we won't get it."

I couldn't argue with that. I also knew, after my last visit to the north, that Travers himself was not going to help incriminate his friends. And that even if he had been willing to, he probably didn't know much more about my kidnappers than I did. So I decided to take another tack.

"What about cell phone records? These two guys, Pete and Jack, probably contacted the kidnappers by cell phone at some point. Both the ones in Minnesota as well as, of course, the relative in California. They may still be doing it. Can't you look at their records, find out who they were calling?"

"That's another gray area," responded Burris. "There was a time very recently when it was possible to buy phone records over the internet, but companies are starting to clamp down on the practice. It would be difficult for me to get the records of these two guys unless we have more evidence of their involvement. I can try, certainly, but no promises." He stopped striding for a moment, deep in thought. "We could probably subpoena Travers's records, though. Since he owns the house where you were taken."

I shrugged helplessly. "What good will that do? I don't think he's had any contact with the kidnappers."

Burris stopped wandering and faced me from across the table.

"But he does have contact with his friends, of course. You told me you think he called them the day you escaped from the house, to come and get him out of the cellar. If we could establish that, at that point we would have a better basis for arguing we need to subpoena his buddies' records. Worth a try."

I had to be content with that. I wasn't really happy, though. I had worked very hard at all this DNA analysis, and if Burris was right, it wasn't going to help me convict anyone. Maybe the cell phone records would be a different story, but of course I appreciated from personal experience how difficult it could be to trace the actual user of a cell phone.

So I was leaving, I asked Burris, "Have you personally ever convicted someone on the basis of cell phone records?"

He laughed. "No, but I myself was once convicted on that basis."

I stared at him in shock. "You were *convicted*? Of a *crime*?!?"

He opened the door of the room to the hall. "I was convicted of the crime of adultery, my boy," he said, clapping a hand on my shoulder in a show of intimacy he had never exhibited before. "And let me give you a little prosecutorial advice: if you ever go through a divorce, make sure you use a cell phone that your wife doesn't know about."

The following day, in the early afternoon, I went to see Candy about my grant application. The last time I had visited her office, I had suggested that someone in the lab was selling information about my research. In response, she had become noticeably uncomfortable. I was more and more convinced she was hiding something. But how to bring it to light?

I couldn't flat out accuse her of anything, in the first place, because I didn't know what, if anything, she was actually hiding, and in the second place, because, based on her earlier response, she would just clam up. She didn't like confrontation. So what did I say to her? How did I approach her non-confrontationally, but at the same time insisting that she open up to me?

The solution to the problem hit me just as I was walking into her office, smelling all those fragrances in the jars on the shelf along one

189

wall, seeing the statue of Buddha, the pictures of saints. Candy was the one who was always talking about being open, being in the present. So that was exactly what I would do. I would set the example, and expect her to reciprocate.

So I didn't say a word as I entered her office, showed no sign of being rushed or under stress as I usually did in that situation. I sat down in front of her desk, put the grant in my lap, held my back straight up, and stared at her. I tried to appear as peaceful, as beatific, as possible. Still without speaking, or even moving.

At first, it was very difficult; it felt forced, very unnatural. I was embarrassed, as though I were trying to parody her. I was about to give it up as a dumb idea. Even Candy would think I was acting ridiculous, pretending to be someone or something that I clearly was not.

But then, out of the blue, I remembered that night in the lab, just before I was kidnapped, when I knew I had discovered a new test for colon cancer. I remembered how *high* I had been, how clear and alive everything in the lab had appeared to me. It was not that I had completely forgotten that moment until now; I had occasionally *thought* about it. But this was the first time since then that I had *re-lived* it. It was as though I had gone back in time to re-visit that moment. Not even that, really. It was as though that moment were eternal, and I *always* was living in it. It was just that sometimes I forgot that. Now I remembered.

Now everything in the office came alive to me, just as everything in the lab had that night. I seemed to see objects directly, rather than through the filter of my thoughts and pre-conceptions of them. And none more so than Candy herself.

I don't mean that I could stare into her mind, and see everything that was there. But for maybe the first time in many years I was sensitive to what someone was feeling, rather than what I thought they were feeling, or what I thought they should be feeling, or what I thought I should be feeling. I could see her emotions as clearly as though they were pages in a book I was reading—not really pages so much as pictures, or patterns. And what I saw was that she was hiding something from me. And feeling very, very guilty about it.

"You have something to tell me, Candy," I said, quietly, but not

190

exaggeratedly so. I was surprised at how gently the words came out of my mouth, in their own good time. At how much power words could have when the speaker was peaceful, and not competing with his own message.

She said nothing, but I could see the emotions sweep across her face in response to my words. I was actually conversing with those emotions, asking them questions and listening to their answers. And so I was not surprised when Candy finally spoke without any further words from me. There was nothing chancy or spontaneous about it. She was responding to forces I had just never been aware of before.

"Do you remember a few days ago we were talking about who might have kidnapped you and why?"

"Yes, of course."

"And you suggested there were a lot of people in the lab who had information about your work, information that would be valuable to someone working in another lab?"

I said yes without speaking, without moving.

She was silent for a moment. I could see how difficult this was for her.

"I...er, showed part of one of your grants to someone."

I felt as though 880 volts had just gone through me. I had expected something like this, wanted something like this. But I was totally unprepared for the effect it had on me in my current state. The price for heightened sensitivity to someone else's emotions was of course more vulnerability to my own. I felt my peace beginning to shatter.

"You *showed* someone part of a grant..."

"Well, actually I did more than that. I gave him a copy of the whole grant."

"Who?"

"Alex Pignatti."

It all made sense now. Finally. He hadn't independently identified my three genes, he had stolen them. Even if they weren't explicitly identified in the grant, there was enough information so that Alex could have put it all together. That was when he came to me, pretending he had a gene that he thought might be mine. He had known all along it was mine. He pretended not to know, to keep up the appearance that he had discovered it independently. Because if he had discovered it on his own, he couldn't have known it was mine.

So there was no secret at all to his successful bluff. Anyone can bluff when he holds a royal flush. Or when he knows what all your cards are.

All of this logical train of thought blazed through my mind in probably less than a second. Then I exploded.

"Goddamn it, Candy, you swore to me you wouldn't sell confidential information like this to anyone. You *swore* to me!!"

It was very, very weird. I could hear those words being spoken, yet I wasn't speaking them. Someone was, certainly, but it wasn't I. I was watching those words being spoken. Powerless to stop them, yet so powerful in observing them.

"But I *didn't* sell him anything."

"You just—"

"I *gave* it to him. It was a *gift*. It was *free*."

"You gave it to him for free? Why?"

"Because we're lovers, Alan. I'd give him anything."

She spent the next ten minutes or so confessing her heart out, saying how very, very sorry she was, not just for giving Alex the grant behind my back, but for withholding the information at the very time when I desperately needed to know anything and everything that might be related to my kidnapping. Though she was *certain* that Alex had *nothing* to do with my kidnapping—and of course, *she* had nothing to do with it—she *completely* understood how it had to appear to me. I think if I had taken off my shoes and commanded her to wash my feet, she would have done so immediately.

"Alan, if there is *any*thing I can do to make this up to you..."

I was in a daze. I felt bad that I had broken the spell, raised my voice against her. But if I hadn't, wouldn't I have been sending the signal that what she did was no big deal? At the very least, she had given Alex the means to join Mitch and me on the patent. It wasn't easy to forgive something like that.

But I tried to remain calm, to continue observing her directly, rather than just reacting to her words. She appeared very vulnerable to me, her offer of help genuine. I made a quick decision. I told her about the text I had received from Marissa's cell phone the night I was kidnapped. I didn't go into a lot of details, bringing in Bernie and Bill Tye and all the rest. I just made it very clear to her that whoever used Marissa's cell that night must have been involved in my kidnapping.

"I've talked to Marissa, who denies using it. She says it was in her desk at the time, but I don't think it was. If you can find out anything at all about that..."

Back at my desk, while still recovering from the shock of what Candy and Alex had done, I tried to fit these new pieces into the puzzle of my kidnapping. So Alex had lied to me and taken advantage of Candy, but was there anything more to it than that? With the knowledge of my three genes, plus his share of the patent, he would seem to have no incentive to get me out of the way. Unless, of course, he wanted not merely to join me on the patent, but to supplant me.

What Laurie had suggested about Mitch applied as well to Alex, I now realized. If he shared the patent with me, he would stand to make more if I were out of the way. And to replace me on the board of OS as well.

What about Candy herself? She had lied to me, or at least not told me something she should have, but was she hiding anything more? Even assuming she was capable of hiring someone to kidnap me, what motive would she have? Alex knew what the three genes were now, and she was close to Alex. Was she ambitious for him? Did she want to see him rise to the top at OS?

Candy, who seemed to think a lot of cancer research was a waste of time?

I was still stewing over this when Laurie appeared. She knocked gently on the side of my cubicle. I looked up.

"Hi," I said. "How's it going?"

"Pretty good. Are you doing anything tonight?"

No, I thought. And I really needed to be with someone I trusted right now.

We went over to my place a little while later. I had a one bedroom apartment about a mile from campus. I gave her the tour, such as it was. I lived very simply. I didn't have much furniture, other than a kitchen table and chairs, a sofa and armchair, a TV, and a desktop computer on its own table. The walls were virtually bare, except for a couple of posters of national parks. I had no photographs of anyone, myself included, displayed anywhere. My closet, full, could have been mistaken for some closets found in just-vacated apartments. Laurie commented that I lived like a monk, which I guessed was true.

We sat in the kitchen, and I poured some red wine. I told her all about Candy's confession.

"Candy's a good person," commented Laurie. "I mean, she's a little New-Agey, she has some really crazy ideas, but I like her. She's always very nice to me."

I nodded. I couldn't disagree with that assessment. "But she did lie to me," I pointed out.

"In a way, that's a point in her favor, isn't it?"

"Huh? How do you figure that?"

"Well, for one thing, she admitted to it. Maybe you suspected she was hiding something, maybe you pressed her, but people lie when under far more pressure than that. You yourself said you thought she was guilty. That's a sign of innocence, isn't it? Or at least of someone who has a lot of trouble committing a crime."

She paused for a moment to take a sip of wine. Her hair was down and gleamed in the kitchen light, flowing over the back of her chair, almost to the floor. Just knowing that I would be feeling that hair in a very short time—really, about any time I wanted—made me feel excited. When we were alone together, I had begun to call her Laurie Juicy Fruit.

"OK, I'll buy that, I guess," I said. "But still, if she hid that, what else might she still be hiding?"

"Probably nothing, I'd say," Laurie replied. "When people want to hide something really important, Alan, they often cover it up by confessing to something minor. You admit to taking a few dollars that were lying around on someone's desk, you don't admit to graft. But this was not minor. This was not a token admission offered to convince you that she is basically honest." She finished her glass of wine, and reached out to pour herself another. "In my humble opinion, of course."

I thought about that for a few minutes. I wasn't sure I agreed with her. While Candy herself felt she had committed a major transgression, in actual fact there was nothing illegal about showing someone a grant proposal. Maybe not even unethical, if money was not involved. So she could have been hiding something worse.

"What about Dick?" I told her briefly about my last encounter with him, how I had tried to bait him into giving me information from another grant, and he had rejected me unequivocally.

"Dick? Very smart, very clever. A bit of a dandy, of course, all those expensive clothes. I think he's basically unhappy, though. A very lonely person."

"Really? Why do you say that?"

"Just my impression. It seems like everything he says or does is directed towards others. Some kind of show that he's putting on. There's nothing left for himself."

I shrugged. "OK, how about Bill Tye?"

She frowned, and took another sip of wine.

"Bill…hmmm. I don't know him that well. Very hard worker, seems to me very reliable. Certainly I have nothing against him."

I couldn't resist asking her if she found him attractive. She burst out laughing, almost spilling her wine.

"What's so funny?"

"He's gay, Alan. Can't you see that?"

I flushed, and not just because the wine was beginning to take effect. Of course, I thought, that explained why he showed no interest in Marissa.

"How about Marissa?"

She started laughing again. This was beginning to annoy me a little.

"What is it?" I said.

She flashed me a devilish grin. "I don't have to ask if you find Marissa attractive."

I put my head down on the table. Covered my head with my arms.

"Jesus, is it that obvious?"

She reached across the table and squeezed one of my arms.

"To me, yes. To her, yes. To anyone else in the lab, probably not."

I lifted my head up again. "OK, what are your impressions of her?"

She was thinking very carefully about this one, I could see.

"Hmmm...I don't think I can be objective about her..."

It was my turn to wear a wicked grin. "Oh, really?"

"Marissa..." she pondered. "I find her a little aloof, preoccupied. I mean, she's very helpful, will always answer questions I have about some procedure. But she seems...oh, I don't know, a little uptight, maybe. Doesn't share herself freely with others. I don't want to call her arrogant, but..."

So it's not just me, I thought.

"OK," I said. "One more. What about Mitch? You were the one who pointed out to me that he might have a motive," I added.

"Mitch..." she said thoughtfully. "Yes, I certainly think the motive is there. But he just seems too...preoccupied to plan a

196

kidnapping."

"You mean with his divorce."

"For sure. I can see it wearing down on him. I don't know any of the details, but I've heard his wife is giving him a pretty rough time. Following his every move."

"So you think he's too busy to do anything else?" I took another sip of wine. By now, I had enough of a buzz so I could talk about Mitch in ways I probably wouldn't have had I been completely sober. "Wouldn't that be a motive, if it came to that? He needs all the money he can get now."

"Sure, but she'll just get half of it, won't she? I mean, the more money that patent is worth to him, the more he has to pay her. It can't be a lot of fun knowing that."

I wondered if that could be a motive for delaying filing of the patent. Or was it when the provisional patent was filed that mattered? I had no idea how divorce law worked in that regard, and I doubted that Laurie did, either. But then something else occurred to me.

"Anyway, I have a better reason for eliminating Mitch."

"What's that?" she said.

"That text that was sent to me from Marissa's cell phone. I don't see how he would have known where her phone was, and even if he had, he wasn't around then. He had a seminar that night until nine. He hadn't gone home yet, but he wouldn't have been in our research wing at that time, either."

Later, when we were in bed, it occurred to me that she had never actually told me who she suspected most, and why. I asked her what she would do if she were in my situation.

"I would start by picking the one person I was most certain was innocent. The one who I simply could not believe was capable of committing the crime."

"And that's the one who did it, right?"

"No, no, Alan, this isn't this some mystery novel where the

criminal is the person no one suspects. In real life, the person you are most sure is innocent almost always is. You have to trust your gut instincts here. At least, I would, if I were in your position."

"OK," I said. "So you eliminate that person. Then what?"

"Then I would go in the opposite direction, and decide who I thought was most suspicious, who I thought was most likely to have committed the crime."

"And that's the perp."

"Nope. Wrong again. I would eliminate that person, too."

"What!?" I separated myself slightly from our embrace, so I could see her face in the pale light coming in through the bedroom window.

"You would eliminate the person you're most suspicious of? Why in the world would you do that?"

"Because that is where I wouldn't trust my gut instincts. When it comes to being suspicious of someone, all sorts of factors creep in, some of them very personal, some of them maybe having nothing to do with the crime. If I'm really suspicious of someone, I'm probably not being objective enough about them."

"It still sounds weird to me," I said. "Very counter-intuitive. It seems to me you run the danger of ignoring one of the prime suspects."

She reached out and stroked my back gently.

"Think of it as eliminating the outliers," she said. "The person who appears most innocent, and the person who appears most guilty."

I raised my head and upper body, resting their weight on my elbows.

"But a criminal *is* an outlier, Laurie," I protested. "A criminal is a deviant, someone whose behavior differs from normal, civilized behavior by several standard deviations."

"Yes, but a good criminal *hides* that deviant behavior. He or she tries to act as normally as possible, to blend in with all the innocent people. So though his actions may be deviant, the way he appears to everyone else around him won't be."

She thought about this for a moment longer. I could almost feel the thoughts run through her mind in the way they subtly broke up the rhythm of her strokes on my back.

"Innocent people usually make no effort to broadcast their innocence, to make it appear they are innocent, because it doesn't really occur to them that they have anything to worry about. So it's likely that someone who appears really suspicious is just someone who hasn't made any effort not to appear that way."

She finally stopped stroking, put both her arms gently around me, and pulled me back to her.

"You know all details better than I do, Alan. But if I were in your position, I would throw out both the least suspicious person and the most suspicious person. Whoever's left—one of them's the one you're looking for."

16. A SUSPECT IS ELIMINATED

Alex was planning to attend our next board meeting, which was conveniently the very next day. I couldn't have been more pleased with the timing. At first, I planned to announce and denounce him in front of the full board. I thought it was exactly what he deserved. But thinking it over, I thought it would be better if I confronted him in private. It would be embarrassing and humiliating for him to be exposed in front of everyone.

I wasn't really sure, though, why I cared. He was a slimeball, no question about it. He had not only stolen data from me, that was bad enough. Using these ill-gotten gains, he had then misrepresented himself and his value to me, trying to leverage his way onto the patent. And as if all that weren't enough, he had gained all this by still another act of fraud, committed towards Candy. As far as I could see, she really cared for him—a classic attraction of opposites, I thought--whereas I had only needed to see Alex in action at that party in San Francisco to know that she was just another conquest for him.

Still, this meeting I planned with Alex was not going to be easy for me. Despite everything he had done to deserve my undying enmity, I liked him. I had always enjoyed my discussions with him, despite or even to some extent because of the underlying tension, our knowledge that we were competitors in a high stakes game. He in turn seemed to genuinely enjoy talking to me, and to have great respect for my work.

I told myself over and over not to look at him in that way, that I was being as duped by him as surely as women like Candy were. He was charming, of course, but that was the whole problem. Charm was not something solid like love, respect or friendship. It was superficial. That was not to say that it had no purpose or use, that it was not a valuable tool in the arsenal of social interactions. But it was all too easy to conflate it with something far more meaningful, reliable and enduring, and people like Alex depended on others making just this mistake.

We met outside again. Even if his smoking wouldn't have been a problem, I did not want to have this discussion at my desk, where others in the lab might overhear. I also liked the wide open space surrounding us. The wrath that I felt would radiate out into the open air, rather than hovering over both of us like a poisonous cloud. I wouldn't have much cared if that cloud suffocated Alex, at least I told myself I didn't, but I knew I was far more the likelier one to suffer from its toxicity.

I got straight to the point.

"Alex, I talked to Candy. She said she gave you a copy of my grant."

Alex did not reply immediately. He looked surprised, but it was not the surprise of someone who has been unexpectedly caught with his hand in the cookie jar. It was, rather, the surprise of someone learning for the first time that there are cookies to be had.

Indeed, he really looked at sea. For one very bad moment, I thought he was going to deny even knowing who Candy was. Had he done that, I swear to God I would have hauled off and slugged him. I really would have.

"She might have. Yes, that's possible."

"No, Alex, not *might* have. She did." I started to stand up, already fed up with his bullshit. "If you really want to deny this, we can go over to her office and see her right now."

Alex waved me down. "OK, Alan, OK. I will take your word for it. If she said she gave me this grant, then she did." He took a drag on his cigarette. By a sort of unwritten agreement between us, he usually put it out when I arrived, not wanting to inflict on me any second-had smoke. I hadn't objected, but it was all I could do now not to slap it out of his mouth. "So what?"

I hadn't known how Alex would react to this conversation, but I definitely had not expected this.

"Alex, let me spell it out for you, all right? You stole my data. That's how you learned the identity of my three genes. You pretended to have isolated them yourself. You pretended not to know that they were my genes, that you wanted me to verify them. You did that so that I would feel certain that you had actually isolated them. Then, when you had convinced me that you were a co-discoverer of these genes, you used that, together with the two genes you did discover on your own, to persuade me and Mitch to take you aboard the patent."

Alex stared at me in silence for a long time, actually forgetting his cigarette.

"Is that really what you believe, Alan?"

"Of course that's what I believe! Candy told me!"

"She told you she knew the identity of these three genes, and also that she told me what they were?"

He was being deliberately obtuse, I thought. The last refuge of the intellectual scoundrel.

"No! Of course not! She doesn't have a clue about these genes, and you know it as well as I do. But she gave you the grant, which is all the information you needed. You were able to put the rest together from there."

Alex finally seemed to understand something he hadn't understood before. Now at last he began to relax.

"Which grant, Alan?"

"The one I'm writing right now. The one Mitch and I will be submitting at the end of the month."

He took another puff of the cigarette.

"She told you this? That this was the grant she gave me?"

"No, but what other – "

I stopped instantly, my words dead in the water. I had assumed that Candy had given him the grant I was currently working on. I had assumed that because that was the one that was constantly on my mind, because that was the one that had sensitive data on it, that was the one that someone might kidnap me to get a hold of. That was the one that would provide the most clues, indeed the only clues, to the identity of my three genes.

"Alan, what I suggest you do is go back and talk to Candy again. What you will learn from this very nice lady is that she did not give me the grant you are currently writing. What she gave me is one of the previous grants, the renewal application. Everything in it is either published, or data that you no longer are interested in."

Oh, my God, I thought. Oh, my God.

Prior to my joining Mitch's group, one of the grants supporting the laboratory had been for five years. This is a typical time period, and in principle when the grant is awarded, the investigator is guaranteed support for this length of time. In practice, though, the grant must be renewed each year. The scientist must summarize all the progress that has been made towards fulfilling the specific aims, to justify the expenditures made to date and to rationalize continued funding for the following year.

This was what Alex was referring to. The previous year I had written the renewal for the final year of that old grant. The grant I was currently writing was to supersede that. At the time I wrote that renewal, I had not yet discovered the three genes, so there was nothing about them in it.

Candy, of course, would not know the difference — that a current grant had far more significance to certain people outside our laboratory than a former one did. To her, one grant was about the same as any other. While she probably should not have given Alex the older grant without at least notifying me, I would certainly have given her permission. As far as I was concerned, it was ancient history.

I sagged down on the little stone border. I had come here expecting Alex to be embarrassed and apologetic, and suddenly it was I who was in that position. The words that I had just used to accuse him now stung in my mind. I had not simply been wrong, made a mistake. Mistakes happen. But in doing so, I had revealed myself to be untrusting, paranoid, really, and all too willing to jump to very serious conclusions without thinking about what I was doing. All in all, a miserable performance.

So what did I say now?

"Jesus, I'm sorry, Alex. The way Candy said it" — I paused. No, I thought, don't try to lay the blame on her. "I mean, I've been preoccupied with that grant. I thought that was the one she was talking about."

"It's OK, Alan."

I sighed, and looked around the courtyard. It was another lovely summer day. Lots of people had come out to sun themselves. To enjoy themselves. And somehow, I never did when I was out here. "All this time, I thought you stole those three genes from me."

Alex smiled, a warm, friendly grin of the kind he rarely directed at members of the same sex. "I didn't steal those three, Alan. I stole the other two."

I turned around and stared at him. "You mean those two new genes of yours?"

He nodded.

"Yes. That's the information I got from the grant Candy gave me."

I couldn't understand what he was talking about. "But those two genes aren't mine. I never identified them."

Alex shook his head. "Yes, you did, Alan. They were on that old grant. They were part of your preliminary data. You had a table in there, from a microarray, in which both those genes had fairly high activity. You just weren't interested in them."

I was racking my brains to recall those data. "The activity couldn't have been too high, or I would have noticed."

"Not too high, that is right. But high enough. And what I noticed about them was that they both had been previously described as active in certain diseases of the lungs. I remembered that when I saw them. That's what caught my attention."

I would have to go back and look at that grant again, I decided.

"You never bothered to follow them up," Alex repeated. "And when you found the three others, you forgot all about them."

He took a last puff of the cigarette, then crushed it under his heel.

"But I did follow them up. Very interesting genes, they are.

204

Associated with both colon cancer and lung cancer. I don't know any other genes like that, do you, Alan?"

He got up.

"Thanks, Alan."

It was nice having Alex with me at the board meeting. Though he would not become a member of OS, I hoped he would be allowed to attend regularly, since his work was so critical to our project. For the first time, I felt I had someone on my side, someone who knew what it was like to work in a lab and actually get the data that the others just played around with.

I opened the meeting by introducing Alex to everyone. As he walked around the table, warmly shaking everyone's hands, I could indeed see the value of charm. Even crusty old Alvin Duistermars beamed at him. And when he approached Stella Luhrman, the CEO of some large mail order business and the board's expert on computers, I thought he was going to bend over and kiss her hand. He didn't, but from the look she gave him, I was sure she wished he had.

Alex then gave a little talk, basically discussing the same studies that he had presented in the poster session in San Francisco. He was collaborating with Bill Tye and me in the search for a sensitive, reliable blood test for lung cancer. I figured since he was on our team, I might as well let him run interference for me in front of the board. Let him try to persuade them to fund these studies. Sure, it was throwing him to the lions, but it was the least he could do for me. I hadn't just discovered all five of those genes, really, before he had. I had had to endure all those card games with him.

So I had mixed emotions watching him. On the one hand, having been in the same place myself so many times, I had to feel sympathy for him. A blood test for lung cancer that really delivered would be a marketing bonanza, probably an even bigger deal—thanks to Philip Morris—than a stool test for colon cancer. But currently it was pie in the sky. The ones out there had yet to survive a definitive, large-scale clinical trial, and we had barely got our efforts past the planning stage. We had a very clear idea about what to do, but precious few results so far to confirm our strategy. The board, for all its scientific illiteracy, would have no trouble figuring that out. There is nothing that is more certainly the kiss of death to a businessman than pure, unadulterated theory.

On the other hand, I secretly enjoyed it all. Watching Alex make his case, our case, was like watching myself, only completely objectively. I was with him up there at the front of the table, gesturing towards the screen, right alongside him, not physically, of course, but in spirit—in solidarity, as the radicals say. He was making basically the same points I would have made, yet I was not taking any of the heat from the other board members that he was. In other words, I could immerse myself totally in the intellectual aspects of the argument without any direct emotional investment in the outcome. For a scientist, this is as good as it gets.

"What makes you think you can develop a better blood test than those already out there?" asked one of the board members. "You yourself just admitted that one scientist claims he has identified a single protein marker that can identify lung cancer with 99% specificity."

"But this marker is also associated with other forms of cancer," Alex pointed out. "It may also be associated with other diseases. We don't know yet how selective it is for lung cancer. It may have a high false positive rate. If it does, we are back to square one, just like CT scans."

"A successful blood test will almost certainly require multiple protein markers," I pointed out. "Several labs are zeroing in on some of these markers, but there are many yet to be discovered. And please keep in mind, folks, that there will always be room for more than one test. Because there are so many things that we want, not all of them likely to be furnished by a single test. First and foremost, high sensitivity, the ability to identify virtually everyone with the disease. Second, high specificity, a low false positive rate, so we minimize the number of people who are erroneously diagnosed. Third, the ability to detect the cancer at the earliest possible stage, certainly before it has metastasized, but also, hopefully, before it has even grown to the point where treatment is expensive, prolonged and maybe damaging to the patient's body..."

The board listened to the presentation politely enough, but declined to offer any funding at the moment. I was disappointed, but of course not surprised. We spent the rest of the meeting discussing the large-scale study of the colon cancer test. Alvin Duistermars reported that the study was now underway, and that the results were expected the following week.

We were in the process of adjourning when Andrea Davies opened the door. Everyone looked up in surprise at this unexpected intrusion.

"Bill Tye," she said breathlessly. "He was just taken to the hospital. He may be dead."

Back in the lab, I learned the details, such as they were, from Andrea and Laurie. Bill's roommate, a woman, claimed she had returned to the house they shared late the previous evening, and found Bill in his car inside the garage, with the engine running. She had dragged him, unconscious, out of the car, then called 911. She had not heard from the hospital since, but she didn't think he would survive. It appeared to be a suicide.

Was it possible that Bill had been the one behind my kidnappings, and had killed himself in an agony of guilt? I didn't really think so, and granting I didn't know the guy that well, I found it hard to believe he would kill himself for any other reason. It seemed to me almost immediately upon hearing the news that a more likely alternative was that Bill had actually been murdered — because he knew who my real enemy was. By making a murder look like a suicide, the perp would not only remove someone who threatened exposure, but shift the blame onto him.

The roommate said there was no suicide note, but I wasn't sure how to interpret that. On the one hand, if this were a murder staged to look like a suicide, it seemed to me that the killer would want to provide such a note. But then again, if Bill were the innocent victim of the person behind my kidnappings, it might be hard to write a note that would believably tie him to these crimes. Perhaps the murderer thought it better to leave the situation ambiguous. The most important point was to remove the threat to being identified.

I suggested all of this to Officer Burris, whom I visited later that afternoon. Since Bill lived off campus, Burris and his University police colleagues were not investigating the case. In fact, he had not even heard about it when I told him. But he listened with interest when I told him about my talks with Bill Tye the previous week.

"I think he knew who the person was who sent that text," I explained. "At the very least, he came close enough to be seen as a threat."

"So if Dr. Tye was telling you the truth, the cell phone was not in that desk drawer at the time it was used. Someone must have removed it from the drawer some time earlier." He moved his head back and forth as he thought that over, but was not yet ready to reject categorically the suicide scenario. "Isn't it possible that Dr Tye was just trying to remove suspicion from himself?"

"I don't see how. Whoever used that cell phone might very well have removed it from the drawer for a while. I don't see how knowing that shifts the focus to anyone in particular."

"Yet his statement seems to contradict what the young woman— Ms. Cheng—told you. Maybe he was trying to implicate her?"

"But he seemed to support her for the most part. She told me she never carries that cell around with her when she's working in the lab, and Bill said he had noticed that himself. He also backed up her statement that the phone was normally kept in the drawer. His point was just that it was not in the drawer at that time. And she herself did not deny that that was possible."

Burris looked at me speculatively. "But wouldn't she have some idea of who took it? Doesn't it make her look like she's hiding something?"

I couldn't deny that. I had felt that all along. I thought of mentioning her reaction when I reminded her after the group meeting, but I felt that it really didn't prove anything.

"She acted like she might have her suspicions. She never said flat out that she had no idea. But after what happened to Bill, I can't blame her for being afraid to say any more. Everyone in the lab is scared now. There has been no official word on the cause of this, but I think everyone understands that it could have been a murder attempt. No one thinks Bill would try to commit suicide. And if someone did attempt to kill him, I'm not the only target any more. Anyone else could be next."

Burris wandered about the interview room in silence for a moment.

"We could bring Ms. Cheng in for questioning, if you like."

I didn't like. I hated to involve others in the lab in the crimes committed against me. If my suspicions were right, Bill Tye had attracted a killer's attention because he knew too much. Not only knew too much, but told me some of what he knew. Maybe Marissa knew too much, too. It seemed to me that her going to the police would only advertise that fact. I guessed that was, in effect, intimidation of a witness, but who was I to tell her what to do, even if my own life was at stake?

"I'll suggest it to her," I said reluctantly. "But I think she'll say she doesn't know anything that can help.

Needless to say, the lab was quiet and gloomy for the rest of that day. Bill had been reasonably well-liked by everyone in the group, and even if he had been the victim of some unfortunate accident, the news would have been very depressing. Under the circumstances, everyone was on edge. I was working at my lab bench for a while, and I could feel the tension. Every time someone walked by, moved into my peripheral vision, I would look up nervously. At one point, someone slammed the door to the cold room—a foot thick aluminum slab—and I jumped a foot. Even the background humming of a centrifuge managed to conjure macabre images in my mind. It reminded me of the sound of the car approaching the house when I had been trying to escape.

Still, even if a murderer was loose, I felt safer there than anywhere outside. I hadn't been kidnapped while in the lab, and Bill hadn't been killed there. It was inconceivable to me that anyone would try to strike in this environment.

So I didn't look forward to going home. I actually considered sleeping in the lab, something I had done more than once in the past when an experiment went late. I suppose I should have been grateful under the conditions that Burris arranged a police escort for me that night, just as a precaution, but I didn't like it at all. I didn't like having to call the cop when I was ready to leave, I didn't like waiting for him at the door to the building to pick me up, and I didn't like riding home in his squad car. It all just reminded me of how precarious my situation had become.

17. HONOR AMONG THIEVES

The next day was Saturday. Usually I work on weekends, but I couldn't face the lab that day. I wasn't really afraid to go there. Surely the killer was not going to strike in broad daylight, in an environment with other people around. But as far as my case was concerned, I felt impotent in the lab. I wasn't making any progress in identifying either the killer or the motive, and that was no longer acceptable to me. It was clear to me now that if I didn't get to the killer, and soon, he or she would get to me.

So I was drawn back to the one man who I thought could help me: Travers. I knew his buddies had met the men who had kidnapped me in Minneapolis, and I also knew these buddies, through a brother or some other close relative, had tried to have me kidnapped in San Francisco. These buddies, these bootleggers, thus had vital information, and I had to get it.

Laurie was out of town, visiting her family, so I went alone. I thought it was just as well. The first two times we had visited Travers together, I had little doubt that we would return safely. This time I was not so sure, and I didn't want to involve her.

As I drove north, I went over for the umpteenth time the conversation I had overheard the last time I had visited Travers. There was one puzzling thing that one of the men had said, something I hadn't really been aware of until now: "boyfriend". My memory was very fuzzy at this point, but I was quite sure that this word had been used in the context of the person behind the kidnapping. A boyfriend was involved in this in some way. Apparently the kidnappers knew that much and had mentioned it to the bootleggers.

I strained to recall the conversation: a boyfriend knew something. Knew what? The same thing I knew that was so valuable? Or was it that the person behind the kidnapping had a boyfriend who knew what was going on? Or were there two perps, boyfriend and girlfriend?

I immediately thought of Candy and Alex. If Candy were

behind this, and Alex knew or suspected...Or if Alex was behind this, and Candy knew or suspected. But I had already been over the evidence for the involvement of either, and had found it wanting.

I parked the car by the trailhead this time. No point in trying to hide the fact that I was visiting Travers from his buddies, because his buddies were the ones I wanted to meet. As I walked briskly up the path towards the little cottage in the woods, I was carrying no gun, no knife, no weapon of any kind—except the most powerful weapon of all: knowledge. Knowledge that was both a sword and a shield, knowledge so awesome, so terrifying, that it could save someone's life, including my own. At least, I hoped it could. I knew that if I could find the men I sought, men who had once tried to put me in harm's way, this knowledge was the only thing that offered me any protection.

When I reached the cottage, I knocked on the door. No answer. Damn it, I thought, Travers was not home. He was probably tramping around the woods, but good luck finding him. Still, I had driven too far just to turn around and go back home, so there was nothing to do but try the other house. I returned to my car and drove it to the end of the road, to the abandoned house.

It was not abandoned now. There was a pickup parked in front. I shivered at the sight. I wasn't certain, but it looked like the same pickup that had stopped for me that day when I was hitching. In any case, I knew it had to be. That meant my quarry was inside the house. Was Travers with them? I could only hope he was. I didn't want to face them without his help.

I parked my car behind the pickup, got out and walked across the driveway. I guessed the two bootleggers were in the basement, checking on the boxes of cigarettes. Maybe they were preparing to load them into the pickup to take them back to Canada, or maybe they had just unloaded a fresh haul. I mounted the squeaky wooden steps to the porch, and my heart in my mouth, rapped loudly on the door.

A moment later, the door opened. It was the red-haired, beer-bellied man who had first spotted me when I had visited Travers' cottage the last time, who had caught me just as I was trying to leave. He was sober now, which was good news and bad news. He would be more likely to understand what I had to tell him, to offer him. But he also recognized me now.

"You!" he ejaculated. He looked over my shoulder at the driveway, searching, I guessed, for possible signs of police. Seeing none, he turned around and called over his shoulder, "Hey, Jack, get your ass up here. We got a little visitor up here."

There was still no furniture in the house, so we sat outside on the porch steps. I felt much, much better that way. I'm not sure I could have handled being inside that house again, not with these two guys between me and the door.

"I have come to help you, one of you, and in return I need your help," I began.

"What kind of help?" the one called Jack said suspiciously. He was skinny and short with a narrow, pimply face and the nervous, menacing undulations of a ferret, and I took an instant dislike to him. I found myself talking more to Pete, not that I felt much more comfortable about him, than to Jack.

"Let's clear the air first, OK? I know what you two guys store in that basement, and I don't give a shit. As far as I'm concerned, it's none of my business. I also know that you rented this house to the two men who kidnapped me. I need to know who they are." I turned towards Jack. "And finally, I know that you have a—what, brother?—who tried to kidnap me in San Francisco."

I had been counting on the shock value of all this information unloaded at once to catch them off balance, and it worked. For a moment, both men were too surprised to speak. Then Jack, who was actually standing in front of the steps, blocking my way out, reached down and put a hand on my throat, which absolutely terrified me.

"Why, you snot-faced son-of-a-bitch, who the fuck—"

"Wait a minute, Jack, wait a minute," interrupted Pete, putting a hand on his friend's arm, and somehow persuading him to remove his grip.

213

"OK, you need our help. What's in it for us?"

When I had planned this, I had thought this would be the hard part. I had thought they wouldn't understand me, or wouldn't believe me, or wouldn't take what I said seriously. In other words, I had thought they wouldn't react the way anyone who received this information in a doctor's office would react. But they did. They might have been scum--smugglers, would-be kidnappers, connected to someone who had committed or tried to commit murder--but they weren't fools. When a doctor spoke, they listened in respectful silence.

"The man who abducted me in San Francisco has a serious genetic disease. He is virtually certain to get colon cancer in the next ten or fifteen years. I know this because in the process of escaping from him I picked up a blood sample, which I was able to analyze in my cancer research laboratory at the University of Minnesota. I was looking for ways to ID him, but I also discovered this genetic disorder."

I couldn't believe what pussies they turned into, both of them. Jack backed off from me a few steps, gaping in astonishment. Pete, too, shifted slightly away from me, as if unable to bear hearing this news at close range. Then I administered the *coup de grace*.

I looked directly at the Weasel. I felt sorry for him, and hated myself a little for that. Not because he didn't deserve the same compassion that anyone else did, even if he was scum. But because I felt I was showing more than compassion, something more personal, and I felt I had no business relating to him on that level.

"You have the same genetic disorder. Don't ask me how I know, you can take my word for it. You and your brother both need to see a gastroenterologist, a specialist in the colon, and both of you will probably need a colectomy—removal of your large intestine. The good news is that colon cancer is a preventable disease. It doesn't have to kill you. But it almost certainly will if you don't do something about it."

Jack really took this hard. He began whimpering to me about occasional stomach pains he had, diarrhea, begging me to tell him if they were signs of the cancer.

"Maybe, maybe not," I said. "What I'm going to do is give you my card. After I return to Minneapolis, I will make an appointment for you to see a specialist. And I want you to get in touch with your relative in San Francisco and tell him the urgency of the situation. He needs to see a doctor, a gastroenterologist, probably a colonoscopist."

I let this sink in, then continued. I knew that as the shock wore off, they would be less willing to bargain with me.

"In return, I'm asking you to give me all the information about my kidnappers that you can. What they look like, their names, anything you know."

This was asking a lot, I knew, even with all the good will I had accumulated. Jack the Weasel was obviously reluctant to rat on his brother, well aware that by doing so he was implicating himself. In fact, without that brother in the picture, neither man had any provable connection to either of my kidnappings. I couldn't establish that they had rented the house to the Minnesota kidnappers, and by giving me any information at all about them, they were unnecessarily incriminating themselves. So now I played my other trump card.

"I know that your brother was not connected with the two men who kidnapped me and brought me to this house. He was not being paid by whoever ordered the original kidnappings."

Both of them looked in wonder at me. Both of them were smart enough not to ask me how I could be so sure that something incriminating about them was not true.

"He was acting on his own," Jack insisted. "I never told him to do this."

I didn't believe that, of course.

"I don't care about your brother, except, as I said before, he needs to see a doctor. But I don't have to know anything more about him. What I do need to know is something about the guys who brought me to this house." I looked entreatingly from one to the other. "A name? A description?"

Pete and Jack looked at each other. Pete shrugged.

"Zell," said Jack finally. "One of the guys' names is Zell. Swear to God, that's all I know about that."

"You can't tell me what he looks like?"

Jack muttered something about sunglasses. This time I believed him.

"He wears them all the time, doesn't he?" I said. "Even indoors."

Jack looked at me in astonishment. "How did you know that?"

"He has a genetic eye disease," I said. "People with this disease are often very sensitive to light."

Both of the men were regarding me with awe, as if I were some witch doctor with unfathomable powers. I tried to ride the crest of this wave as far as it would take me.

"Cell phone number?"

They didn't like this. The question was, why? Did they realize that if the police could access Zell's records they could implicate Jack and Pete—or did they just worry that I was going to stir the pot?

"I'm not going to call him," I said carefully..

"Why else would you want his number?" Pete asked suspiciously.

I told him. They looked at me in wonder. There must have seemed to them no end to the miracles I was capable of.

"You can really do that?" they said, almost in unison.

"Sure," I replied, realizing I was probably a sort of accessory to a new crime down the road.

I was glad to get out of there. I thought I now had enough information to crack the case, but even if I didn't, it was not as though I had given away my valuable knowledge for nothing. I had very possibly saved two people's lives. I would have freely given that information to anyone else, how could I not give it to them? And these three men, I was pretty sure, would make no further attempts to kidnap me. I had no more to fear from them.

I was about halfway back to Minneapolis when I received a text on my cell phone, from an unknown number:

Can we meet soon? I have very important information for you.

Who is this? I replied.

Someone sentenced to death, but still alive. No one must know about this meeting.

Jack, I thought. My cell phone number was on the card I had given him. Maybe he was going to tell me something more about my kidnappers. Or could it possibly be his brother, already contacted by Jack? But did I really want to meet with him? The guy in the van who had fired a gun at me when I was hanging for dear life onto that cliff? And why would he want to meet me?

When and where?

Tomorrow. I'll text you later.

OK.

By the time I returned to Minneapolis, it was late afternoon. Tired as I was from all the driving, I still missed the lab. I was not accustomed to not being there. Maybe it was just my imagination, fueled by the news of what had happened to Bill Tye, but there seemed to be fewer people around than usual. Or maybe it was just the great summer weather. It was Saturday, after all.

I went to my desk and worked on the grant proposal for a while. It was almost done, I just had a few recent results to add. I was relieved that I would make the flexible but still important deadline of the middle of the month, two weeks before the real deadline at the end of the month. That was when it actually had to be submitted.

I was now ready for Mitch to look at it. This was one of the main reasons I had set a personal deadline for the middle of the month, so that he would have time to make comments and adjustments. In fact, he had reminded me of this just a few days ago.

His door was open, as usual, but he was not around. I decided to wait. I didn't sit down, but wandered around his office restlessly, thinking about my meeting with Pete and Jack. I knew I should contact Burris soon, but decided it could wait till tomorrow or Monday.

I glanced at some of the articles that were lying on Mitch's desk. They were piled up in one place, and I began removing them one by one, glancing at the titles, just to see if there was anything I should be reading. And there, on the bottom of the pile, was a cell phone. Marissa's cell phone.

Though I had seen it only once, that day she had showed me that the text was deleted, I recognized it instantly. And in that moment of recognition, I of course also realized its significance. She had left it here in his office today. Wasn't it possible that she had also done so the night of my kidnapping? That the person who sent that text had accessed the cell phone here?

I picked it up. I knew that text had long ago been deleted, that even if the person who had sent it hadn't done so, Marissa would have. Still, irrationally, I had a burning desire to confirm that, to see what was really on this cell phone that seemed to hold a central clue to my kidnapping.

I didn't dare go through the texts here in Mitch's open office, where anyone could walk in at any moment. So I slipped the cell phone in my pocket, left the office, and ducked into a men's bathroom down the hall. With one of the stalls safeguarding my privacy, I began to invade Marissa's.

Almost immediately I wished I hadn't. The first sent text I opened began with the word "honey". She had a lover! I couldn't believe it! I slumped down on the seat of the toilet, feeling thoroughly humiliated. I had thought I was mostly over her now, as I grew closer to Laurie. Instantly, this text reminded me that Marissa still had enormous power over me, that I still fantasized about her. Yet at the same time this text was reminding me of this, it of course also delivered the message that all my desires, as if I hadn't known long ago, were futile, that it was useless even to dream of having a relationship with her.

Was it anyone I knew? Despite the shame, the sliminess I felt in doing so, here in the obscurity of a toilet stall no less, I began to read through the text, looking for clues. The ones that I found were

218

like nothing I had expected. In fact, at first they made no sense at all: "at the OS meeting", "my kids", then "my wife". Wife? How could Marissa be talking about—

Then the realization hit me with full force. *Mitch* was the author of these texts! Mitch was using Marissa's cell phone to text his secret lover, who could therefore only be…Marissa herself.

Even now, when I look back on this, I wonder how I could have been so incredibly blind, deaf and dumb. Girls like Marissa Cheng may admire sexy young men like Bill and Alex, but they gravitate to the older guys, the ones with power. Why had it not been obvious to me long ago? The clues—hell, the blatant evidence— were out there for me to see, all I had to do was look at it. The group meetings, when she looked at him constantly, and he in turn praised her work extravagantly. The seminars, when they sat close to each other, and always seemed to leave together. And of course, that night at the conference in San Francisco, the party in Mitch's suite, when she never left his side. And why was she still there when virtually everyone else had gone home? Because she was home. She was staying there with him.

But the logic of my discovery did nothing at all to ease its shock. I began to feel dizzy, disoriented. I was in fact forced to confront two horrible truths. Mitch, the most important man in my life after my father, my professional father, was Marissa's lover. And even worse, that he must have been the author of that text sent to me the night of my kidnapping. Didn't he have to be?

But why was he using her cell phone to text her? My mind instantly fastened on this little puzzle, anything to blunt even temporarily the enormity of the emotions I was now experiencing. Mitch had his own cell phone, why would he use Marissa's?

Then I recalled what Burris had said to me about divorce: "make sure you use a cell phone that your wife doesn't know about." Mitch, in the process of splitting up with his wife, would have been afraid to use his own cell phone to text Marissa, because his wife could have found out—she could have obtained records of everyone he called or texted. Of course, if she had any suspicions about Marissa, she might have been able to subpoena her records, too, but only the numbers called and texted from her phone—from her two cell phones if she could learn about both. So Mitch could use one of Marissa's phones to communicate with her using the other one. A list of numbers that each phone called would reveal nothing incriminating. Maybe someone would notice there was communication between the two phones, but that proved nothing — as long as, of course, no one knew that Mitch was using one of those cell phones.

So he had to have been the one to send that text that night. Didn't he? And Marissa had to know that. Didn't she? Of course she pretended not to know. Of course she lied to me when she said the cell phone was in her desk. At the least, she would have known who removed it from her desk. But she protected him — from both his wife, and from implications in the kidnapping case.

I felt absolutely devastated. My world was crumbling around me. Nothing made sense any more. If I couldn't trust Mitch, who could I trust? I wanted more than anything else just to stay in the stall, not face the world outside. But I had to return this cell phone to his desk before he missed it. Reluctantly, I got up, and walked hurriedly out of the restroom.

I was too late. As I walked down the hallway back towards Mitch's office, I heard voices from inside. He was there with Dick and perhaps Candy. For an instant, I thought of marching in there and confronting him. But of course he would deny everything. I still lacked proof. I needed to think.

So I turned around and headed towards the lab. I went into the cubicle area. Marissa was not at her desk, and no one else was nearby. I thought about keeping the cell phone as evidence, but I was more interested now in hiding my tracks. Quickly, surreptitiously, I slipped the cell phone into her desk drawer. If I were lucky, Mitch would think Marissa had needed it and taken it back.

Whenever I get depressed, I know there's one thing that always helps. Get busy with my hands. Get into the lab, do something, do anything.

So I started an experiment. I devised it on the fly, working all the numbers out in my head as I moved around the lab, gathering up reagents, tubes, pipetters. It didn't matter if I got some of the volumes wrong, because I didn't care in the slightest how the experiment turned out. I didn't care if I didn't even finish it. I just had to be physically active.

As I worked, my mind loosened up a little. I stopped obsessing over Mitch and Marissa, and began to consider this new piece of information from every conceivable angle, to place it into the context of everything else I knew. I thought of all the puzzling things that had happened in the past few weeks. That my desk had been disturbed in some manner when I returned from the first kidnapping. Why Alex lost his patent to the government. When several pages from my lab notebook went missing.

I also thought of what I had overheard that day when I had eavesdropped on Travers' friends. That I knew something valuable. That I had to be held out of action until the end of the month. That the person behind my kidnapping was under pressure to act soon. Something about a boyfriend.

And most of all, I thought about Officer Iris Hamilton's words that night she drove me back to San Francisco. That the most successful crimes, like the most successful cancers, don't kill their hosts. They keep them alive, so that they can continue to suck the life juices out of them indefinitely.

For a long time, I had had the germ of a theory to explain these facts, but it didn't quite work. There was one thing in particular that didn't make sense. Motive. Someone was stealing something from me, from everyone in the lab, yet the theft was so minor, so trivial, that it hardly seemed worthwhile calling it theft. I had discarded the theory many times, certain that it couldn't be right, but it remained the only thing that fit all the other facts. I remembered a cardinal principle of science: *the successful theory is what remains when everything else has been falsified.* Or as my mother used to say, when you've lost something, you look for it first in all the obvious places. If you don't find it in any of them, then you look in the places that are not obvious, even places where you feel certain that it could not be.

Just thinking all this over helped calm me down, helped me

forget my feelings about Marissa and Mitch, and as I calmed down, I focused more carefully on my experiment. Into each well in the plate had to be placed several reagents, at different concentrations. Each reagent occupied just a few microliters in the well, but rather than place it in each tube separately, there was a much easier way, known to any laboratory technician in the world. You made up a large volume containing each of the reagents in the right concentration, then pipetted that volume into each well.

For example, suppose each tube needed to have 2 microliters of buffer, 2 microliters of each of four nucleotides, two microliters of DNA, and so on. Rather than laboriously put each and every one of those very tiny volumes into each and every tube, it was immensely easier and more practical to make up a large volume which contained buffer, nucleotides and DNA, in the correct proportions. Then one only had to make a single addition of this solution to each tube. The proportions were the same throughout. If each individual tube contained 2 microliters of buffer in a total volume of 20 microliters, then the large volume might contain 2 milliliters of buffer in a total volume of 20 milliliters. Or 20 milliliters of buffer in 200 milliliters total. The exact volume you make up doesn't matter, as long as the proportions are the same. Two microliters in twenty is the same as twenty milliliters in two hundred...

I had just entered the cold room, where many temperature-sensitive solutions and reagents are stored in the laboratory, when it hit me, in a single flash of insight. The motive. I had been looking at microliters, when milliliters, maybe even liters, were involved. I had been looking at these really trivial crimes, so trivial they couldn't even be crimes, and hadn't seen what was literally the larger picture: that they added up to something far more immense.

And as soon as that insight flashed into my mind, I *knew*. I knew who had tried to have me kidnapped. And why. All of the pieces of the puzzle fell into place.

But it was too late. I was just picking up the bottle of reagent and turning to leave the cold room, when I heard something click outside. Before I even rushed to the door, I knew it would be locked, trapping me inside. Then the lights went off. And I was left there in the cold and the dark.

18. THE AGONY AND THE ECSTASY

I didn't panic. At first, I really wasn't too worried. A typical laboratory cold room has a temperature just above freezing, say, 36-40 degrees Fahrenheit. As anyone who lives in Minneapolis knows, a human being can survive for a long time at that temperature, even lightly dressed, as I was. Granted, I wished I had a little more clothing on. There was a large heavy coat hanging on a rack just outside of the cold room, that the technicians put on when they had to run an experiment inside the cold room, and therefore might have to spend an hour or more there. But I had just nipped in to pick up the bottle of reagent, so I hadn't bothered.

I was shivering almost immediately, of course, had been the moment I had walked in the door, but though I was uncomfortable, I didn't feel in any imminent danger. I started to do exercises to keep warm. First I ran in place, did some pushups, jumping jacks, anything I could think of. But some of this activity made me sweat a little, which I knew would only make me colder, so I stopped doing those and exercised more slowly and deliberately. I finally settled on isometrics.

I had not been in the cold room too long when it occurred to me that, lightly clothed that I was, I could do a little more to insulate myself. Stumbling around in the pitch black, I came upon a large cardboard box, one of the shipping containers. I dumped everything that was in it out onto the hard cement floor. Then I ripped the box into little pieces of cardboard, which I shoved down my pant legs, tucking the bottom of my pants into my socks to make a closed system. I put more of these cardboard fragments into my shirt.

I remembered stories of people dying out in the cold because of failure to take very simple precautions like wearing a hat. A large proportion of the body's heat is lost from the head. I stumbled around in the dark, searching for something to cover myself there. I finally settled for a smaller cardboard box, as it was better than nothing, and at the very least, would trap air between itself and my head, forming a warm buffer between myself and the air beyond.

All of this I did within the first hour that I was there. Beyond the effect it had on slowing the inevitable cooling of my body, it gave me something to do, so that I did not have to dwell too directly on my plight. But eventually I had done everything I could do, and there was nothing, bar some isometrics that I all too quickly tired of doing, to occupy my time and my mind.

At that point I realized that my enemy did, in fact, intend to kill me. There was no point in trying to pretend otherwise. Locking me in the cold room was not simply sending a message, trying to scare me, to get me to back off, to get me out of the way temporarily. The plan now was to get rid of me for good, because I knew too much, and could no longer be tolerated alive. The reason for that, too, I had understood in that flash of insight.

I also had to concede that the plan looked good, very likely to succeed. It was Saturday night. I should have been with Laurie, but she was out of town. It was quite possible that no one would come to the lab the following day. I knew there was absolutely no chance I could survive at this temperature for thirty-six hours, till Monday morning. Even if someone did come into the lab tomorrow, Sunday, they would probably come relatively late, ten or eleven in the morning at the soonest. Could I survive even until then?

As I stood there in the middle of the cold room, on the frigid, unyielding cement floor, surrounded by blackness, trying to stay warm, I could see very clearly what the plan was. I was expected to die or be so close to death as to be incapacitated by the following day. My enemy would come into the lab at some point in that day, unlock the door to the cold room, and look in on me just to make sure I was either dead or so far gone that I could not escape. Then leave. When the next person finally came into the lab and saw me lying there dead in the cold room, he or she would assume there had been some kind of accident. Since the door would be unlocked, all evidence of murder would have vanished, along with my last breath in this frigid air.

Still, I clung to the belief that I could survive. What else could I do? All living organisms have been designed by evolution to survive. They do whatever it takes. What I didn't yet understand is just what it does take, under the conditions I was entering.

I didn't start to get really scared until I began shivering. When I say shivering, I don't mean the kind I did when I first entered the cold room. The kind when you feel cold, and you shake a little, and say, Brrrr. When I shivered like that, I still felt reasonably in control of my body. The shivering I now encountered was like nothing I had ever experienced before. It was as though some gigantic dog had picked me up by the scruff of my neck and begun to shake the living daylights out of me. My muscles flopped this way and that as though I were a rag doll. My teeth chattered so badly I thought they were going to fly out of my mouth. My body was totally out of my control. I really thought for a while that I was going to die then and there, not from hypothermia, but just from being shaken to pieces.

I knew, of course, that shivering is the body's way of trying to keep warm, that it's a life-saving mechanism that had evolved in humans and other mammals. But knowing that didn't make me feel any better. On the contrary, it was a warning. My body's core temperature had begun to drop dangerously, and it was going to continue to drop unless and until I escaped this icy prison. Moreover, as the shivering got worse, I lost virtually all control of my body's major muscles. It became very difficult for me to stand up or move around. I began to stumble around like I was drunk, a couple of times crashing into steel racks placed against the wall of the cold room, knocking over bottles of reagents. Several of these bottles tumbled to the floor and shattered, sending liquid and glass all over the place. I struggled to avoid stepping on the glass, and even more, to avoid getting wet, for I was still aware enough to realize that being wet would greatly accelerate the cooling process.

By now I was terrified. I felt totally alone and hopeless in a manner I was utterly unfamiliar with. I had always been a very independent person, as scientists generally are, accustomed to relying on myself. Of course like any social creature, I depended on people for some things, but I had never before felt that my fate was completely in someone else's hands. I had been kidnapped twice after all, and though I had a little help the second time, had escaped largely through my own wits.

But now I really was helpless. I knew there was no way I could get out of this icy hell on my own. I was not enough, I was not sufficient, I was not complete.

"Oh, God," I moaned, "someone please help me."

But there was no answer.

When you get really, really cold, though, there is one thing that is even worse than shivering. That's not shivering. At a certain point, my shivering started to slow down, and eventually ceased altogether. This was not because it had been successful in warming me, of course. On the contrary, my body was essentially giving up on the muscles. They were wasting energy, taking blood that now needed to be concentrated on my internal organs — the last line of defense.

I was now approaching paralysis. My muscles became stiff and virtually useless. Even worse, I was also beginning to lose my mind, literally. It became more and more difficult to think, to concentrate on any idea, indeed, even to know what an idea was. At some point, without really knowing how I got there, I realized I was lying on the hard cement floor, curled up trying to expose as little of my skin to the cold air as possible. But that was about all that I was capable of grasping, of thinking about.

I have no idea how much time passed like this. I seemed to drift in and out of consciousness. Sometimes I was dimly aware of who I was and my predicament. More often I knew only that I was some form of life trying desperately to survive. Like some plant that was rooted to the spot, had no chance whatsoever of moving from one location to another or defending itself against any more intelligent form of life that encountered it, all I could do is lie there and know that I was in some measure alive, if not for much longer.

I knew, to the extent that I had any knowledge at all, that the end was very near. I knew that not because I could rationally, objectively look at myself and say I had spent so many hours in near freezing temperatures, but because I could in some primal manner feel my death approaching. It was as though I were sliding downward into a black pit, and as my surroundings became blacker and blacker, it was clear, by the most basic instincts available even to very primitive forms of life, that the end could only be total oblivion. But just when I seemed to have hit the very bottom, when there was absolutely no lower that I could possibly go, no darker that my surroundings could possibly be, no conceivable way I could possibly survive any longer, I had the most extraordinary experience of my life. I left my body.

I had heard of out of body experiences before, of course. Candy would seize on them as proof of life after death, that there was more to consciousness than the brain. I had found them interesting, but the evidence for them unconvincing. As I pointed out to her, when some scientists had attempted to verify them, they failed. They would put some object, maybe simply a card with a word or number on it, in some position in a room where the subject, lying on his back, could not see them. If his consciousness left his body, and was able to look down on the room from above, as was often claimed, he should have been able to see this object. But no patient I knew about had ever passed this test.

My experience was not like that, in any case. It was simpler, but far more powerful. My consciousness did not shift from one location to another, from one perspective to a different perspective. On the contrary, *it no longer had a location, a perspective. It was everywhere, everything.* I was the entire world, all of it simultaneously.

With this enormously expanded identity came a sense of peace, of fulfillment, of being, that is impossible to describe. There I was, as close to death as it is possible for a living organism to be, and yet I was totally beyond pain, fear or despair. It was not that I felt joy or pleasure, that I now felt comfortable or safe. There was just no feeling of any kind whatsoever. Not because I lacked the capacity to feel, not because the remorseless cold had crushed all living sensation from my body, but because I was somehow far, far beyond feeling. I was in a place where feeling no longer mattered.

I don't know how long this experience lasted. It may have been just the briefest instant, or it could have been an hour or more. Indeed, the experience itself was timeless, a sense of the eternal. But at some point I was aware of its passing, and that was when I had another remarkable experience. I saw an angel.

This vision was preceded by a rush of warmth, the most blessed heat that I had ever felt in my life. And suddenly there was light, too. My eyes, so long adapted to the total dark, were blinded by its brilliance. It seemed to saturate my long-dormant senses, even as the heat began to awaken them. There was light, light, light everywhere, where an instant before there had been none. And in the center of all this heavenly warmth and light was my guardian angel.

As the heat started to flow back into my body, though, and my eyes began to function more clearly, I gradually became aware that it was not really an angel that stood before me. It was a woman. And as the sluggish blood in my brain began to flow again, and awaken a mind that had long been dormant, thoughts, a type of experience I had forgotten I was capable of having, began to creep back into my consciousness. I thought, it can't be her. She wouldn't be here. Not now. Not so soon.

But it was her. My eyes, my brain, were starting to work now, and I could see that it really was her.

Candy Rominger.

19. ESTABLISHING A CONTEXT

She stared in astonishment at me, curled up there on the floor.

"Alan, what are you doing here, lying on the floor? Why was the door locked, why—Oh, my God!"

Seeing that I was totally unable to move, she reached down, grabbed both of my arms, and hauled my out of that icy womb. Without a second's hesitation, she then plopped down on top of me, enveloping my body in her nourishing warmth. She pressed as close to me as possible, tearing off some of her clothes and mine, so that our bodies were fused into one, her heat flowing into mine. Her legs were spread, straddling mine. She cradled my head and my neck in her arms, pleading with me to return.

And while she did this, I cried and I cried and I cried, because after where I had been, what I had experienced, it was so hard to be alive! To be born into a world where there was joy, but also sorrow; where there was pleasure, but also pain; where there was love but also hate; where there was peace but also war; where there was hope but also fear; where there was health, but also disease; where there was triumph but also defeat; where there was good but also evil; where there was I but also you. A world where there was life but also, always, always, always, the shadow of death.

"Alan, please don't die! Please come back! Oh, Alan, please, please, please!"

And slowly I did. The heat flowed into my body like electricity, unthawing my muscles, restarting my internal organs, releasing my mind. It felt strange to possess a body again, this hunk of flesh that moved this way and that when I commanded it to. Indeed, it felt strange to be able to issue commands, to have control over anything.

After a little while, she carefully got off me, and helped me to my feet. I took a few tentative steps, to see if I could balance myself and walk again.

I looked around at the lab in wonder. It was all there, just as it had been when I had left it. I still couldn't quite believe I was here, alive, to see it again.

"What time is it now?" I asked, then added, "And what day?"

She looked at me in amazement and worry. "You don't know what *day* it is, Alan? It's Sunday. And it's five o'clock in the morning."

It was my turn to look astonished.

"Five AM Sunday, Candy? What are you doing here at this hour?"

She briefly explained to me.

"Last night, just as I was getting ready to leave, I saw Mitch go by Marissa's desk and take her cell phone. I remembered what you told me about that text that was sent to you from her phone the night you were kidnapped on campus. I thought you should know about this, but I couldn't find you."

I had gone into and out of the cold room several times, she had probably looked in the lab when I was in there.

"I tried to text you later, from home, but there was no answer. Then Laurie texted me much later, around midnight, I think, saying she had tried to call you several times. That was when we both got worried. She told me to try your apartment first, the manager let me in, you weren't there, of course. So I came to the lab."

I pointed to the cold room.

"It's a wonder you thought to look in there, Candy. Have you ever been in there before?"

"Oh, sure! Lots of times."

I looked at her in surprise.

"Really, what for?"

"I practice *tummo* in there. It's the ancient Tibetan art of generating body heat. You should try it some time, Alan."

I continued to walk about, feeling stronger as time went on.

230

"Alan, we have to get you to a clinic. Are you strong enough to walk, or should I call an ambulance?"

I shook my head. "Later. There's no time to waste. He will be back here any minute now."

"Why are you so sure about that?"

"To unlock the cold room door. If my dead body had been found in there with the door locked, it would have been an obvious case of murder. If the door is unlocked, it will look like an accident, even if everyone would be suspicious."

"So let's get out of here!"

"Hell, no. I'm going to get some evidence—and maybe even a confession. But I need your help."

Moments later, I was back inside the locked cold room, lying on the floor. I had to wait there almost thirty minutes, shivering in the cold, which of course was the last thing my body needed after what it had just been through. I was so relieved when the lights suddenly went on, and the door opened, that it was all I could do not to spring to my feet and bolt back into the warmth of the lab.

His plan, I'm sure, was just to confirm that I was either dead or too incapacitated to open the unlocked door. But as soon as he looked into the cold room, he saw the signs that a desperate man had scrawled during the last moments of his life. Written crudely on pieces of cardboard, the signs named both his killer and the crime the murder had been intended to cover up. He didn't want those to be seen, of course. So he walked right into the trap, stepping carefully past me and going to the back of the cold room.

Between us, Candy and I managed to get much of it on film. Candy, hidden outside, followed his movements as he unlocked the door, examined my body lying on the floor, then continued on inside. I had set up another cell phone camera inside the cold room, activating it when Candy texted me that he was on his way.

A few minutes after he had gathered up all the evidence and left, Candy texted me the all clear signal, and I got up and stepped outside into the welcome warmth of the lab again.

"Now can I take you to the clinic?" Candy asked.

"Yes. I have one more thing to do, but that can wait till we get there."

Inside the clinic, while I was being administered to, I texted him, explaining to Candy what I was doing.

"It's called caller ID spoofing," I said. "Or text spoofing in this case. The text appears to be coming from another cell phone, not mine."

"What number are you using then?"

"It belongs to a guy named Zell."

Can you text me at another number? It's about Rupert.

Having established that I was texting from Zell's number, I then switched over to another number so that I could receive texts.

Rupert was carried out of the research building on a stretcher a little while ago. Did you know that?

What are you talking about?

Rupert is now at the campus clinic. What's going on? First someone else tries to grab him in SF, now he's on a stretcher?

I don't know what you're talking about.

You know what I'm talking about! I want that 25K! Do we still have a deal or not? Did you hire someone else?

I don't know what you're talking about.

I was watching the research building the whole night. Only two people went into it before Rupert was carried out. You and some woman.

What woman?

I don't know. She left with Rupert.

There was no immediate reply to this text, so I continued.

Do we still have a deal? Or do I go to the police with what I know?

You don't know anything.

I know what time you went inside that building last night, and what time you returned there this morning. I want to know if we still have a deal or not.

I will meet you later.

When and where?

In back of that building down by the river in one hour.

OK.

I then called the campus police. Burris wasn't there, so I explained the situation to an officer on duty.

"Do you expect us to arrest this man?" she said when I was finished.

"I'm just telling you the evidence I have. In addition to the film, which clearly shows he left me lying on the floor thinking I was near dead, I have a witness who can corroborate it. At the minimum, I expect you to verify that he does in fact appear there in one hour. Together with the cell phone texts, I should think that would be enough for you at least to bring him in for questioning."

I spent most of the rest of the day in bed at the clinic. Though by the time I got there my body temperature was near normal again, they wrapped me in blankets and gave me plenty of warm liquids. Took my temperature at regular intervals. Monitored my heart and my brain, to make sure they were functioning normally. Periodically I would shiver a little, my body sort of remembering what had happened to it, but it was a far cry from the wet dog shakes I had experienced before. I can't say that I soon felt as good as ever, but then again, in some ways I knew I felt better than I ever had.

My life had been changed forever, I understood that. I had seen something that no scientific experiment could ever reveal. I had known something that I doubted any scientist could ever prove. I had experienced something that, had someone else told me about, I would have refused to believe. And just because I would have refused to believe someone else's words, I knew my own were useless. To describe it at all seemed to me almost a sacrilege, so inadequate was any description. It would be like drawing a circle on a piece of paper and telling someone, that's the sun. Drawing a stick figure, and saying, that's a human being. Drawing two figures, and saying, this is love.

But telling stories is, after all, what human beings do. I could no more resist this than anyone else. And of course, I had a very receptive audience.

"I saw God in there," I told Candy. "I mean I experienced God. I mean, I was God. I mean, there was no I and no God. I mean..."

She smiled at me. "I know. I was afraid you weren't coming back."

"I had to come back. Did you really know that?"

"Of course. You weren't ready. If you aren't ready, you die. If you are ready, you move on."

"Are you ready?" I asked her.

"Oh, no, not even close."

"But how do you know if you're ready?"

"You don't know."

I looked at her, puzzled.

"You mean, you can never know if you're ready?"

"No, I mean, you *don't know*. That's when you're ready. When you don't know. When you know that you don't know anything. When you stop asking questions like that."

I heard from the police later. They had gone to the Ice Palace and verified that our perp was there. They had taken him back to the station for questioning, but felt they couldn't hold him without further evidence. I was disappointed, but not really surprised.

"I can't prove he locked me in the cold room," I said to Candy. "I can only prove that he was guilty of gross negligence in leaving me there. But since I survived, with no apparent physical infirmities, I don't really have a case even for negligence. Of course it's extremely suspicious, only a psychopath would refuse to try to save someone's life when it required so little effort on his part. But it's not clear that he can be prosecuted for this."

"What about the texts you sent him?" Candy asked.

"Same deal, I guess. Very suspicious, but not compelling evidence. We'll need the testimony of this guy Zell himself."

She looked at me in astonishment.

"So you have *nothing*?! This monster gets off scot-free?"

"Oh, no," I replied. "I have documentation of the original crime. The crime he was trying to cover up."

In the excitement and chaos of the past twenty-four hours, I had completely forgotten about the text I had received the day before, while driving back to Minneapolis after meeting with Travers' bootlegging friends. I remembered it only when I received another text from the same source.

You must have found out something. I see the police were questioning him.

How did you know that? I replied.

I was watching. I followed him there, down by the river.

You knew who he was? How did you know that?

I'll explain it all to you tomorrow. Just be very careful. And remember, no one must know that I'm around.

I had to be content with that.

20. LIFE AFTER DEATH, DEATH AFTER LIFE

Monday morning, bright and early, I waited outside of Mitch's office to see if he would show up. I thought at the very least he might be unsettled enough to take a day or two off to start planning his defense, thinking about how he would respond to the charges he knew I would make against him, but I guess I underestimated his confidence in himself. Or maybe he just thought that by coming to work he could squelch a lot of the gossip that was sure to take place if he were absent. I managed to hide myself a little so he didn't see me as he walked up and unlocked the door. When he started to go in, I followed right after him.

He had to expect this confrontation, he must have prepared himself for it, but he was betrayed by his expression, which was drawn and tired in appearance. Truth be told, he looked a lot more like someone who had barely survived a night in the cold room than I did.

"Alan," he said weakly. "How have you been?"

"Hello, Dick," I said. "I've been chilling out."

I knew there was no point in going over what had happened yesterday. He was smart enough to realize that I had won a battle if not the war. Even if I couldn't make an attempted murder or kidnapping charge stick, after Candy spread the word he would be so obviously guilty in the eyes of everyone in the lab that he wouldn't be able to touch me again. He was going to lose his job, and a lot more.

"I know everything, Dick," I said, waving the invoices in his face.

He didn't respond. He had probably already consulted a lawyer, I thought.

To his credit, Dick had tried to warn me off. How many times had he pleaded with me to let him take care of the budget section of the grant? He knew if I kept comparing the old invoices with the actual delivered products, I would start finding discrepancies. And so I had, almost from the beginning.

But the differences were so minor. Ten dollars here, twenty-five there. In a million dollar grant, how could someone worry about chump change like that? I thought I must be making a mistake, that I had either added wrong, or had missed some shipment. For such a long time, the thought never crossed my mind that the discrepancy was real, and intentional.

There were signs, of course, had I only been alert enough to notice them. When I had been kidnapped the first time, I had left a pile of invoices on my desk. Dick had made sure to collect them while I was away. When I asked Alex how he could have overdrawn on his budget, necessitating the use of a federal grant to cover expenses, he insisted that he had planned his expenses carefully. And not long after I suggested to Dick that the kidnapping was an attempt to steal information from me, he removed a few pages from one of my notebooks, in an attempt to reinforce that theory.

At first, Dick had only wanted to get me out of the way for a few weeks, until the deadline for the grant's submission: July 31. Once that deadline had passed, he figured the threat would be over. Of course, I would apply for more grants in the future, but probably not as a member of this research group. And even if I did, I would not again delve so deeply into the lab invoices.

All of that changed, though, when I asked to see invoices from another lab. In retrospect, that was what had sealed my fate in his eyes, why I could no longer simply be temporarily removed from the lab, but had to be killed. I was just trying to see if he would sell me information from another lab. But the way Dick interpreted it was that I had noticed the financial discrepancies in our own laboratory's grants, and now wanted to see if they were present in the grants of other laboratories as well. That I was expanding my investigation.

Because that was the key to the game, the key I had finally

grasped just before I went into the cold room that night. That though the amounts were small, they added up. A few dollars here, a few dollars there, totaled to maybe several thousand dollars overall in one grant. Still not a lot. But how many grants came through his office? How many grants were currently being funded, year by year? Twenty? Thirty? If he skimmed off a similar amount of money from all these other grants, soon we would be talking about as much as $100,000 - $200,000 or more *a year*. That was the kind of money people committed crimes for. Like kidnapping. Like murder.

I slapped the stack of invoices against my free hand.

"Bill Tye never knew about these, did he, Dick? All he knew was that you had to be the one who texted me that night. He realized that was very suspicious, that it strongly implicated you in my kidnapping, but he refused to believe that you—his lover, his boyfriend—could possibly have a motive for kidnapping me. So he told you what he knew, asked you for an explanation. Right up to the night he died he was probably convinced there was a harmless explanation for it all, wasn't he?"

I found Dick's continued silence—his unwillingness even to look up at me-- enormously frustrating. I don't know what I expected. Was he really a psychopath, someone with no conscience, who felt no remorse, who even on the dock would not admit to any regrets? Who would kill me right now, on the spot, if he thought he could get away with it? Or was he—as I desperately wanted to believe— just another human being who wanted a little more money than he was actually capable of earning, and in the process of pursuing it, dug himself into a deeper and deeper hole?

I understood that he couldn't admit what he had done, even if at that moment he was possibly overwhelmed by the need to confess. He was as much bound by the rules of law as I was. Rules that dictated what suspects could do, should do, were entitled to do. And that, I decided, was the problem. I was treating him as an adversary, an enemy. Just as I had treated Candy, until that day in her office I realized there was another way to approach her.

I fell silent and tried to look at Dick non-judgmentally, as just another human being. Of course it was an impossible thing to do under the circumstances, really, under any circumstances, but I tried nonetheless. Maybe it was because the silence made him uncomfortable, he wasn't sure what I was doing or trying to do, but for the first time he looked up at me. I caught his eyes, still trying not to show anger or hate or fear, or even curiosity or confusion. Just trying to experience his presence, our presence. No more, no less.

So the two of us just stood there, six feet apart, only Mitch's desk between us. I had read the guilt in Candy that day so easily that I thought I would be able to read it in Dick, too. I thought I would see the remorse, the regret, the wish to make amends, the desire to apologize. But that was not what I saw. I saw only anger and fear. So much anger that I was more scared at that moment than if he had drawn a gun and pointed it at me. So much fear that I realized instantly that he was capable of doing absolutely anything, that he was trapped in a corner, literally and figuratively, a wild animal that had nothing to lose.

I found myself backing slowly out of the office. I felt an utter fool for what I had just done—confronted someone who had tried to kill me, as if admitting that was no more difficult than apologizing for losing one's temper. What was I thinking? I also felt humiliated. I had put up such a bold front, challenging him so confidently because I had evidence on my side, I had witnesses on my side, I had law and the full force of society on my side. Yet without all those, just alone, one-on-one with this man, what was I? It wasn't just that I feared for my life. Even if he made no move to physically threaten me, even if he just stood there, I was no match for his fear and his anger. It overwhelmed me.

I still had not reached the safety of the hall when, to my horror, he did pull out a gun and pointed it at me. I couldn't believe he was going to shoot me here, in broad daylight. I froze instantly, reading in his expression that another step, any movement of any kind on my part, would be deadly.

For what seemed like an eternity, nothing happened. Though I realized I was a fraction of a second from death, that my fate could be decided by a lightning-quick series of neural messages in a brain I couldn't control, I experienced a little of the peace I had known in the cold room thirty-six hours earlier. I knew now, not with all my heart and soul, yet with a memory that had not yet faded, that though I might die, something would live on. That realization calmed me, and though it might have been my imagination, I thought it calmed Dick, too. The fear and anger I saw in his face receded slightly.

Emboldened, I tried to dissolve the fear that still contorted my own face. Without saying a word, I somehow reached across the room, placed my will on the barrel of the gun, and began to push it so that it pointed towards the floor. I felt the tension ebb out of his body. I tried to will him to set the gun down harmlessly on the desk

Then I felt rather than heard or saw someone come up behind me, from outside the office.

"Put the gun down, Dick," said a familiar voice.

Dick stared past me as if he had seen a ghost. And indeed, he had.

"You're dead!" Dick screamed. "I killed you! I killed both of you!"

Then he turned the gun on himself, pulled the trigger, and crumpled to the floor behind Mitch's desk.

The man who had been standing behind me quickly came around, and went to examine the body, shaking his head sadly. It was Bill Tye.

Later, after the police had arrived and Bill and I had given our statements, everyone in the group assembled in one of the conference rooms. I described how I had been locked inside the cold room Saturday night, and was barely alive when Candy rescued me early Sunday morning. I continued on to explain very briefly the evidence I had accumulated of Dick's embezzlement. I did not discuss any of my meetings with Travers or his friends.

When I was done, I turned to Bill, bursting with curiosity.

"Why would you fake your own death?"

"Hey, my death was pretty close to being real! Like yours, I

240

guess. I was still unconscious when they took me to the hospital on a stretcher. But I came around, and when I did, I asked the staff not to say anything about my condition, to encourage people to think I was dead, or at least in a coma."

"But why?"

"Partly for my own protection—and for yours. I realized it had to be Dick who had tried to kill me, and that if he knew I was still alive, he would try again."

"Because you knew he was the one who sent that text to me using Marissa's cell phone."

Bill shook his head.

"Uh-uh. Sure, I guessed he must have, but I had no real evidence that he did. What I did know, or strongly suspect, was that he was playing fast and loose with the grant money."

I looked at Bill in surprise. "How did you find that out?"

Bill didn't say anything for a moment, but looked around the conference table at the others. When he began speaking again, it was in a quieter tone.

"Dick and I were…well, close. I guess some of you knew or guessed that. We went out to dinner a few times, did some other things together. When Dick picked up the tab, as he usually did, he used one of several different credit cards. I never thought much of it, until one day when I was in his office, I happened to notice that one of these credit cards was used to pay certain departmental expenses. It was the same one I had seen him use in the restaurant."

A murmur of surprise swept around the room.

"In other words, he was using a university account to pay personal bills," Mitch pointed out.

"Yeah. And when I mentioned that to Dick, he said it was no big deal, because he always paid off the bill later with his own money, money drawn from his own personal account. He actually showed me a transaction he had made where he did that. I thought it was a little strange, using a university account to pay a personal bill, then reimburse the expense later, but it all seemed on the up-and-up."

"You didn't tell anyone else about this?" I asked.

Bill shook his head.

"But later, I got to thinking. Dick is...was in charge of a little financial empire. He oversaw a lot of departmental accounts, so he probably had a bunch of these university credit cards. Not only that, but he regularly transferred federal grant money into and out of these accounts. As I understand it—he actually explained it to me once—every grant awarded to the university by the federal government, or some other external source, goes into its own separate account. But sometimes, if there is a temporary shortage of funds—for example, if a grant has been awarded, but the funding has not yet arrived--a university account may be used to pay off some item that is officially charged to the external source of funding. When the external funding becomes available, it's used to pay off the expense in the university account. So money gets shifted into and out of these accounts a lot."

Mitch nodded. "Yes, there are strict rules about such transfers, but they can be done."

"So it dawned on me that he could have been playing a complicated shell game. Draw money out of a university account for personal expenses, then reimburse the university account by transferring money into it from a federal account. The deficit in the federal account is paid off by transferring money from a second federal account. That deficit is paid off using money from a third federal account. And so on."

"A game of musical chairs," someone remarked.

"Yeah. Kind of a pyramid scheme, except one in which the number of suckers—in this case, the federal grants—doesn't grow much over time. I think he got the idea from one of his mistakes, actually. Alan, you just pointed out that his fake invoices resulted in using up all the private funds in one of Alex Pignatti's grants, so that he had to shift some federal money earmarked for another proposal into that grant. I think it occurred to him that he could keep taking money out of one grant if he replaced it with money from another grant. Then he would use money from a third grant to replace the money taken from the second grant. And so on."

"In the end, though, he balanced the books by creating fake invoices."

Bill bobbed his head in agreement. "Anyway, I had a hunch he was embezzling big-time, but I wasn't sure. I also didn't understand how Alan was involved, why Dick would want to have him out of the way. I guessed, though, that it had something to do with the grant that Alan was working on. And that was the second reason why I wanted people to think I was dead. I wanted to set up a sort of trap for Dick, and it depended on his thinking I was dead, or at least unable to leave the hospital."

"A trap?"

"Yeah. See, Dick has the key to my house. I knew that with me out of the way, he would search my place to make sure I had left behind no incriminating evidence. So I planted some. I have a little office at home with a desk. On this desk, along with a bunch of other papers, I left two folders. One of them was labeled: "Alan's Patent. Supporting Information". The other was labeled: "My Grant. Current Records.""

"You wanted to see which one he would take."

"Uh-huh. If this had anything to do with the patent, if Dick was trying to get you out of the way because of that, he would have taken the patent folder. On the other hand, if, as I guessed, it had to do with grant funding, he would take the other folder, since it might contain records that could implicate him."

"And in either case," I realized, "leaving the folder that was not relevant to him might incriminate you. By leaving the patent folder, for example, he could suggest to anyone who searched later that you might be trying to obtain proprietary information about my patent."

"Right. And that's just what happened. Dick took the grant folder, while leaving the patent information right where I left it."

I thought this over carefully.

"One thing I don't understand, Bill, is why you didn't tell me what you were up to. Didn't you trust me?"

Bill looked surprised. "I did contact you. Don't you remember that text I sent you Saturday afternoon? I told you I had some information that I wanted to give you."

It was my turn to look surprised. I now remembered the text from someone who said he was "sentenced to die".

"That was *you*? But why the mysterious way of referring to yourself? Why didn't you just tell me who you were? That wasn't your regular number."

Bill shrugged.

"I wasn't sure you'd believe me. I was supposed to be dead or at least hospitalized. I thought that if I told you I had left the hospital, you might have suspected it was Dick, setting up a trap. I had begged the staff there to tell everyone who inquired that I was still there. By referring to myself as "sentenced to die", I thought you would understand it had to be me. Dick of course would never refer to me in that manner."

We discussed Dick's financial schemes for a few minutes longer. As we did, people began to get up, returning to experiments in the lab. I stopped Marissa before she could go, though.

"One of the key clues for me was finding your cell phone right here on Mitch's desk last night. You knew that phone was here the night of the first kidnapping, or at least that it could have been. Yet you never said anything to me." I didn't say, though I hoped she understood, that she had in effect interfered in the investigation of a crime. I also didn't point out that, had I had this information sooner, both Bill and I might not have had attempts made on our lives.

She tried to rationalize her actions.

"I didn't know the importance of that text until you told me a few days ago. That was when I asked Mitch. He remembered that he had a seminar that night—it's every Monday night at that hour. So he was not in the office at that time. It couldn't have been him."

Yes, I had eventually realized that, too.

"But that didn't mean it could have been anyone else. It was more likely to have been some people than others. Who would know that your phone was here? Who had the most access to this office?"

I let that question hang over their heads, as well as the issue of Marissa's relationship with Mitch.

I spent the rest of the day in the lab, liberated by the knowledge that the growing fear I had lived in for the past several weeks was now gone. Laurie returned from out of town in the early afternoon, and thus had missed all of the excitement. I gave her a brief summary, then later, at my apartment that evening, filled her in on all the details. It was not lost on either of us that had she not been away, she probably would have come looking for me in the lab much sooner than Candy did.

"Candy told me you almost died in the cold room."

"I did die in there," I replied. "And that is a mystery no one will ever solve."

EPILOGUE

The kidnapping cases are still ongoing, but a big break occurred when Jack, the bootlegger, found that he did indeed have a mutant form of the gene *adenomatous polyposis coli* (APC), just like his brother. Both he and his brother learned that had their condition not been diagnosed, they probably would have developed colon cancer by their early forties. Jack was so grateful to me for saving his life and his brother's life that he provided a full description of my original kidnappers. Though the police still have not found them, they believe it's only a matter of time.

The large clinical trial of the colon cancer screening test passed with flying colors. It worked so well that we really didn't need to use the one gene that the federal government had claimed title to. My other two genes, plus those Alex contributed, were sufficient. However, I convinced Mitch and Alex to add that other gene, anyway, because it made the test even better. We finally settled with the government. They will get fifteen percent of the patent royalties. The university settled for slightly more than fifty percent. Mitch, Alex and I each got about ten percent. Though the test has not yet gone on the market, I anticipate that when it does, I will be able to fund my own laboratory.

Mitch and Marissa broke up. That was inevitable, I suppose. She got her degree and moved on, joining a biotech company in California, I believe. I miss her a little, but not too much. I'm sure I concentrate better at work now. And my relationship with Mitch has never been better.

Laurie and I are not living together, but we do see each other a lot. She's close to finishing her Ph.D., and looking for postdoctoral positions. She has no interest in working in industry, but plans to keep her career academic. Wherever she goes, I'm sure we'll stay in touch.

In some ways, though, I feel closer to Candy. After all, she did save my life—or as she puts it to me, she saved my death. We continue to disagree about a lot of things, but they don't seem very important to me now. She still practices *tummo* in the cold room, now going there early every Sunday morning to honor my experience there. She urged me to join her, but for a long time I wouldn't go back in there, not even during the course of laboratory experiments. It wasn't because I was afraid to. I just regard that place now as sacred, a place not to be entered casually, frequently, or without preparation. Whenever I do go in there, I get goose bumps, though that could be just because it's so cold.

All diseases, I think, ultimately result from some form of alienation. Cancer, for example, occurs when some cells alienate themselves from the rest of the body. They forget where they came from, what nourished them into being, where they used to belong. In a funny sort of way, we humans are like that, too. To rediscover that we are sacred is the only cure for this disease that I know.

Books by Andrew Smith:

The Dimensions Of Experience: A Natural History of Consciousness (2009) Andrew P. Smith ISBN 978-1436370837 Hardcover, (Also in Paperback and Kindle editions), Xlibris Corp. 504 pp This book tells a plausible story of how consciousness evolved, beginning with the simplest forms of existence. Citing recent studies in animal learning, perception and behavior, together with molecular biology, cell biology and neurophysiology, the book shows how dimensions of experienced space and time, together with increasing awareness of self and other, emerged in association with hierarchical complexity of information processing entities. This is the first complete history of consciousness ever written..

Killing for the Cure – A Biomedical Technothriller (2012) ISBN 9781159630781 Andrew P. Smith. Suspense thriller Everyone wants a cure for cancer. Is someone willing to kill for it? BeachHouse Books published in 2010 as **A Cure for Cancer**

BeachHouse
Books

www.beachhousebooks.com

An imprint of

𝕾𝖈𝖎𝖊𝖓𝖈𝖊 & 𝕳𝖚𝖒𝖆𝖓𝖎𝖙𝖎𝖊𝖘 𝕻𝖗𝖊𝖘𝖘

PO Box 7151

Chesterfield MO 63006-7151